SHOOT HIM
IF HE RUNS

BOOKS BY STUART WOODS

FICTION

Fresh Disasters[†]

Short Straw

Dark Harbor[†]

Iron Orchid[*]

Two-Dollar Bill[†]

The Prince of Beverly Hills

Reckless Abandon[†]

Capital Crimes[‡]

Dirty Work[†]

Blood Orchid[*]

The Short Forever[†]

Orchid Blues[*]

Cold Paradise[†]

L.A. Dead[†]

The Run[‡]

Worst Fears Realized[†]

Orchid Beach[*]

Swimming to Catalina[†]

Dead in the Water[†]

Dirt[†]

Choke

Imperfect Strangers

Heat

Dead Eyes

L.A. Times

Santa Fe Rules

New York Dead[†]

Palindrome

Grass Roots[‡]

White Cargo

Deep Lie[‡]

Under the Lake

Run Before the Wind[†]

Chiefs[‡]

TRAVEL

A Romantic's Guide to the Country Inns of Britain and Ireland (1979)

MEMOIR

Blue Water, Green Skipper (1977)

[*] A Holly Barker Book   [†] A Stone Barrington Book   [‡] A Will Lee Book

SHOOT HIM
IF HE RUNS

STUART WOODS

G. P. PUTNAM'S SONS   NEW YORK

G. P. PUTNAM'S SONS
Publishers Since 1838
Published by the Penguin Group
Penguin Group (USA) Inc., 375 Hudson Street, New York, New York 10014, USA • Penguin Group
(Canada), 90 Eglinton Avenue East, Suite 700, Toronto, Ontario M4P 2Y3, Canada (a division of
Pearson Penguin Canada Inc.) • Penguin Books Ltd, 80 Strand, London WC2R 0RL, England •
Penguin Ireland, 25 St Stephen's Green, Dublin 2, Ireland (a division of Penguin Books Ltd) •
Penguin Group (Australia), 250 Camberwell Road, Camberwell, Victoria 3124, Australia (a division
of Pearson Australia Group Pty Ltd) • Penguin Books India Pvt Ltd, 11 Community Centre,
Panchsheel Park, New Delhi–110 017, India • Penguin Group (NZ), 67 Apollo Drive, Rosedale,
North Shore 0745, Auckland, New Zealand (a division of Pearson New Zealand Ltd) •
Penguin Books (South Africa) (Pty) Ltd, 24 Sturdee Avenue, Rosebank,
Johannesburg 2196, South Africa

Penguin Books Ltd, Registered Offices: 80 Strand, London WC2R 0RL, England

"Black Mountain Blues": Words and music by J. C. Johnson. © 1965 Record Music Publishing Co.
c/o Songwriters Guild of America. All rights reserved. Used by permission.

ISBN 978-0-399-15444-7

Printed in the United States of America

BOOK DESIGN BY NICOLE LAROCHE

This is a work of fiction. Names, characters, places, and incidents either are the product of the author's
imagination or are used fictitiously, and any resemblance to actual persons, living or dead, businesses,
companies, events, or locales is entirely coincidental.

While the author has made every effort to provide accurate telephone numbers and Internet addresses
at the time of publication, neither the publisher nor the author assumes any responsibility for errors,
or for changes that occur after publication. Further, the publisher does not have any control over and
does not assume any responsibility for author or third-party websites or their content.

This book is for Barbara Ellen.

Goin' to Black Mountain
Take my razor and my gun;
Gonna cut him if he stands still
Shoot him if he runs.

"Black Mountain Blues," by J. C. Johnson

E laine's, late.

 Stone Barrington blew into Elaine's, later than usual. Dino Bacchetti, his former NYPD partner, sat having dinner.

"Where the hell have you been?" Dino asked.

"Spokane, Washington," Stone replied. "I told you, remember?"

"I don't remember anything anymore," Dino said. "That's Genevieve's job, now." Genevieve James was his new girlfriend, his first regular since his divorce. "What were you doing in Spokane?"

"I'm having the engine ripped off my airplane and replaced with a turbine—that's a jet engine, turning a propeller."

A waiter set a Knob Creek on the rocks before him, and he sipped it gratefully.

"But why are you late? Dinner was two hours ago."

"Because my flight was late."

"You don't take the airlines; you have an airplane."

"Dino, having sex again is addling your brain. I left the airplane in Spokane; the work takes three months. It's a big job."

"Right."

Stone put several letters on the table and began opening them.

"You getting your mail here now?"

"No, I stopped to drop off my bag, and I just grabbed the mail on the way out the door."

Elaine came over, allowed him to kiss her and sat down. "You getting your mail here? We charge extra for that."

Stone put down the mail. "No, I brought it with me. Any charge for opening it here?"

"Don't make a habit of it," she replied. "People will think you're living in my back room."

"You don't have a back room."

"That won't stop them from thinking it."

"Your logic is unassailable," Stone said, shoving the mail aside and sipping his drink.

A waiter appeared with a menu.

"Green bean salad, hold the peppers, spaghetti carbonara, half a bottle of the Chianti Classico," Stone said.

"You look hungry," Elaine said. "You're late, too; where you been?"

"Spokane, Washington; Dino will explain it to you."

"He's turning his airplane into a jet," Dino said.

"Sort of," Stone replied. "A jet with a propeller. It's called a turboprop."

"Why are you doing this to your airplane?"

"Faster, quieter, more reliable, climbs faster."

"Oh."

Elaine had never evinced the slightest interest in his airplane, Stone remembered. He waited for the next, inevitable question.

"Only one engine?" Elaine asked.

"One's all you need."

"What if it stops?"

"Extremely unlikely, but I'd find a place to land it."

Elaine nodded. "Yeah, sure."

"Where is Genevieve?" Stone asked Dino.

"Late shift; she'll show soon. She might bring Eliza."

"Good idea." Eliza Larkin was an ER doctor Stone had been seeing occasionally since he had been run down by a car and she had treated him.

The two women, on cue, breezed into the place, exchanged kisses with everybody and sat down.

"Bring 'em a menu," Elaine said to a waiter.

"No, thanks, I had dinner in the cafeteria earlier," Eliza said.

"Me too," Genevieve said.

Elaine looked at them incredulously. "You ate food from a hospital cafeteria instead of here?"

"I would have fainted if I hadn't," Eliza said. "Maybe I'll have dessert."

"Dessert is good," Elaine said, pointing at a tray of samples and motioning for a waiter to bring it over.

"Cheesecake," Eliza said.

"Make it two," Genevieve echoed.

The two women excused themselves and went to the ladies' room.

Stone turned his attention to the mail again, and a large white envelope caught his attention. He turned it over to read the return address. The White House, Washington, D.C., it read.

Stone opened the envelope.

"You look funny," Dino said.

"I've been invited to dinner at the White House," Stone said, gulping. "Holly Barker and me."

"On the same invitation?" Elaine asked, taking it from him.

"Why you and Holly?" Dino asked.

"Yeah, Eliza is gonna want to know the answer to that question, too," Elaine said.

Stone took the invitation and stuffed it into his pocket. "Let's not discuss it with her," he said, "especially since I don't know the answer to that question."

His cellphone vibrated on his belt, and he flipped it open. "Hello?"

"It's Holly." Holly Barker was his friend and sometime lover, a retired army officer and chief of police in a Florida town, now doing something or other for the CIA.

"Speak of the devil."

"How was Spokane?"

"Fine. How did you know I was in Spokane?"

"I have a computer program that tracks the flight of any airplane. You went yesterday; I figured you came back today. You're doing the engine conversion?"

"How the hell did you know that?"

"I know lots of stuff. You got the invitation?"

"Just now."

"You getting your mail at Elaine's these days?"

"I picked it up on the way here."

"I have further instructions for you about the dinner."

"Okay."

"It's going to take five days, maybe a week of your time."

"Huh?"

"Listen to me carefully, and don't argue. Dinner, you will have noticed, is tomorrow night; it's black tie."

"I got that from the invitation."

"Pack a bag with warm-weather clothing and bring your passport."

"Holly . . ."

"Shut up. I told you not to ask questions."

"I'll have to see what's on my calendar for the next week."

"Nothing; I checked with Joan this afternoon."

Joan Robertson was his secretary. "A conspiracy," he said.

"You don't know the half of it, kiddo," she replied, then hung up.

"What?" Elaine asked.

"I don't know what," Stone replied. "Weird, is what."

2

The following day, Stone, as per directions included with his White House invitation, took the Acela to Washington and a cab to the Willard, the restored grande dame hotel of the mid-nineteenth century. He was led by a bellman to an elegant suite and was a little surprised to find the luggage and clothes of a woman there. He tipped the bellman, then explored.

The clothes in the closet were few, but from fashionable designers, and slinky. He reflected that Holly was tall, but not particularly slender, and a little on the butch side, with short, light brown hair. She was certainly very attractive, but these clothes could not be hers. He called the front desk to inquire as to whether he was in the right suite and was assured that he was. He looked at his watch: four hours until he was to present himself at the White House.

He phoned the concierge and arranged for a massage, and while he waited for the masseuse to appear, he sent his dinner jacket and other clothes out to be pressed.

After an hour and a half of prodding and pummeling, he soaked in a hot tub and took a nap. He was in front of the hotel at the appointed time and was met by a black Lincoln and a driver, who knew the way to the White House.

The mansion and its grounds looked very beautiful with the moonlight on its six-inch blanket of new snow. At the gate he identified himself with his invitation and his passport and was driven to a portico, lit by a huge, hanging lamp, with Marine guards on either side of the door. Inside, he was greeted by name (they must have a photograph, he thought), his coat was taken, and he was asked to follow an usher. They walked down a portrait-hung hallway, took a couple of turns and stopped before a pair of double doors. The usher rapped lightly, and the door was opened by a man in a tuxedo. "Mr. Barrington," the usher said, and stepped back to allow Stone to enter.

Stone walked into the room and was astonished to find himself in the Oval Office. The president of the United States, William Henry Lee IV, sat at the desk, on the phone, in his shirtsleeves, his dinner jacket resting on a valet stand beside his chair.

The president waved and pointed at a couch.

Stone sat down, and it was a good thing, too, because he felt a little weak in the knees. He had never been in this room, nor in this house, nor had he ever seen its occupant face-to-face.

A uniformed butler materialized and asked his pleasure in drink.

"A Knob Creek on the rocks," Stone said automatically. "But if you don't have that . . ."

"We have it, sir," the man said, and he was back in a trice, with not one, but two drinks on a tray. He served Stone, then set the other glass on the president's desk and dematerialized.

"I'll expect to hear from you before noon tomorrow," the president said, then hung up. "Mr. Barrington," he said, rising and slipping into his dinner jacket. "I've heard a great deal about you." He walked toward Stone, his hand out.

Stone rose and shook his hand. "Have you, Mr. President?" He couldn't imagine how.

"Bill Eggers is an old friend, and Woodman & Weld have been very helpful to the Democratic Party and to me over the years." His accent was softly Southern. "Bill has told me some of the things you've done for them since becoming of counsel to the firm."

What Stone did for Woodman & Weld was the things the firm did not want to be seen to be doing themselves, and he was a little embarrassed that the president knew about that. "I see," he said.

"Oh, don't be embarrassed, Stone," Lee said. "Every law firm needs that sort of work"—he paused—"as does every administration." He waved Stone back to his seat.

Stone sat down, uncertain as to what might come next.

"I asked you here a few minutes before the arrival of the others to thank you in advance for your help. I'm aware of your campaign contributions over the years, and I'm grateful for those, too."

Stone had made a few thousand-dollar donations, but he couldn't imagine why the president would be aware of that.

"I'm also aware of your honorable and very capable service to the NYPD for the fourteen years before you became an attorney, and as a citizen, I thank you for that, too."

"Thank you, Mr. President." Stone gulped. He took a long sip from his bourbon.

"Good stuff, Knob Creek," the president said. "Knob Creek was where Abraham Lincoln spent his early years, in Kentucky, you know."

"Yes, sir."

The president raised his glass. "It's the patriotic thing to do," he said, taking a sip. "Though I mustn't be patriotic too often these days, given the nature of the work."

"I suppose not, sir."

The president sat down on the sofa beside him. "Let me come directly to the point; the others will be here soon."

Stone waited and listened.

"I believe that, some years ago, you were involved in a widely publicized criminal trial, on the island of St. Marks, way south of here."

"Yes, sir, I was."

"I believe I even caught a glimpse of you on *60 Minutes.*"

"Yes, sir, it was important to the outcome of the trial that we obtain as much media coverage as possible."

"I forget; what was the outcome of the trial?" The president asked, raising his eyebrows.

Stone had the distinct feeling that he had forgotten nothing. "My client was hanged," he replied.

President Lee burst out laughing. "I'm aware that you believed her to be hanged, until some years later, and I'm aware of your most recent encounter with her. Where is she now?"

"In a Florida prison, Mr. President."

"Ah, yes, and she's been asking me for a pardon every year since; for her husband, too. Tell me, Stone, if you were in my position, would you pardon them?"

"Since I don't represent her anymore, I can say candidly, absolutely not. Both she and her husband deserve worse than being where they presently are, and the country is better off for having them there."

The president chuckled. "We are of one mind," he said. "Stone, someone is going to ask you to go back to St. Marks for . . . a visit."

"That would not be unpleasant duty, Mr. President. It's a beautiful island."

"I hope you can take the time to go."

"I was requested to pack my bags, Mr. President, and I have done so. May I ask why you want me to go back?"

"Oh, I haven't asked you to go back," the president said. "Someone else will, but I will not. And I must ask you to recall this meeting, this room, this bourbon and this conversation as wholly imaginary."

"As you wish, Mr. President."

"Stone, I'm sure you know that I am up for reelection in the autumn, and I wanted to tell you personally that your visit to St. Marks may, in one way or another, have a profound effect on my chances. Since, in light of your campaign contributions in the past, I have some reason to believe you think it might be important for me to finish my administration's work, I wanted to tell you personally that you may soon be in a position to contribute to my campaign in a larger way than you imagine, and I want you to know, in advance, that you have my deep gratitude for your help."

Stone was too baffled to speak, and he was relieved of that obligation when a door behind him opened and a woman's voice said, "Will, honey, it's time for us to go in."

Stone sprang to his feet and turned to see the first lady, who was also the Director of Central Intelligence, standing in the open door.

"Kate, darling, this is Mr. . . . ." the president started to say.

"I know who he is, Will," she replied, walking over and shaking his hand. "And I'm glad to have the opportunity to thank you for your efforts in solving the death of your cousin, Dick Stone, last summer. Dick was about to assume an important post at the Agency, and I had hopes that he might one day succeed me, when I've played out my string. Lance Cabot has told me how helpful you were to him during the investigation."

Funny, Stone thought, and I was laboring under the apparent illusion that Lance was helping *me*. "You're very welcome, ma'am."

"Good luck on St. Marks, Mr. Barrington." She turned and walked out the way she had come in.

"I must go," Will Lee said, shaking Stone's hand. "And by the way, the woman you just met was entirely imaginary, too. Have a seat; someone will come for you."

The president followed his wife out the door, closing it behind him.

Stone stood in the center of the Oval Office, alone with its ghosts. He recognized the President's desk as the one John Kennedy had used, and he remembered a photograph of John-John playing under it. He took in the portraits and the model of a yacht on one side of the room, and the rug under his feet with the Great Seal of the United States woven into it.

Then the door through which he had entered opened and Lance Cabot walked in.

"Oh, shit," Stone muttered to himself.

3

L ance smiled and extended a hand. "So nice to see you, Stone."

Stone had not seen Lance for several months, and that had been all right with him. Every time he saw Lance he found himself in the middle of some sort of problem, and it seemed to be happening again. He shook the hand. "Hello, Lance," he said. "What the fuck am I doing in the Oval Office, about to go to St. Marks?"

Lance arranged himself in a chair and motioned for Stone to sit. "Relax, Stone, all is about to be revealed."

Stone couldn't wait. "Please start revealing."

"Have you ever heard of a man named Teddy Fay?"

"Of course; everybody's heard of him. He killed several right-wing political figures a couple of years ago, and when they were about to catch him, he killed himself by exploding the small airplane he was flying."

"You're half right," Lance replied.

"Which half?"

"The first half. Teddy didn't die in the aircraft explosion. He got out, made his way to New York and spent some time last year killing Middle Easterners whom he believed to be enemies of the United States."

"*That* was Teddy Fay?"

"Indubitably, it was."

"Was he the guy who died in the collapse of the building he bombed, then?"

"Not quite. At the time there was every indication that the body found in the ruins of the building was that of Teddy, but a woman who had reported her homeless father missing gave the NYPD a DNA sample last week, and it matched that of the body we found."

"So Fay is still alive?"

"I'm afraid we don't know, but we have no conclusive evidence that he's dead."

"And what does this have to do with my going to St. Marks?"

"Let me begin at the beginning, Stone, since there's a lot you may not know about Teddy from press reports."

"Please do."

"Theodore Fay was a career employee of the CIA, joining in his twenties and retiring at age sixty-five. He worked in Technical Services, which is the rather bland name of the department that supplies all sorts of things to agents going into the field: clothing, disguises, false passports, driver's licenses, insurance cards, credit cards and other documents an agent requires to establish a legend— that is, a false identity—in the field. The department also supplies weapons—some of them quite exotic—communications equipment and, well, you get the picture."

"I do. What did Teddy do there?"

"Teddy, over the course of his long career, did *everything*. He was the most skilled technician and inventor the Agency has ever employed. Twice, he was offered the job of heading his department, and he turned it down both times, because he enjoyed his work too much to become a manager.

"For the last twenty years of his career Teddy ran one of several teams that supplied the tools of their trade to, for want of a better word, spies. He was expert in virtually every area of his work, and he trained other specialists."

"So that would make him able to change his own identity with documents, et cetera, with some ease?"

"It would, which is why it has, so far, proved impossible to catch him."

"Is he on another rampage now?"

"No, not that we know of. My guess is that he is living quietly in retirement."

Stone frowned. "In St. Marks?"

"Perhaps. That is what we want you and Holly to learn."

"Why St. Marks?"

"There is another Agency employee named Irene Foster living there. She retired after twenty-five years, shortly before Teddy's most recent vanishing. Another former Agency employee has told us that many years ago, she and Teddy had a rather torrid affair. We've not been able to establish that there has been any contact between them since then, but still . . ."

"That's a pretty slim connection, isn't it?"

"Irene's last post was as Assistant Deputy Director for Operations, and she was in a position, had she chosen to do so, to provide Teddy with a great deal of information that he would have needed to conduct his campaign in New York."

"Wasn't she investigated at the time?"

"There was a full internal investigation into who, if anyone, might have been helping Teddy."

"And?"

"No culprit was discovered. Irene Foster conducted the investigation."

"Oh."

"Irene told her colleagues at the time of her retirement that she had bought a house on the island of St. Barts, but not long after her retirement, she sold the house and left the island."

"For St. Marks?"

"We've only recently learned that she bought another house on St. Marks."

"Why Holly and me?"

"Three reasons: one, Holly was the only member of the New York team who thought Teddy was still alive after the building collapsed, and she has actually seen him twice, though he was disguised; two, you are under contract to us as a consultant, and you are an experienced investigator with some experience of St. Marks; and three, a couple would excite less interest in such a setting than a single person, and you are the only man Holly would agree to share . . . ah, quarters with."

"I have a feeling there's another reason," Stone said.

"Ah. Yes. I take it you have a personal interest in seeing President Lee reelected."

"I support him, yes."

"You did not know that Teddy Fay had survived the aircraft explosion, did you?"

"No."

"Neither does anybody else outside the FBI director's office, my director's office and those designated by the current occupant of this room. The president was persuaded to conceal his knowledge of Teddy's survival, in the interest of helping catch him. He shared that knowledge with only three other people—all members of Congress."

"So?"

"Since we now believe that Teddy may still be alive, and since the president knows this, he is vulnerable if it should become known. In effect, he has kept from the public, on two occasions, the knowledge that a wanted criminal is still at large. His wife, as director of Central Intelligence, shares this vulnerability. Should Teddy's continued existence become known in the months remaining before the election, Katharine Rule Lee would be forced to resign from the Agency. Since she was always an unpopular choice with the political opposition, they will make much of it, and the ensuing uproar might very likely torpedo the reelection of the president."

"I'm uncomfortable with this," Stone said.

"*Everyone* is uncomfortable with it," Lance replied, "not least the president and the first lady, but there it is, and we have to deal with it."

There was a knock on the double doors. "More of this tomorrow." Lance called out, "Come in."

The door opened and a tall, very slim woman with shoulder-length red hair wearing a striking evening gown entered the room. "Hello, Stone," she said. Stone and Lance got to their feet.

It took Stone more than a moment to absorb the change. "Holly?"

"Amazing what losing a little weight, a dye job and a tan will do, isn't it?"

"You look gorgeous." Stone had hardly noticed the man who had followed her in, but now he did. "Dino? What the hell are you doing here?" He had never seen Dino in a tuxedo before.

"I got the same invitation you did, pal."

Lance spoke up. "I forgot to mention that Dino will be going along, too."

"I believe we're due at dinner," Holly said.

"That we are," Lance replied. "There'll be a further briefing for you and Dino tomorrow, Stone, but right now, the president awaits." He led the way out of the Oval Office and from the West Wing to the White House proper, where they joined a receiving line. When Stone was introduced to the president and first lady, they greeted him without reference to their earlier meeting.

Shortly, they were seated at one of many tables in the East Room, sipping California champagne. Stone looked around. "Who are all these people?" he asked Lance. "I don't see any familiar faces."

Lance smiled. "In fact, this is probably the most anonymous group ever to dine at the White House. These are the approximately hundred and fifty highest-ranking people at the Central Intelligence Agency, the National Security Agency and the Federal Bureau of Investigation, and their spouses. This is the first time such an event has occurred, and it appears on the White House daily schedule as a personal dinner party given for friends of the president and first lady."

"Wow," Dino said. "If a bomb went off here . . ."

"Don't even think that," Lance said.

4

S tone woke slowly, momentarily disoriented by the strange surroundings. He lifted his head and saw a naked, red-haired woman coming out of the bathroom.

"Good morning," Holly said. "You'd better shower and shave; Lance and the others will be here in forty-five minutes. I've ordered breakfast."

Stone continued to watch her; he liked the changes. "Why red hair?" he asked.

"You'll find out at the briefing; now get moving!" She goosed him in the ribs, then dodged his grasp and started dressing.

Stone and Holly were just finishing their coffee when there was a knock on the door. Holly let them in: Lance, Dino and Genevieve James.

Stone gave Genevieve a kiss. "You're in on this, too?"

"I would do *anything* for a vacation on a tropical island," she said. "And don't worry, I've been sworn to secrecy."

"Genevieve just came to say hello," Lance said. "She's going shopping now."

"I believe I've been dismissed," she said, and with a little wave, left the suite.

"Anybody want coffee?" Lance asked.

Nobody spoke.

"Good. Now, let's get started; you have a plane to catch this afternoon."

Everybody took a seat.

"Stone, let's begin with you: tell us—briefly, if you will, since there'll be time to fill in details later—about your experience in St. Marks, and especially, about the people you know there."

Stone took a deep breath. "I was on vacation there several years ago, when a yacht entered English Harbour, sailed by a woman alone, causing something of a kerfuffle. The following day, she was charged with killing her husband at sea and shoving his body overboard. I somehow got involved and defended her at her trial. I lost, and she was hanged—or at least I thought she was. She turned up later, alive in Florida, but that's a different story."

"Tell us who you know on St. Marks," Lance reminded him.

"I spent most of my time at the English Harbour Inn, near the harbor, run by a retired NYPD cop named Thomas Hardy, who was born and raised on St. Marks."

Dino spoke up. "I met him a couple of times on the job, years ago."

"Right. He's a good guy; I think we should stay there, if he has room."

"You've already been booked into a cottage there," Lance said. "The four of you. Who else did you know?"

"An elderly barrister named Leslie Hewitt was assigned to work with me on the trial; he may be dead by now."

"He is not," Lance said.

"And there was Sir Winston Sutherland, the minister of justice on the island, who decided to prosecute the case himself."

"Sutherland is now prime minister," Lance said, "so you know people in high places."

"Sir Winston would have a poor opinion of me," Stone said, "since I made him look bad a number of times during the trial, and since I cast him as the villain in the considerable publicity we managed to generate, in an attempt to save my client's neck."

"Duly noted," Lance said. "You should make a point of not running afoul of the law in St. Marks, partly because of Stone's unsatisfactory relationship with Sir Winston and partly because, as prime minister, he has run the island in a more authoritarian manner than the previous administration did. Questions?"

"Why does Holly have red hair?" Stone asked.

Lance smiled. "I think I told you that Holly has seen Teddy Fay twice, although he was heavily disguised, but that means that he has also seen her twice, so I thought that a change of appearance was a good idea, and a change of identity, too. Teddy may still have computer access to the Agency mainframe computer, and he probably read Holly's personnel file at the time he met her. She is taking the identity of Virginia Heller, her father's girlfriend, whom you met on Islesboro."

"Why Ginny?"

"Because it's faster than creating a legend for Holly. Since Ginny is a real person, she can be researched by Teddy. We've changed the photographs on Ginny's website and substituted Holly's—Ginny runs a flying school in Florida—and in the Florida driver's license database and the U.S. Passport database. This should hold up, because should Teddy become suspicious of her, he doesn't have any resources on the mainland to investigate Ginny. He'll have to be content with electronic investigation. Any other questions?"

Dino spoke up. "What do we do when we get to St. Marks?"

"Find Irene Foster, and go from there. You should know, Dino— all of you—that this is not an official Agency operation; it's purely a seat-of-the-pants thing to learn whether Teddy Fay still exists. It's being paid for through a front travel agency operated by the Agency, and the funds will be untraceable. Just be who you are when you get there, except for Holly, who will be Ginny. Any other questions? No? Then I'll give you some basic info on St. Marks."

Lance set up a large laptop computer and began displaying maps of the island and photographs of the terrain. "The island is made up of a central, dormant volcano, known as Black Mountain, surrounded by tropical forest and fine beaches. St. Marks is a former British possession that gained its independence about twelve years ago. Since that time, one political party has held power, and Sir Winston is only the second prime minister. It is, ostensibly, a parliamentary democracy, although Sir Winston, as previously noted, wields more personal power than most elected officials.

"The government is stable and the island safe for tourists. Ninety percent of the population is black, as are all the people Stone knows there; the rest are mostly descendants of the former British settlers, whose accents are British. There are a few dozen expatriates who've bought homes there because of the stable political atmosphere and the moderate real estate prices."

"So finding Irene Foster shouldn't be hard?" Stone asked.

"No," Lance replied.

"Why did she leave St. Barts for St. Marks? I mean, the real estate prices on St. Barts would have been higher, but she already owned a property there. What made her move?"

"We investigated her existence in St. Barts thoroughly, before she left the island. What we picked up was that she didn't speak any French, which is the local language, and she preferred an English-speaking island. Also, she got an unsolicited offer for her house, and she jumped at the chance to move. Incidentally, before she moved, we had a close look at the inside of her house, and we found no indication of a co-habitor—only one toothbrush, et cetera. She had a local reputation for picking up suitable men at local bars and having them over for a night or two—always tourists, who would be leaving in a few days. From that, we deduced that she was not being sexually satisfied by a regular lover—i.e., Teddy." Lance looked at his watch. "You have a flight from Manassas, Virginia, in three hours, and you have to get packed. Any other questions?"

Stone spoke up. "What do we do if we find Teddy Fay?"

Lance closed his laptop, put it into his briefcase and closed it. "Holly will inform me, then you will all go home."

"And what will happen to Teddy?" Stone asked.

Lance stood up and walked to the door. "You needn't concern yourself with that," he said. "Have a nice trip." He walked out and closed the door behind him.

5

W hen they got out of their car at Manassas Airport, Lance was waiting for them, standing beside a small jet.

"Is that the new Swearingen J-30?" Stone asked.

"It is," Lance replied.

"I've been reading about it for years, so I guess it's finally certified?"

"Just barely. This is the first one bought by the government; we're anxious to see if it flies."

"Oh, great," Dino said. "We're an experiment?"

"Relax, Dino," Stone said. "The airplane has been through the whole gamut of tests, and only one has crashed."

"Where can I get the nearest commercial flight?" Dino asked.

"Dino," Lance said, "shut up, put your luggage in the locker, and get aboard." Everybody started to climb aboard, but Lance pulled Stone aside. "I don't want you to draw any inferences from what I said yesterday."

"And what was it you said?"

"I said to let me know if you find Teddy Fay, and that I would take care of it. I meant just that. You should know that Teddy is dangerous when he's cornered, and you are not equipped to deal with him."

Stone felt his ears starting to get hot. "Lance, I've dealt with more cornered rats than you've had hot dinners. While you were sitting behind your desk at Langley or wandering around Europe, Dino and I were putting away heavily armed bad guys, whether they liked it or not, and we never needed help from the Central Intelligence Agency."

"Calm down, Stone; this is a special case, and it has to be handled carefully. We don't want this hitting the papers, or the president and the director could end up as collateral damage."

"You've already explained that very thoroughly," Stone said. "We'll be in touch." He turned around and got aboard the airplane, followed by a single pilot. "Mind if I fly right seat?" Stone asked.

"Not today," the pilot replied. "Maybe on the return trip." He began starting the engines and running through his checklist.

Stone shrugged, took off his jacket and found a seat. It wasn't hard, because there were four seats and only one was available, facing aft, opposite Holly.

"I hope you don't mind sitting there," Holly said. "I sometimes throw up when I travel backward."

"I'll be fine here," Stone said. He settled in and fastened his seatbelt. The airplane began to move.

"What were you and Lance talking about?" Holly asked.

"Oh, it was just the usual stuff with Lance, the control freak."

"Well, he is that, but he's good at it."

"Great."

The airplane turned onto the runway without slowing down, and a moment later they were in the air, climbing fast.

"Are you going to be able to recognize Teddy Fay?" Stone asked. "You've met him twice, is that right?"

"Sort of. The first time I met him at the opera, and he invited me to sit with him; since he had better seats than I did, I accepted. Problem was, he was well disguised. Second time, I'm not even sure it was him; it was an old man on crutches, with one leg."

"Since there are no photographs, do you have any idea what he looks like?"

"He's about six feet tall, slender, balding or bald. We had a sketch done with the help of people in Tech Services who had worked with him." She fumbled in a large handbag and handed him a sheet of paper.

Stone looked at the face. "This looks like Larry David from the HBO TV show."

"Everybody says that, so it must be true. He's pretty bland-looking, so he disguises easily, and he's good at it."

"Is he likely to go armed?"

"I've no idea, but he certainly knows how to use—even build—weapons of all sorts."

Dino and Genevieve looked at the drawing. "I've seen this before," Dino said. "I doubt if it's worth the paper it's drawn on."

"There's something else you both need to know," Holly said. "Every time we've gotten close to him, Teddy has always had a well-planned escape route. Expect him to be slippery."

"How about Irene?" Stone said. "Is she going to be difficult to deal with?"

Holly dug out a photograph of a handsome woman, apparently in her early fifties, her brown hair streaked with gray. "She was an agency drone for a long time, working her way steadily up the ladder."

"Do you know her?"

"I think I passed her once in a hallway at Langley," Holly replied.

"Any chance she'll recognize you? Or will Teddy, for that matter?"

"Stone, *you* didn't recognize me, until I spoke to you."

"Touché," Stone said. "Will Teddy recognize your voice?"

"I don't think there's anything all that distinctive about my voice, do you?"

"I suppose not," Stone said.

"For what it's worth," Dino said, "I didn't recognize her either, even when she spoke to me."

"The transformation is remarkable," Stone said. "Like two different women."

"For better or worse?" Holly asked archly.

"They're both gorgeous," Stone replied, diplomatically.

"I could get used to this," Genevieve said waving an arm at the airplane's interior.

"Don't," Dino replied. "Stone's airplane isn't as nice as this, and I can't afford the rental on jets."

"I'm going to get used to it, anyway," she said, putting her head back and closing her eyes.

The pilot's voice came through an overhead speaker. "Ladies and gentlemen," he said, "we're at our cruising altitude of forty-one thousand feet, making a little over four hundred knots. We'll arrive at St. Marks in three hours and forty-one minutes. The toilet is forward, if you need it; please remember to close the curtain."

"What's the cabin altitude?" Stone asked.

"A thousand feet," the pilot replied. "The pressurization is very good."

Stone picked up a magazine and read until he was drowsy, then he napped. He was awakened by the pilot's voice in his head.

"Landing at St. Marks in five minutes," he said.

In exactly five minutes, Stone felt the airplane touch softly down. A couple of minutes later they taxied to a stop, and the pilot shut down the engines and opened the door, which was forward of the wing, then he went back to the cockpit for something.

Stone was first off the airplane, and he found himself facing half a dozen uniformed police officers, all black, pointing guns at him.

"Get on the ground," a man in plain clothes and sunglasses said.

"What?" Stone asked.

"*Get on the ground!*" There was the sound of guns being racked.

Stone got on the ground.

6

Stone heard the others being ordered down, then he felt cold steel pressed against the back of his neck.

"Identify yourself," a voice said.

Stone was about to do that when he heard a car screech to a halt and the door open and slam. "Stop that!" a man's deep voice commanded.

The barrel of the weapon left Stone's neck.

"Help them up," the driver of the car said.

Someone put a hand under Stone's elbow and helped him to his feet, along with the others.

"These people are my guests."

Stone turned and saw Thomas Hardy walking toward him, smiling, his hand out.

"Thomas, I'm very glad to see you," Stone said.

Thomas shook his hand and gave him a hug. "Let's get your luggage into the car," he said.

The policeman wearing dark glasses stepped up. "I require to see their passports," he said.

"Of course, captain," Thomas said. "Stone?"

Everyone produced a passport and handed it over. The captain motioned to a policeman who ran over and made a desk of his back while the captain stamped each passport, then handed them back to their owners. "My apologies," he said, then with a wave for his troops to follow, walked away toward the small terminal.

"Thomas, let me introduce my friends: this is Dino Bacchetti, who used to be my NYPD partner; his girlfriend, Genevieve James; and my friend, Holly Barker." He felt an elbow in his ribs. "Oh, uh, I'm sorry, this is Ginny Heller."

"I'm very pleased to meet you all," Thomas said. "Hop in, and I'll drive you to the inn." He leaned close to Stone's ear. "Stone, you'd best learn the names of your women."

"Right," Stone whispered back. "I'll explain later."

The pilot finished loading the luggage into a Volvo station wagon. "Contact Mr. Cabot when you need me," he said to Stone, "and on the way home you can fly right seat. That was my first solo flight in this airplane, and I didn't want any witnesses."

"Great job," Stone said. Thomas started the car, and they drove away. "What was that all about, Thomas?" Stone asked.

"You'll find that things have changed a bit in St. Marks," Thomas said. "Since Sir Winston Sutherland became prime minister, the police take a greater interest in everyone than they once did."

"It can't be very good for tourism to do that to everybody who arrives."

"No, it's not, but they don't bother the folks on commercial flights quite as much. They tend to look at every private airplane as a conveyer of drugs, and there is no faster way to get in trouble on this island than to possess illegal drugs."

"Well, thanks for your help."

"You'll find things quite different at the English Harbour Inn, too. I'm a member of Parliament now, and I've prospered since the advent of Sir Winston, mostly because he likes my conch chowder, and, of course, because I pay him well under the table. I was allowed to buy some beachfront property from the government that's adjacent to my own, and I've built a dozen cottages. You're all in the nicest of them, and you'll have your own housekeeper and butler."

"Sounds wonderful."

"I bought the marina, too, and I've made improvements. You can even get wireless Internet on your yacht these days. The restaurant has been enlarged, and I got a new chef from England last year. I also started a liquor distribution company, so the wines are better than when you were last here."

"Sounds like the advent of Sir Winston has brought all sorts of improvements."

"He hasn't been all bad," Thomas said. "I've never learned to like the man, but he's cracked down on crime, the roads have been improved, and the national income from tourism is up and headed higher, I think."

"What's the downside of Sir Winston?"

Thomas shrugged. "The payoffs are higher than with the last PM, but then so are the profits, and the police are more . . . observant of the citizens." Thomas nodded toward the island's central mountain in the distance; its top was shrouded in fog. "The old man is wearing his gray hair today," he said. "Did you ever go to up to the top of Black Mountain?"

"No, I seemed to spend most of my time in a courtroom last time."

"Ah, yes," Thomas said, smiling. "I read about the exploits of the lovely Allison and her evil husband in Palm Beach a couple of years ago. They've been put away, I believe."

"That's so, and I'm glad to have had a hand in it. I had dinner with the president of the United States last night, and he told me that she requests a pardon every year."

Thomas looked amazed. "You had dinner with the president?"

"Along with about three hundred other people," Stone said, "but I did get to chat with him for a couple of minutes."

"You're coming up in the world, Stone."

"Not really; it was my first White House dinner, and I expect it will be my last."

Thomas turned through a pair of large stone gateposts with a brass plaque bearing the legend "English Harbour Inn," and below that another plaque identifying the inn as a Relais de Campagne hotel.

"You got in the Relais? You're coming up in the world, too." The Relais was an international organization of luxury hotels and country inns and restaurants.

"Well, at least I didn't have to bribe anybody," Thomas said. "I applied, they showed up and inspected the place, and I got that little plaque for my gate."

"You didn't even have a gate last time I was here."

Thomas laughed and turned off the main drive onto a smaller road. A moment later he stopped the car beside a stone cottage with a roof of palm thatch. The sea lapped against a powdery white beach a few yards away. "Here we are," he said.

A man wearing a white cotton jacket and a black bow tie materialized next to the car and opened the doors.

"This is Jacob Marlow, your butler," Thomas said. He nodded at a plump woman in a white dress, standing in the doorway of the cottage. "And that is Hilda, his wife, who will help take care of you. I've booked a table for you in the restaurant at eight; I'll see you then." Thomas shook Stone's hand, got in the car and drove away.

The cottage consisted of a large, comfortably furnished living room with a well-stocked bar in one corner and two bedrooms, en suite. There was also a small, book-lined study with a desk and a sofa. Ceiling fans kept the air moving, and air conditioning seemed unnecessary. A large flat-screen television set was built into a wall unit in the living room, and each bedroom had a smaller set.

"Mr. Barrington, would you and your guests like a drink before Hilda and I unpack for you?"

"Thank you, Jacob, you go ahead, and I'll do the drinks."

"Would you like something pressed?"

"The blue blazer and the white linen trousers," Stone asked.

Jacob took similar instructions from the others, then dematerialized.

Stone went to the bar, made a batch of vodka gimlets and served them from a tray. Everyone relaxed.

"Well," Genevieve said, "I don't know about the rest of you, but I'm glad I came." She gave Dino a kiss.

"I'll drink to that," Holly/Ginny said, raising her glass. "And here's to Stone remembering my name."

As they took their first sips of their gimlets two gunshots rang out, at a not very great distance. Holly started to get to her feet, but Stone stopped her.

"Holly, never run *toward* gunfire, unless you're the police, and you are no longer the police."

They continued to sip their drinks, but the mood had changed.

7

At seven-thirty they walked up to the main building and into the open-air restaurant. A long bar occupied one side of the room, and a steel band was playing at one end of it. Stone estimated there were about fifty tables in the restaurant, and three-quarters of them were already full.

They were having a drink at the bar when there was a stir in the room and Stone looked toward the door to see Sir Winston Sutherland, clad in his usual white linen suit, enter, accompanied by his wife. He was halfway to his table when he spotted Stone. He seated his wife, then walked back toward the bar, a small smile on his face. "Ah, Mr. Barrington," he said, "welcome back to St. Marks."

"Thank you, Sir Winston, or I should say, Prime Minister. Congratulations on your election."

"Thank you, Mr. Barrington. We are glad to have the opportunity to apologize to you for the treatment you received at the airport this afternoon."

"I confess I was surprised; I thought there might be hard feelings left over from our courtroom appearance together some years ago."

"Certainly not; your conduct was professional at all times, at least when you were wearing the robes and wig. Though it seems we were right about the lovely Allison, after all."

"Well, you weren't right about her murdering her husband, but I must admit you were a better judge of her character than I. She had me fooled, but not you."

Sir Winston beamed.

"May I introduce my friends? Mr. Bacchetti, Ms. James, Ms. Heller."

Sir Winston shook their hands. "We welcome all of you to St. Marks and wish you a most pleasant stay. Now, if you will excuse us." He returned to his wife at their table.

"He was very cordial," said Thomas, who had walked up behind the bar.

"Surprisingly so," Stone said.

"You notice he has adopted the regal first person plural, instead of the more democratic first person singular?"

"I did notice that," Stone said. "I would have thought that more appropriate for a king than for a prime minister."

"Quite so," Thomas replied, "but Winston tends to blur the line between the two. Your table is ready; will you follow me?" He stepped from behind the bar and led them to a table in a sort of gazebo in one corner of the dining room, with a fine view of the sea in the medium distance. "Will you allow me to order for you?" Thomas asked.

"Thank you, Thomas; we'd like that," Stone replied.

Another round of gimlets arrived.

"I have a feeling," Genevieve said, "that by the time we leave here I will be thoroughly pickled in vodka gimlets."

"Just think of them as a preservative," Dino said.

The steel band was replaced by a pianist and a bass player, who played soft jazz and ballads through the evening.

A first course of conch chowder arrived, followed by an enormous paella, made from local seafood. After dessert, Thomas brought them a pot of espresso and a bottle of good cognac and they invited him to pull up a chair. Dino and Genevieve repaired to the dance floor, and Thomas poured them all a brandy.

"All right," he said, after they had raised their glasses, "what's going on here?"

Stone and Holly exchanged a glance.

"Holly, I know who you are. I shot pistols against your father in the nationals some years ago, and you were there; I think we even were introduced. As I recall, you were just out of the army and serving as police chief in some little Florida burg."

"Well, yes," Holly said.

"I'll admit that I wouldn't have immediately recognized you had Stone not blurted out your name. Why are you here under an assumed name?"

"I think I'd better bring Thomas up to date," Stone said to Holly.

"If you think it's a good idea," she replied.

"I think it's a good idea, because we're going to need Thomas's help."

"And that means you have to tell me everything," Thomas said. "I don't want Sir Winston's police breathing down my neck."

"It's nothing illegal, Thomas," Stone said. "We're looking for a man named Teddy Fay."

Thomas blinked. "I read in the *New York Times* that that gentleman was killed in some sort of airplane incident."

"He certainly was not killed in that incident," Stone said, "and he may still be alive."

"And you think he's alive *here*?"

"Possibly. Do you know a woman, an American, named Irene Foster? Fiftyish, attractive?"

"Of course," Thomas said. "Irene bought an old house up on Black Mountain and renovated it. She lived in the inn for a couple of months in the off-season, while the work was being done. Do you think she might have something to do with Fay?"

"They knew each other when they both worked for the Central Intelligence Agency, and Ms. Foster retired about the time Teddy disappeared for the second time. It's thought she might have been helping him, though there's no hard proof of that."

"So Irene was CIA? And she told me she was a retired college professor," Thomas said.

"Has she been spending a lot of time with any particular man?" Stone asked.

"Just the opposite," Thomas replied. "Irene has a propensity for picking up single men, tourists, of a certain age, and doing what comes naturally. I've never seen her with the same man for more than two or three evenings."

Stone produced the drawing of Teddy Fay. "Seen anyone who looks like this?"

Thomas looked at the picture. "Larry David? I always TiVo his show."

"We're hearing that a lot, but this is as close as we've been able to come to what he looks like. He destroyed every photograph of him ever taken."

"No, no one like that. Who are you working for on this little search? The FBI?"

"We'd better not go into that," Holly said.

"If you want my help, I want to know it all," Thomas replied.

"All right, I work for the CIA now, and Stone and Dino are helping out. Genevieve is just along for the ride."

"How long are you planning to be here?" Thomas asked.

"A week or so," Holly replied. "Longer, if necessary."

"Well, stick around here and you'll see Irene in a day or two; she comes in a lot. You'll probably get to see her in action."

"Thomas," Stone said, "we heard gunfire near the cottage earlier this evening. What was that about?"

"A man came ashore in a rubber dinghy from a larger boat offshore. The police shot him no more than a hundred yards farther down the beach from your cottage."

"Drugs?"

"Probably. Certainly, they thought so; I don't know what they found in the dinghy."

"I get the impression that the police here might shoot first and ask questions later."

"That is not a false impression," Thomas said. He nodded toward Sir Winston, who was leaving the restaurant. "That's the way he likes it."

8

Stone woke up with his head in "Ginny's" lap, and he took a moment to investigate how thorough the Agency's makeover of Holly had been. He was impressed to find that she was a redhead all over. Lance was not taking any chances.

"What are you doing down there?" she asked.

"Easy, Ginny; just checking out your disguise."

She laughed. "Check it out all you like," she said, pushing his head down.

They had breakfast on the cottage's patio, overlooking the beach. Stone and Dino were particularly interested to see that there was, apparently, no prohibition of nudity on the strands of St. Marks.

"Try looking at your eggs," Genevieve said to Dino.

"As an investigator, I'm expected to be aware of my surroundings at all times," Dino replied.

"Me too," Stone added.

"Now you understand why Lance insisted that my disguise be complete," Ginny said.

"I won't ask," Dino said.

"You won't need to," Ginny replied. She stood up, dropped her robe and ran for the water.

Stone swallowed the last of his coffee and followed her, just as naked. He caught up with her a few yards off the beach, and she splashed water in his face. "I didn't think you'd do it," he said.

"Well, Ginny is just full of surprises, isn't she?"

Stone heard splashing and saw Dino and Genevieve running into the water. "You know, for as long as I've known Dino, I've never seen him naked?"

"I'm a little disturbed that you're looking at him instead of Genevieve," Holly said, ducking him.

Stone sneezed salt water and headed back for the beach. He walked back to the cottage, passing a naked couple along the way, and stood under the outdoor shower, washing off the salt. Holly joined him after a moment, and they soaped each other.

"So," she said, "how do you like being a spy so far?"

"I'm not the spy, you are. I'm here under my own name, remember."

"So you are." She grabbed a towel and began drying herself, while Stone dried her back.

"What do you want to do today?"

"I want to have a look at Black Mountain," she said, "from the top."

They borrowed Thomas's station wagon and drove out of the resort and along the beach. When they came to a fork in the road, with a sign pointing to Black Mountain, Holly said, "Stick to the beach; let's not be too obvious. You have to be sneaky when you're a spy."

"Whatever you say." Stone drove along the beach road, and they entered and left a small village.

After half an hour of sightseeing Holly said, "Okay, now let's head for Black Mountain." She looked up at the mountaintop. "The old man seems to be shedding his gray hair."

Stone made his way back to the fork and took the other route. The road rose quickly as they made their way, and soon it was more humid, and the vegetation changed. "St. Marks seems to have a rain forest," Stone said. "I never knew that."

They passed a construction crew working on the road. "Looks like they started at the top and worked their way down," Holly said as the road wound back and forth toward the peak over new tarmac.

They passed a few houses, most of them set close to the road, but as they climbed, the houses got larger and were set farther back. Near the top of the mountain they came to a roundabout with a parking area. Stone pulled over, and they got out of the car and looked at the view. They could see all the way back to English Harbour and could have counted the yachts in the marina if they had wished.

Holly put a hand on Stone's shoulder. "Don't turn around, but there's a gate on the other side of the roundabout, and a driveway going up a little higher. When we walk back to the car, follow the road with your eye, and you'll see a bit of rooftop in the trees. I'll bet that's Irene Foster's place."

"Does Irene have money?" Stone asked. "Because this has got to be prime real estate up here, and Thomas said she renovated the place. I wouldn't think she could do that on a government pension."

"I'll ask Lance when I talk to him later today," she replied. "Why, do you think she's getting money from Teddy?"

"I don't know, what do you think?"

"Teddy has never been strapped for funds. He's an inventor, has a bunch of patents on various things, including some of that stuff you see sold on the television shopping channels, choppers and slicers. Word is that over the years, he's gotten nice royalty checks

every year, and after his so-called death, they were paid to an offshore bank."

"You said Teddy has a history of always having an escape route?"

"That's right. When they found him at the cottage in Maine, he
got out through a tunnel and made his way to the little airport there
before they could catch up to him. That's why the navy fighters
were ordered after him."

"Well, as far as I can tell, there's only one way up and down this
mountain, and that doesn't augur well for an escape plan."

"Good point."

They looked at the view for a few more minutes, then drove back
down Black Mountain.

"I'll ask Thomas about other routes up and down the mountain,"
Stone said. "He'll know."

B ack at the cottage, Holly produced a satellite telephone and
went outside to call Lance. She returned after a few minutes.
"Irene has some savings besides her pension and an inheritance from
her father, for a total of a little over two million dollars," she said.

"That ought to be enough to buy a house here and renovate it,"
Stone said. "We'll ask Thomas; he probably knows what she paid;
he seems to know everything else around here."

T hey had lunch served by Jacob on their terrace, and in the middle of it their telephone rang.

Jacob came out of the house with a cordless phone. "It's Mr.
Hardy for you," he said, handing the phone to Stone.

"Hello?"

"I thought you'd like to know that Irene Foster just came into the
dining room for lunch," Thomas said, "and she's with a man I've
never seen before."

9

Stone and Holly walked into the dining room, took seats at the bar and, without looking around, ordered piña coladas. They made a point of gazing into each other's eyes and touching a lot, then Holly turned toward the tables and leaned against the bar.

"See them?" Stone asked.

"Give me a minute," she said. "It's crowded." She looked some more. "Don't turn around, but I've got 'em. I think."

"Well, is it they, or is it not?"

"Okay, it's Irene. I've never seen the guy before."

"Describe him."

"Don't know about height; he's sitting down. Mid-fifties, red-dish brown hair, gray at the temples. It's like that color when men use something to cover the gray? I don't know why they bother, it's so noticeable. He's heavier than Teddy."

"People gain weight."

"They don't grow hair," she said. "From here, it doesn't look like a wig, and the first time I saw Teddy—both times, I guess—he was wearing wigs. But his colleagues at the agency said he had been going bald for years, and the last time they saw him, he was nearly completely bald on top."

"Hair transplants?"

"On St. Marks? Before that, I don't think he had the time; he was a busy fellow, killing people."

"Did he really kill the speaker of the house, Efton?"

"The FBI thinks so, but there was no physical evidence to connect him to the crime. The Agency thinks he killed that Supreme Court justice, the young one who died in the auto accident."

"The one who drove off a mountain in Maryland?"

"Right."

"And a Secret Service agent was driving his car?"

"An SUV."

"Why does the Agency think he was murdered? I never read anything about that in the papers. It was an icy road in the mountains."

"It took nearly a year to figure it out, but the secret was in the chip that controlled the car's electronic stability system."

"A faulty chip?"

"Not faulty; altered."

"Altered how?"

"The stability system works by applying the brakes selectively to the wheels when it senses a skid. It does it faster than a human can, and it can brake just one wheel. The chip had been altered so that when it sensed the skid, it applied the brakes not to the correct wheels but to the opposite wheel or wheels. So instead of defeating the skid, it made it immediately worse. The driver couldn't keep up with it."

"Are they sure it wasn't a manufacturing fault?"

"No, but this sort of thing had never happened before."

"That the chip company would admit."

"Right."

"Well, it's a very clever way to murder somebody, but that kind of attempt would have a very low success rate. I mean, the killer would have to know that the car would be in conditions conducive to an accident."

"It was public knowledge that the justice had a house in the mountains, and the weather report for the day is all the information Teddy would need."

"Okay, I buy it. Can I turn around and look at these people now, please?"

"You can look at the guy up close; he's headed this way."

Stone turned and looked at the man, who had come up to the bar on the side opposite from Holly. She was right about his hair; colored, but real.

"Morning," the man said to everybody.

"Good morning."

"Bartender, do you have any Alka-Seltzer back there?" the man asked.

"Yes, sir." A glass of water was placed on the bar and two tablets began to fizz.

"I've got to stop eating my own cooking," the man said. His accent was mildly southern.

"You're eating your own cooking on vacation?" Stone asked, grateful for the opening.

"I came in on a boat last night," the man said. "Sailed it down from Lauderdale."

"Singlehanded?"

"Yep. A lot of fun."

"I've done a little of that. I sailed a fifty-footer from here to Lauderdale a few years back."

"Mine's smaller than that," the man said. It's a Hinckley Bermuda Forty."

"Nice boat. Easy to singlehand?"

"Well, I improved the deck layout a little for singlehanding, and GPS sure makes the navigation easier."

"How'd you pick St. Marks?"

"Well, I was going sailing, anyway, and . . ." He stuck out his hand. "By the way, my name is Harry Pitts."

Stone shook the hand. "Stone Barrington."

"Lady I used to go out with has a place here, so I dropped in to see her, thought I'd rest up for a week or two. Where you from?"

"New York."

"I'm from a little town in Virginia you never heard of. What business you in?"

"Attorney. You?"

"I had a very nice home improvement business; sold it a couple of years ago and retired. Bored out of my skull, until I went sailing. A friend took me out on the Chesapeake, and I kind of went nuts about it. Excuse me." He picked up the glass, drank the fizzy liquid, belched, and set the glass down. "Nice to meet you," he said. "I'd better rejoin my lady. If you're around later, I'll buy you a drink."

"I'd like that," Stone said.

"You staying here?"

"Yes, cottage number one, down on the beach. Why don't you both join us for a drink around six?"

"That's mighty nice of you; let me check with Irene, and I'll get back to you." He gave a little wave and went back to his table.

"What do you think?" Stone asked.

"He's not Teddy, but that was good about asking them for a drink; at least we'll get to talk to Irene. He's waving at you."

Stone looked over at the table. Harry Pitts was making a circle with his thumb and forefinger and nodding, then held up six fingers.

Stone gave an acknowledging wave and turned back to his piña colada. "It would be a plus if they didn't turn out to be awful bores," he said.

"I don't see how anybody who rose as far in the Agency as Irene could turn out to be a bore," Holly replied.

"Any way you slice it," Stone said, "she was a bureaucrat."

10

Their guests arrived at ten minutes past six, laughing. It seemed that they had already had at least one drink, but Stone poured vodka gimlets that he had made the night before and stored in the freezer. Introductions were made.

"So," Stone said, "are you both from Virginia?"

"How did you know that?" Irene Foster asked.

"Harry said he was from a small town in Virginia that I never heard of."

"Well, I'm from Virginia, but not from a town you never heard of, or from any other town," Irene replied, taking a big sip of her gimlet. "I'm a country girl."

Harry Pitts laughed. "She's the slickest country girl you ever met," he said. "She worked for the CIA for more than twenty years."

"*Harry!*" Irene exclaimed.

"What's the matter? Is it still a secret?"

"Sort of," she muttered.

"It wasn't a secret when you worked there," he said. "Why is it a secret now?"

"I'm sorry," Stone said. "I didn't mean to pry."

"You're not prying," Irene said. "It's just that when you work for the Agency for so long, you get used to not discussing your work. I used to tell people I worked for the Agriculture Department; that usually stopped the conversation in its tracks."

Everybody laughed.

"This is one hell of a good drink," Harry said, taking another sip and savoring it. "How do you make it?"

"Pour six ounces out of a fifth of vodka, replace it with Rose's sweetened lime juice, and put it in the freezer until it hurts to hold the bottle. If you make it in a cocktail shaker, you just water it down."

"Well, I'll be damned," Harry said. "So easy!"

"Certainly is."

Dino jumped in. "What part of the CIA did you work for, Irene? Were you a spy? Or is my question a no-no?"

"It's not a no-no," Irene said. "I worked in the operations section, but I wasn't a spy; I just worked with spies. I was an administrator."

"Was it exciting?" Genevieve asked.

"Sometimes it was dull as dishwater," Irene replied. "And sometimes it was way too exciting. It was kind of fun doing work that nobody knew about, only the people you worked with. It was sort of like a club." She held up her glass. "May I have another of these?"

"Of course," Stone said and went to the freezer for the bottle. He came back and poured both Irene and Harry a drink.

"Did you ever work with that guy who killed all those people?" Holly asked. "I forget his name; something about a Teddy Bear."

Stone tried to keep a straight face. "I know the one you mean," he said. "He got blown up in an airplane explosion."

"Oh, yes," Irene said. "Teddy Fay. Teddy worked with people all over the Agency; he was a technical expert. I knew him, but mostly ten or fifteen years ago."

Harry chimed in. "What does a technical expert do?"

"All sorts of things: communications, documentation, weapons—you name it."

"I would have liked to do something like that," Harry said wistfully. "After you've been in the home improvement business for a few years, there aren't any surprises; one kitchen or bathroom looks pretty much like all the others."

"You make it sound boring, Harry," Stone said. "Was it?"

"Well, not really. Once I was doing well enough to hire people it wasn't so repetitive. After that I just went around and worked up estimates, then inspected the work. I like to think I had a reputation for quality."

"That's hard to come by these days," Stone said. "I did most of the work on the renovation of my house, and every time I hired somebody else, I had to watch them like a hawk to make sure the work got done right."

"You're good with your hands, then?" Harry asked.

"You're pretty good with your hands, too, Harry," Irene said, leering at him.

Harry seemed embarrassed.

"My father was a carpenter and a cabinetmaker and a furniture builder, to his own designs," Stone said. "I worked in his shop part-time as a kid."

"You can learn a lot from the right man," Harry said.

"He started out by slinging his tool kit over his shoulder and going around, door to door, in Greenwich Village, asking people if they had any odd jobs. He could fix anything. I still have some of the furniture he made."

"I would have liked to know him," Harry said. "I admire people like that."

"Irene," Genevieve said, "is it true that the CIA can listen in on just about anybody's phone conversations and read their e-mail?"

"You're thinking of the National Security Agency," Irene said. "They're the electronics wizards. Most of what the Agency does is just collect information, sort it and analyze it. Of course, there are actual spies, some of them in embassies around the world, pretending to be diplomats, others out on their own spying on people and cultivating sources in foreign governments and societies."

"I would have liked to be a spy," Genevieve said.

"Well, you're beautiful enough," Dino responded.

"What kind of law do you practice, Stone?" Harry asked.

"I'm of counsel to a large law firm in New York, but I work out of a home office."

"Why is that?"

"I handle the stuff the firm doesn't want to be seen to handle, a lot of it personal, for their clients."

"That sounds as interesting as the CIA," Irene said.

"Probably not. I had a cousin who was in the CIA, but I didn't know that until after his death."

"Who was that?" Irene asked.

"His name was Dick Stone."

"Jesus, I knew Dick; everybody knew Dick. He had just been appointed deputy director for operations when he was killed. A lot of people who should know thought he was on track to be the next Director of Central Intelligence when Katharine Rule Lee retires, which she probably will do when her husband leaves office."

"I didn't know that," Stone said.

"You must know Lance Cabot," she said. "He led the investigation into Dick's death."

"Yes, we, ah, worked together on that. I used to be a homicide detective on the NYPD; Dino still is."

"You were up in Maine, then?"

"Yes."

"Then you probably met Ed Rails, who's retired from the Agency."

"I did."

"How did you meet Lance?"

"He came to see me when he heard that I was Dick's cousin, told me Dick was dead. I was also the executor of his will."

"So you only met him recently, then."

"Yes," Stone lied, "last summer, for a couple of weeks."

"Who's Lance Cabot?" Harry asked.

"He's just a guy at the Agency who wants Dick Stone's job," Irene said. "He might even get it."

"I didn't know that, either," Stone lied again. He raised his glass. "Well, good luck to him."

Irene did not raise her glass. "Fuck him," she said.

11

The following afternoon, while the others were napping, Stone took a stroll down to the marina. The place had been expanded since his earlier visit; there were probably three dozen berths, as opposed to the previous dozen, but there was only one Hinckley Bermuda 40. He walked down the pontoon and looked her over.

Harry said he had changed the deck layout, and Stone saw that the halyard winches had been moved to the top of the coachroof, a sensible change, since it allowed sails to be hoisted from the cockpit, and two large electric winches had replaced the original equipment. A windvane self-steering system was attached to the stern, with its attendant lines, and both the headsail and main were roller reefing.

"Hello there," a voice behind him said. Harry had appeared with a couple of shopping bags.

"Hello, Harry; I was just looking over your boat."

"Come aboard, then," Harry said. Yachtsmen were always anxious to show off their boats. Harry unlocked the hatch, set the shopping bags below and waved Stone down.

Stone climbed down the companionway ladder and looked around. He had never seen a more neatly kept vessel; the yacht was the very definition of "shipshape." "I'm impressed," he said.

"Thank you, Stone, I've done a lot of work on her." He began showing Stone his stowage plan, his tool locker and his central heating system. Finally, they sat down, and Harry produced a pair of bloody marys.

"Thanks for the drink last night," Harry said. "I'm sorry Irene got a little snockered; we had a drink before we left the house, and it was all on an empty stomach."

"We enjoyed having you. It was interesting hearing about her work at the CIA."

"Yeah, she's gotten so she likes to talk about it, if she has a good audience. Funny, your cousin being employed there."

"Yes; as I said, I didn't even know that until he was dead. Our respective sides of the family didn't talk much, but the summer I was eighteen, his folks invited me up to Dark Harbor, in Maine, to spend a few weeks. Dick and I got fairly close at that time, but I didn't see him again until eight or nine years ago, when he took me out to dinner in New York. I thought he was working for the State Department. Then, all of a sudden, he sent me a retainer and his will and appointed me his executor. A few days later, he was dead, murdered."

"And you never talked in all those years apart?"

"Just that one dinner."

"What does your girlfriend do?"

"Ginny? She has a little flying school in Florida. We met when I bought an airplane in Vero Beach from Piper some years ago, and we've seen each other once in a while since then."

"And Dino?"

"Dino's a cop, a detective; we used to be partners when I was on the force. His girl, Genevieve, is an emergency room nurse at a hospital in New York."

"You're a mixed group."

"I guess we are at that. Tell me, how is it you have enough power for those electric winches?"

"I put in larger batteries and a second alternator; I never did like grinding winches."

"I'm with you there. Did you enjoy your solo time on the way down here?"

"I did, though I have to admit, I got a little horny." He grinned. "I was glad to see Irene when I got here."

"So you were close back in Virginia?"

"I wouldn't say close; she seemed to work constantly and didn't have a lot of free time, but we got together now and then."

"Did she talk about her work in those days?"

"Not a peep. I didn't even know what she did, until one of my other customers, her neighbor, told me."

"How'd she end up here?"

"Well, when she retired she went to St. Barts, but she didn't like it much. She likes it better here; less highfalutin and they speak English. Real estate prices are lower, too."

"Did you do any of the renovation on her place?"

"No, I just got here a couple of days ago; she hired a local firm, and they did a pretty good job. I'm cleaning up their work here and there and doing a couple of little things for her."

"I'm sure she's glad to have you here. How long are you staying?"

"Oh, a few weeks, I guess; until the wanderlust bites again, or until Irene and I can't stand each other anymore."

"Were you ever married, Harry?"

"Nope; lifelong bachelor."

"Me, too," Stone said. "Not a bad life."

"Not bad at all."

They seemed to have run out of things to talk about. Stone glanced at his watch. "Well, I'd better get back to the cottage; the others are napping, but there was talk of an afternoon swim."

"I hear that's a nudie beach down there."

"I can confirm that."

"I've gotta have a look at that; Irene would probably like it, too. By the way, she's looking forward to having you all for dinner; she's cooking up a storm. I don't think she knows all that many locals, so she's glad of the company."

"We're looking forward, too," Stone said. They shook hands, and Stone walked back to the cottage.

Holly came out of the bedroom, yawning. "Hey, where you been?"

"I took a walk down to the marina; saw Harry's boat, and we had a nice chat. He pumped me a little, but not enough to be unseemly."

"Did you pump him, too?"

"Not much; didn't want to seem too curious."

"Just as well."

"Something interesting, though; Harry turns out to be a neat-freak. I've never seen a boat that well put together: a place for every-thing, and everything in its place."

"You know, when Teddy got away from New York, we found the place he had used as a workshop. It was cleaned out, but I remem-ber one thing: there was a lot of pegboard on the walls, where tools had been hanging, and he had painted the outline of every tool, so he'd know where to replace it after he'd used it. That's being pretty neat."

"I think that's pretty obsessive. I didn't see anything like that aboard his boat, but I guess he has neatness in common with Teddy."

"He's not Teddy; he's an entirely different physical type. And then there's the hair, of course. I don't think Teddy could have learned how to grow hair since he left New York."

"I have to agree," Stone said.

"Feel like a swim?" she asked, unbuttoning her blouse.

"Oh, yeah," Stone said, shucking off clothes.

12

L ance Cabot sat in his borrowed office at Langley, sifting through his notes. The phone rang. "Lance Cabot."

"Mr. Cabot, this is Eileen, in the director's office. The director would like to see you."

"Of course. When?"

"Right now, if you're available."

"I'll be there shortly."

Lance closed his notebook, checked his hair in the mirror and slipped into the jacket of his pinstriped suit. He walked swiftly down the hallway, across the building to the director's office, which was on the same floor, and presented himself to her secretary.

"Go right in, Mr. Cabot," she said.

"Please, Eileen, it's Lance." He flashed her a smile, rapped lightly on the door and opened it.

"Come in, Lance," Kate Lee said. She rose and walked to a seating area on the other side of her large office and waved him to a chair next to her.

"Good morning, Director."

"Please, call me Kate, when we're not in meetings. It makes me more comfortable."

It made Lance more comfortable, too. He wanted to be on an informal basis with her. There was an office down the hall that he very much wanted to fill. "Thank you, Kate." Lance liked the idea of working for a woman; he got along very well with women.

"Lance, I believe you're the best-dressed man at Langley," she said, smiling.

Lance laughed. "It's all those years of working out of London."

"I'm sure if you're here long enough, you'll raise the sartorial level among the other gentlemen in the building."

"I doubt it," Lance said.

"So do I. Where are we on the Teddy Fay matter?"

"Moving along. Holly and her group are ensconced in St. Marks, and they've already made contact with Irene Foster."

"How did they go about that?"

"It turned out to be quite easy. They're staying at an inn that has the best restaurant on the island, and Irene came in for dinner. Her companion introduced himself, and Stone invited them for drinks."

"Her companion?"

"Yes, but it's not Teddy; it's someone she knew in Virginia before she retired, a building contractor named Harry Pitts."

"Tell me why you believe he is not Teddy."

"A different physical type, and he has hair, which Teddy was short of."

"Are there any photographs of Teddy when he was younger, when he had more hair?"

"There are no photographs of Teddy at all."

"Oh, yes, I knew that."

"Have you checked out this Pitts fellow?"

"Yes, and he's who he says he is. He was well known in the area for remodeling work—kitchens, that sort of thing. He sold his business last year and took up sailing. He sailed into St. Marks earlier this week and is staying at Irene's."

"As long as you're satisfied."

"If Teddy is on St. Marks—and I'm inclined to believe he is—then he's not going to be very visible, and he's certainly not going to be living at Irene's house, not this soon. He would not just show up, but go to some lengths to insinuate himself gradually into the landscape."

"I suppose. What has Holly learned about Irene?"

"That she's lonely and probably drinks a little too much."

"She didn't when she was still here."

"She's acquired a reputation for picking up men and taking them home. She didn't do that here, either."

"Not that we know of."

"It's my assumption that if she did, you'd know it."

"Well, she went through the usual periodic vetting and polygraph; we didn't spend a lot of time spying on her. She was a trusted member of the Company for a long time, and she was bloody good at what she did."

"That means if she was helping Teddy, she was good enough to hide it."

"Certainly."

"Holly and her crew are having dinner at her home tonight; perhaps they'll turn up something new there."

"I'm impressed," Kate said.

"Holly's a very bright girl; what she lacks in formal Agency training, she makes up for in her personal experience in her military and police careers, and her ingenuity."

"You think she'll make station chief someday?"

"She's smart enough; I think it will depend on whether that's what she wants. She seems happiest in the field right now."

"What about you, Lance? Do you think you'd make a good deputy director for operations?"

Lance hadn't expected that, but he didn't hesitate. "I believe I would, Kate."

"Certainly, everything in your career points to that; you've done very well."

"Thank you, Kate."

"There's an attitude among the older hands here that makes them suspicious of younger men who seem to want things a little too much. It's almost British; the Brits don't like naked ambition."

"I've tried to keep my ambition very well clothed," Lance replied.

Kate laughed aloud. "Yes, well, there is that." She rearranged herself in her chair. "During the next four years—assuming my husband is reelected—I want to replace retiring senior people with very high quality younger people who will set the tone at the Agency for years, perhaps decades to come."

"I've no doubt that he will be reelected, and I think there's ample talent here for you to do that."

"I must tell you that Dick Stone's murder knocked a big hole in my plans. I thought he had it in him to be the best DDO in the history of the Agency, and that, after some time had passed, he might replace me when I go."

"I'm in complete agreement on Dick's brilliance; I worked for him for seven years, and I saw it at first hand. I learned a lot from him."

"I believe you did, Lance, and that's one of the main reasons you're under consideration for the job he never had a chance to fill."

"Thank you, Kate."

"I know it's difficult working for Hugh English, but he was kind enough to postpone his retirement and keep doing the job until our vetting procedure is complete. Be nice to him, won't you?"

Lance had always found Hugh English grating, but he had been smart enough to keep it to himself and not join in the chorus of complaints from the other, younger men in his former station. "Of course; he's a good man."

"Lance, are you going to leave in a huff if you don't get the job? Go out and make some money as a consultant for the networks and the oil companies?"

Lance was considering doing just that, if he didn't get the job. He took a deep breath. "No," he said. "I'm a career officer; I'm here for the long haul."

"Good," Kate said, getting to her feet. "Thank you, Lance; keep me posted on progress in St. Marks."

"Certainly, Kate," Lance said. He returned to his office more slowly than he had come. Could Lee really be considering him, or was that just a ruse to keep him pumped on the business in St. Marks?

The balance could tip either way, he thought. He'd have to do something to get a thumb on the scale.

13

Teddy Fay's cell phone vibrated against his ribcage. "Yes?"

"Mr. Elliot?"

"Yes."

"This is Tito, the maintenance manager at Nevis Aero Services."

"Yes, Tito?"

"We're just about done with the annual on your airplane. You need a new set of spark plugs—I'd suggest the platinum ones— and your starboard main gear tire is pretty close to needing replacing."

"The platinum plugs are fine, and go ahead and replace the tire. Do you have a replacement from the same manufacturer of the other two?"

"Yes, sir; they're Goodyears, and we stock those. Will you be picking up the airplane when we're done? It should be ready tomorrow."

"What's the bill going to come to?"

"A little under three thousand."

"Charge it to the credit card number I gave you, and leave a copy of the bill on the seat. I've rented hangar number four, so put the airplane in there and lock it up. The combination on the lock is 4340."

"Yes, sir; it'll be in there by tomorrow night."

"Thank you, Tito."

"Let us know if you need anything else."

"Will do."

Teddy hung up and continued driving. Less than a minute passed before the phone vibrated again. "Yes?"

"Mr. Martin?"

"Yes?"

"This is Cornwall Shipping Agents; the shipment you told us to expect arrived this morning. It should clear customs by noon tomorrow."

"Oh, good; what's the tariff going to be?"

"Around eight hundred dollars."

"All right; charge it to the credit card number I gave you."

"Do you want it delivered?"

"How large is it?"

"Two wooden crates, one about eight feet long, the other about five feet. Not all that heavy, though."

"I'll pick them up tomorrow afternoon, then. Will they be ready to go?"

"Yes, sir, just back up to our loading dock and tell the man on duty you want shipment number 00028, and make sure he gives you both crates."

"See you then." Teddy hung up. This was all coming together very well, he thought. His purchase ostensibly included all the tools he would need, but he was going to have to buy a chain saw.

Right now, though, all Teddy needed was a drink.

14

Kate Lee was dropped by her driver at the White House entrance, and, led and followed by her Secret Service agents, she took the elevator to the family quarters. The two agents remained at the downstairs elevator door. It was nearly eight o'clock, and she was exhausted.

As she got off the elevator she was grateful for the smells coming from the family kitchen. She flung her coat at a living room chair, dropped her bulging briefcase on the floor beside it, then walked into the kitchen.

"Excuse me," she said to the man in the apron with his back to her, "who do I have to fuck around here to get a drink?"

Will Lee looked over his shoulder, turned the steaks on the grill of the Viking stove and came toward her. "You're looking at him," he said, kissing her and dragging a stool up to the kitchen island for her. He went to the freezer and extracted a full bottle of premade, very dry martinis, poured her one in a crystal glass and dropped in two olives. He handed her the drink. "My new speciality," he said, picking up his own glass. They raised their glasses, gazed into each other's eyes and took large sips.

"Mmmmm," she said, "and what is the secret of this libation? What gives it that interesting *something*?"

"That interesting *something* is that the olives are stuffed with anchovies."

"But I hate anchovies," she said.

"That's why it was a secret."

"This is the second time you've fooled me with anchovies: the first was when you put pureed anchovies into a hollandaise sauce."

"You're forgetting the caesar salad dressing," Will said. "Anchovies are an important ingredient of that. I think that what you are learning here is that you absolutely *love* anchovies."

"Only when I don't know I'm eating them," Kate said.

Will turned the steaks. "How was your day?"

"Like all my days: unrelenting."

"Anything special?"

"I spoke with Lance Cabot about the business in St. Marks."

"And?"

"He says things are going swimmingly. Holly Barker has made contact with Irene Foster; in fact, she and the others are having dinner at her house, presumably as we speak."

"Well, I'm glad they're all getting along together so swimmingly. Is this going to help find Teddy Fay?"

"Maybe, and we should never speak that name. The Republicans may have bugged our kitchen."

"I find a little paranoia a good thing in a director of Central Intelligence," Will said, "but not *that* much paranoia."

"I'll try to tamp it down," Kate said.

Will put the steaks on large plates, added baked potatoes and *haricot verts* and motioned for Kate to follow. He led her into the living room to a table for two in an alcove overlooking the White House grounds, their favorite place for dining alone. He seated her, lit the candles and poured the California cabernet that he had already opened, then sat down. They raised their glasses and dug into their food.

"This is the best steakhouse in the world," Kate said.

"You certainly know the way to a fellow's heart," Will replied.

"Did the new polls come in today?"

"Yes, and we're looking good. I've got at least a twelve-point lead over any one of the three likely Republican challengers."

"I wish it were more."

"Who doesn't? But I'll take twelve points."

"That lead could vanish in the blink of an eye if it became known that . . . what's-his-name is alive, having escaped two huge federal efforts to capture him, especially since the public has been repeatedly assured that he's dead."

"If that happens, I'll deal with it," Will said. "It will help that the ranking Republican senator on the Senate Select Committee on Intelligence knows the truth."

"It won't help if he decides to leak the information to some right-wing talk show host."

"If he does that, he'll have to explain why he waited for so long after he found out to tell anybody. I don't think he would enjoy that; he's up for reelection too, you know."

"Thank God for that."

"I know you don't like to talk about this, Kate, but suppose Lance's people find Teddy and capture him? What then?"

"We could build a special prison for him at Guantánamo Bay."

"He'd break out of it inside a week. What instructions have you given Lance in the matter?"

"I've given him no instructions whatever."

"And is he going to interpret the lack of instructions as a license to do whatever he feels like doing?"

"I haven't told him to do that, either."

"You're hoping Lance will just make it go away."

"I'm hoping all sorts of things: I'm hoping Teddy is in a block of ice in Antarctica; I'm hoping he was eaten by a shark the last time he went swimming; I'm hoping he'll put a bullet in his brain, then fall into an active volcano."

"Yes, Teddy is an inconvenient person."

"I'm also hoping he wishes to remain dormant, because if he took it into his head to start killing people again . . . Well, I don't know how we would handle that."

"Perhaps leaving him alone wherever he is is the best move."

"We'll have that option, if Lance's people find him on St. Marks. We could just keep him under surveillance and hope for the best."

"I like that option best," Will said, "except the surveillance part; he'd twig immediately."

"You never give me official orders when we're drinking."

"Just think of it as a firm suggestion."

"I think that, tomorrow morning, when we're both entirely sober, you might give me a written finding to that effect that I can log and store in my safe at Langley."

"But then I would be on record as saying that a murderer, having been found, should remain free. God knows," Will said, "I would hate to see him tried. I think I'd rather invade Iran or Korea."

"Remember, we don't have an extradition treaty with St. Marks, yet."

"State has been working on that since their new prime minister took over."

"Do you think you could possibly slow them down?"

"I think it would be impossible to slow them down, since they're already going as slowly as possible, with no help from me."

"If Teddy is in St. Marks, and we sign an extradition treaty, he could bolt for other, less arresting climes."

"And then we'd have to start all over again?"

"Exactly."

"It's the perfect conundrum, isn't it?"

"It is."

15

Thomas arranged for Stone to rent a car for the remainder of their stay, and early in the evening they drove up Black Mountain for dinner at Irene Foster's.

"Funny," Holly said as they climbed the steep road, "I didn't notice before but there are underground power lines running alongside the road, and a pipeline, too. See the markers?" She pointed them out.

"Odd for a small island to go to the expense of putting power and water underground in what seems to be a fairly sparsely populated area."

"The houses may be sparse, but they're expensive," Holly said. "The rich usually are willing to pay for preferential treatment."

Irene's gate was open, but after they drove through, it closed behind them. An SUV and a smaller car with a rental sticker were parked in the paved parking area, and as they got out of their car, Harry Pitts appeared on the front porch to greet them.

"I see you found the place," Harry said.

"It was easy," Stone replied. "There's only one mountaintop in St. Marks."

"You have a point," Harry said. "Come on in, and let me get you a drink." He led them into a fairly large, comfortably furnished living room and waved them to seats. "Irene's busy in the kitchen; she'll be out in a little while. Are you still drinking those vodka gimlets? I made some."

"You betcha," Holly said. "It's easy to sell this crowd gimlets."

Harry produced martini glasses and a frosty Absolut bottle, the liquid inside tinged with green, and poured for everyone. "Cheers," Harry said, raising his glass.

"Wait for me," Irene said from the kitchen door. She entered the room looking cool and well pressed, not like someone who had been cooking all afternoon.

The men stood and greeted her, and Harry handed her a gimlet. "I'm afraid I had one too many of these last night," she said, "but this time I didn't get a head start." Everyone sat down.

"This is a marvelous place," Holly said. "How'd you find it?"

"The usual way, through an agent. Actually, Thomas Hardy was a big help. He knew that Sir Winston Sutherland had bought up here and that he was bringing in electricity and water. The place had been on the market for a long time for lack of utilities. There's a large cistern under the house, and water was collected from the roof, and although the house had been wired in hope of power, it didn't happen until the PM made it happen. Before there were just a small generator and a lot of oil lamps."

"So, you got in ahead of the rise in property values that must have come with the utilities?"

"Thanks to Thomas, yes. I got the place for half what it would bring now."

"Where is Sir Winston's place?"

"Just down the hill a couple of hundred yards, after what used to be the guesthouse for this one. I couldn't afford the guesthouse when I bought, and an expat English couple bought it, but they seem to be rarely here. I've never met them."

"I've noticed," Stone said, "that since the last time I was here the island has taken on an air of prosperity. Has St. Marks attracted some new manufacturing or something?"

"Or something," Harry said. "It's called offshore Internet gambling."

"How does that work?" Genevieve asked.

"A business establishes what amounts to a casino, except it's entirely virtual. Anyone with an Internet connection, anywhere in the world, can play, and winnings or losses are credited or debited to a credit card. There are half a dozen establishments here, and they are hugely profitable. Each of them employs a lot of people, many of them islanders. The managers and computer people are almost entirely from abroad—the States, Europe and Asia—and those people are buying property and building houses. Irene got in under the wire, but it's getting harder and harder to hire construction people. I tell you, if I lived here I'd start a construction company."

"Is there any sort of regulation for the industry?" Dino asked.

"Not really. The United States is trying to ban Internet gambling, but not very successfully. When they started pressing the credit card companies not to process charges from offshore casinos, the casinos just offered their own credit cards, through offshore banks. A gambler can go online, fill out an application and get a credit line in less than two minutes. The card is mailed to him within a week, and he can use it anywhere, like any other credit card.

"The U.S. has arrested a couple of casino operators when they passed through American airports, but as long as they don't enter the States, they're safe. The U.S. and St. Marks have no extradition treaty, and negotiations have been bogged down for years."

"Is there any local regulation in St. Marks?" Dino asked.

"A government department has been set up to regulate the casinos, but rumor has it, the only enforced regulation is to pay Sir Winston Sutherland for the privilege of operating."

"Sir Winston seems to have a finger in every pie," Stone said.

"Indeed he does," Irene said. "There are rumors that he's pulling in over a hundred million dollars a year for himself, and he's established an offshore banking system much like that of the Cayman Islands. He owns his own bank, and his friends own all the others."

"So he's St. Marks's Papa Doc, then?" Dino asked.

"Sir Winston is, practically speaking, almost as much a dictator as Papa Doc Duvalier was in Haiti, but he's smarter and more benign; he spreads the wealth around. The per capita income on the island is said to have doubled within the past few years, and it's expected to double again. Of course, it was pretty low to begin with, but now there are businesses like car dealerships where there were none before. A few years ago, if you wanted a car, you had to go to a dealer in St. Martin or Guadeloupe or Antigua. Now you can buy a Toyota or a Volkswagen off the lot, and there are rumors that Mercedes and BMW dealerships are on the way."

"I can guess who's going to own those," Stone said.

"Sir Winston and his friends, of course," Irene replied.

"So who's getting hurt?" Holly said.

"The suckers," Harry replied, "the losers at gambling. The casinos have a slightly lower profit margin than the Las Vegas establishments, so they're attractive to gamblers, but they still lose, just like in Vegas. The casinos operate without infrastructure—they don't have to invest in building hotels or producing entertainment. There are rumors that those things are in the offing, though, and that will goose tourist income enormously."

A uniformed black woman came into the living room. "Dinner is served, Miss Foster," she said.

Irene rose, led them into the dining room and seated them at a beautifully arranged table, while Harry poured a French wine.

Stone nodded toward the view from the dining room window. "I can see a couple of roofs," he said.

"The big one is Sir Winston's," Irene replied. "The two smaller ones are the former guesthouse, now owned by the Weatherbys, and another small house, owned by the Pembertons; I haven't met them, either."

16

It was nearly midnight when they left Irene's house, after a good dinner and a lot of talk.

"That must be the driveway to the old guesthouse," Holly said, as their headlights flashed over a gate. "And then the Pembertons, and this one coming up must be Sir Winston's place. I wonder why there's no guard."

"Look," Stone said, pointing, "there's a guard shack up the driveway, about thirty yards after the gate."

"So the big man is not unprotected."

"I guess not. This jungle is so thick, there could be a company of infantry hidden in there."

"St. Marks doesn't have an army," Genevieve said. "I read it on the Internet. The island has a police force, but that's all."

"Well, it's not a banana republic, is it?" Dino said. "And I haven't heard anything about a drug problem. If anything, Sir Winston must be guarding against that, if his police are shooting drug smugglers on the beach."

"If he allowed the drug lords in," Stone said, "they'd own him in no time, or they'd kill him and install somebody more cooperative."

"I'm beginning to think this guy is very smart," Dino said. "How'd you manage to beat him in court?"

"Beat him? My client was hanged, or at least, I thought she was. I didn't beat him. She paid a million-dollar bribe to the old prime minister, without my knowledge, and was allowed to leave the country."

"I wonder how the old prime minister met his demise," Holly said.

"Maybe he didn't," Dino said. "Maybe he's rotting in prison."

"I've got to sit down with Thomas and talk with him about this," Stone said. "There doesn't seem to be anything he doesn't know about what's going on here, and he's a member of the local parliament, so he must be knowledgeable about the politics."

"And he's doing very well out of it, too," Holly pointed out.

"Speaking of doing well," Stone said, "how did we do at dinner tonight? What did we learn?"

"A lot about the island," Holly said, "but not much about Irene and Teddy."

"To tell the truth," Stone said, "I'm not sure there's all that much to learn about Irene. If there were, Lance would already have told us about it. There's just the Teddy connection, if it exists."

"Well, we learned how she's able to afford that house," Holly said. "I mean, buying it on the cheap before property values went up. She sets a very nice table, too, and that was an expensive wine."

"My guess is, Harry would have supplied the wine; probably the groceries, too."

"Is Harry rich?"

"He said he had a large home remodeling business, and that he sold it. He seems to have enough money to retire comfortably and buy a very nice yacht."

"How much would the boat cost?" Holly asked.

"I don't know, anywhere from two hundred thousand to half a million, depending on how old it is and how well equipped. Certainly, it's extremely well equipped now, but my guess is that Harry added most of the equipment. He has the kind of stuff that you would more likely find on a yacht costing twice as much—electric winches, big GPS plotter, watermaker, central heating—everything you could cram into a boat of that size. I think she's an inch or two down on her marks from the extra weight."

"So he's a tech junkie," Dino said. "Nothing wrong with that, if he can afford it."

"Teddy's a tech junkie, too," Holly pointed out. "They have that in common."

"Why don't you ask Lance to check out Harry's net worth?" Stone said. "It would be interesting to know where the money is coming from."

"I'll ask him tomorrow," Holly said.

They arrived back at the cottage, let themselves in, and switched on the lights.

"Nobody move," Holly said.

Everybody stood still.

"What?" Stone asked.

"Something's different; things have been moved. That little sculpture was on the other end of the coffee table; the TV was a little more to the left."

"We do have a staff, Holly," Genevieve pointed out. "Maybe they've been cleaning."

"I gave them the rest of the day off late this afternoon," Holly said. "They wouldn't be spending their evening cleaning the house; anyway, it was already clean. Check the bedrooms."

Dino and Genevieve went into their bedroom, while Holly and Stone went into theirs. She began opening drawers, and so did Stone.

"You're right, Holly," he said. "The place has been turned over."

"But not by an expert," she replied. "I mean, it's neat, but it's not the way it was. What could they be looking for?"

"I'll check the safe." Stone went into his dressing room, opened the little safe with his credit card and looked inside. "My cash is still here, and my spare watch," he called, "but my clothes are pushed over on the rack." He went back into the bedroom.

Holly came out of her dressing room. "Same with my stuff; nothing missing."

"A burglar would have taken the TV and stereo and the booze," Stone said.

"Where's your passport?" Holly asked.

"In my jacket pocket," Stone said, feeling for it. "I always carry it when I'm in a foreign place. Yours?"

"In my handbag."

"Was there anything here . . ." He stopped himself, walked over to Holly and whispered in her ear. "Let's check for bugs."

She nodded, and they both went to work. Dino knocked and came into the room. "We're not missing anything," he said, "but you're right; somebody's been through the place." He got no response, but Stone tapped his ear. "Oh," he said, and went back to his own room.

Holly unscrewed the mouthpiece on the phone, then waved to get Stone's attention. He walked over, looked at the small device inside and nodded. Holly left it there and screwed the thing back together. They went into the living room and found the same device on the phone there; there was one in Dino's room, too.

"Why don't we have a nightcap on the terrace?" Stone said. He grabbed a bottle of premade gimlets and some glasses and led them outside. The wind was up a little, and the waves on the shore were making more noise than usual.

They sat down and Stone poured the drinks. "Okay," he said, "who?"

"The way I see it," Holly said, "we've got two choices: Sir Winston's cops or Teddy Fay."

"Any particular thoughts on which?" Stone asked.

She thought for a minute. "Nope, but Lance is going to just love this."

17

S tone walked up to the inn and found Thomas Hardy in his office, working at his computer. He looked up.

"Stone," he said, sounding pleased, "come in and sit down. Would you like some coffee?"

"Thank you, yes, Thomas."

Thomas spoke briefly into the phone, and a moment later, a waiter appeared with a coffeepot and a plate of cookies.

"How is your visit going?" Thomas asked as he poured their coffee.

"Very well, thanks," Stone said, stirring in a sweetener and sipping. "Until last night."

Thomas's eyebrows went up. "Something wrong?"

"We had dinner at Irene Foster's house last night, and when we returned to the cottage we found that it had been ransacked—neatly, but nevertheless, ransacked."

"I'm very sorry," Thomas said, looking concerned. "Was anything missing?"

"Nothing, but some things had been left behind."

"What?"

"All three phone extensions had been bugged."

"*Bugged*?"

"That's right."

"I've never heard of such a thing happening in St. Marks. You're sure about this?"

"Go down to the cottage, unscrew the mouthpiece on any phone, and you'll see the device."

"But who would do such a thing?"

"I was hoping you might have a suggestion."

"Surely you don't think that I . . ."

"No, of course not, Thomas; I apologize if I gave that impression. Our best guesses are Teddy Fay or Sir Winston Sutherland."

"Well, I don't know about Mr. Fay, but certainly Sir Winston would do such a thing, if he thought it in his interest."

"But what could he possibly hope to learn by bugging our quarters?"

Thomas shrugged. "Perhaps you could better tell me. Is there something about your visit to St. Marks that you haven't told me?"

Stone shook his head. "No, there isn't; I've told you everything."

"Let's start with Teddy Fay, then. Is there some reason, assuming he's on the island, that he would bug the premises?"

"I suppose he might want to learn if our presence here has anything to do with looking for him."

"You say the choices of culprit are Fay and Sir Winston; has it occurred to you that they might be combining their efforts?"

"Combining? How?"

"Well, if I were a fugitive living on the island, I might look for some sort of official protection. Mightn't you do the same, if you were Fay?"

"But what would be in it for Sir Winston to hide a fugitive from the United States?"

"Money, of course; does Fay have money?"

"We believe so, but we don't know how much. Anyway, that sort of bribe would be very small compared to the money I understand he's getting from the offshore gambling interests."

Thomas smiled. "It is not my experience of Sir Winston that any sum of money would be too small to escape his attention. But he might have other reasons to assist Mr. Fay; Sir Winston has a supple mind, and it is always attuned to whatever person or information might be useful to him."

"I cannot imagine what use Teddy Fay's presence in his country would be to Sir Winston."

"Perhaps Sir Winston has a more active imagination than you."

Stone laughed. "I'll grant you that. I suppose that could apply to why he might want to listen in on our conversations. Let me ask your advice: should we leave the bugs in place or remove them?"

"If you are guarded in your conversations, perhaps it might be better to leave them in place. If you remove them, it might excite his further curiosity into why you are here—and that would go for both Sir Winston and Teddy Fay."

"That's good advice," Stone said. "By the way, last night the conversation at Irene Foster's house was mostly of Sir Winston's rapidly growing wealth. Anything to that?"

"Ah, there are many rumors, but if they are true, Sir Winston is being careful not to display too much wealth."

"What about his new house on Black Mountain?"

"That's his most visible purchase in the past couple of years, but it's not an ostentatious place. He has always lived well, but he sold his old house for more than he paid for the place on Black Mountain. Of course, the government might have invested in certain improvements to the house, mostly in the line of security."

"Then what's he doing with all his money?"

"You know about his new bank?"

"That came up in the conversation."

"The bank, I'm sure, required considerable capital, and people in Sir Winston's position have always found it useful to own real estate and to warehouse funds in other climes—South America or Switzerland, for instance—in case of the necessity of a quick change of residence. Sir Winston has also been known to visit Miami from time to time, in his newly acquired government airplane."

"He got himself a jet?"

"A more modest King Air turboprop, but I'm told it's very nice and has a lot of range."

"So he has an escape plan?"

"In his position, wouldn't you?"

Stone took in a sharp breath. "Yes, I would, and so would Teddy Fay. Tell me, Thomas, if you had to escape St. Marks in a hurry, how would you do it?"

"Well, there are boats, of course, but if I were being pursued, air travel would be vastly preferable; perhaps a light airplane that could reach Antigua or Guadeloupe or St. Martins. St. Marks has no direct international flights, except to other islands, but international airline connections are available from those places."

"There's only the one airport here?"

"Yes, and a friend of mine now operates the local fixed-base operation and charter service. You'll remember that Chester, who used to own it, died in a plane crash."

"I remember. What's your friend's name?"

"Don Wells, and he would know who on the island owns small airplanes; there wouldn't be many. Please tell him I sent you."

Stone put down his coffee cup. "Thank you, Thomas, for the coffee, the advice and the information."

"Stone, it might be nice if you stopped in to see Sir Leslie Hewitt."

"How is Leslie? He must be very old now."

"My guess would be about eighty-five, but I swear, he hasn't changed a bit in all the years I've known him."

STUART WOODS

"Is he still pretending to be half gaga half the time?"

"Only when it suits his purposes. And you may find that Leslie has a lot of inside knowledge about what goes on in St. Marks."

"Thanks, Thomas, I will go and see him." They shook hands, and Stone headed for his car.

18

Teddy Fay drove down to the docks in Markstown and found the freight shipping company. He followed the signs to the receiving platform, gave the foreman his shipment number and waited. Shortly a forklift appeared, bearing two cardboard-and-wood crates, and loaded them straight into his vehicle. Teddy signed for them and started back.

On his way he passed a large hardware store and turned into their parking lot. He bought a small chain saw and a five-gallon gasoline tank and a can of two-stroke motor oil, loaded them into the truck and went on his way. He stopped at a filling station for gas and filled both his vehicle and the spare tank.

Three-quarters of an hour later he backed the vehicle alongside a pair of cellar doors. Using a hand truck, he managed to get both crates inside, then he went back for the chain saw and the gas tank. He garaged the vehicle, then got the crates open to look at his new toy. It seemed sensible enough. He had ordered the thing to be shipped in a half-completed state, and he read the instructions for completion carefully before beginning work. It never ceased to amaze him that most people never read the instructions, until they got into terrible trouble putting things together. Teddy loved instruction manuals, especially when they dealt with assembling something.

He finished reading the manual, put down a pad for kneeling on the concrete floor and set out the few tools necessary for assembly. There were three basic parts that had to be joined; two had come in the long crate and one in the short one. First, he went through the whole thing, making sure all the bolts had been properly torqued at the factory, then he joined the three parts, tightening the main bolts only with his fingers. When he was satisfied that everything was properly assembled, he removed the main bolts and set them next to the thing in a teacup, ready to be used when needed. He'd have to get it out of the cellar before it could be finally assembled.

That done, he filled the tiny fuel tank of the chain saw, went upstairs and outside and walked around to the other side of the building. A ravine ran along one side, and a concrete spillway about four feet wide, meant to handle the overflow from the cistern during the rainy season, ran from the building down to the ravine. Two fairly tall trees had grown from one side of the ravine and, bracing himself carefully, he started the chain saw with a couple of pulls of the cord and cut down both trees, leaving them to wash down the steep ravine with the next rain.

He went back to the house, cleaned the chain saw, poured the remaining fuel back into the spare tank and put the chain saw away. Everything was ready for when it might be needed.

Finally, he picked up the DVD that had come with the equipment and inserted it in his computer. It took him, step by step, through the operation, and every bit of it made perfect sense to him. He would run the drill over and over in his mind at odd moments of the day, to keep it fresh in his memory.

S tone drove out to the St. Marks Airport and found the fixed-based operations now called Wells Air Services. He found Don Wells in the service hangar, working on the engine of a Cessna 150.

"Good morning, Don, my name is Stone Barrington; I'm a friend of Thomas Hardy."

Don, a short, thick black man, wiped his hands with a greasy rag and shook hands. "Any friend of Thomas's," he said.

"I just need a little information. About how many privately owned airplanes are based here?"

"Well, except for the King Air, which is owned by the government, all of them, I guess."

"How many?"

Don did some counting on his fingers. "Seven," he said.

"Are all of them owned by local residents?"

"Yes."

"How many of the owners are white men?"

"Ah, five."

"Do you know all of them personally?"

"In a manner of speaking. Some of them have been customers since before I bought the business."

"Any new airplane owners in the past few weeks?"

"Two of them," Don replied, "a Bonanza and a Cessna 140."

"Who owns them?"

"The Bonanza is owned by one of the casinos, or, I guess, by one of the people there. His name is Brent; he's one of the top people in the company, I think."

"Can you describe him?"

"About thirty-five years old, five-ten, well over two hundred pounds, dark hair."

"And who's the owner of the 140?"

"He's fairly new on the island, older fellow, a retiree from England. His name is . . . let me think a second . . . Robertson."

"Description?"

"Close to six feet, slim, thick salt-and-pepper hair, early seventies, I'd say. Nice fellow."

"Where is the airplane?"

"I've got four T-hangars," Don replied. "It's in one of them."

"Could I have a look at it?"

"Sure. Follow me." Don led the way outside and down a row of hangars, stopping at one of them and entering the combination for its padlock. He hauled the door upward to reveal the airplane.

Stone walked slowly around the aircraft, then opened the pilot's door and climbed in, looking at the instrument panel. Stone was impressed. The Cessna 140 was the predecessor of the 172, the world's most popular airplane, and it qualified as an antique. This one was in beautiful condition and seemed to be entirely original; all the equipment—radios and flight instruments—was period stuff.

"This is really something. Do you know where he got the airplane?"

"He said he had owned it for more than forty years, since it was new. When he bought his house here, he had the wings taken off, then shipped the whole thing in a container to St. Martin, where they put the wings back on. Then he flew it over here."

"Well, thanks, Don. It was a treat just to look at this machine." Stone made a note of the airplane's British registration number.

"Anything else I can do for you?"

"No, I don't think so."

"You a pilot?"

"Yes, I am."

"What do you fly?"

"I've had a Piper Malibu Mirage for a few years, and I'm having it converted to a turboprop right now."

"Sounds hot."

"It will be."

"Well, I've got to get back to work; gotta have that 150 finished today."

"Thanks very much for the information," Stone said. "I'd appreciate it if you'd keep our conversation to yourself."

"Sure, I will. Say hello to Thomas."

"I will, Don. Good day."

Stone got back into his car and headed back to the inn. Holly could get Lance to check out the registration number of the 140.

19

As Stone drove back toward the inn he recognized the turning to Sir Leslie Hewitt's cottage, and he swung left into the road. As long as he was out this way, he might as well stop in. He drove up a long hill then turned into the drive, marked by a mailbox, then parked the car in the gravel turnaround and knocked on the door. No answer. He tried again, then he walked around the cottage and let himself through the garden gate. Sir Leslie was a few yards away, kneeling on a gardener's stool, digging in the soil with a trowel.

"Leslie?"

The old man turned and peered at him through thick, steel-rimmed eyeglasses. "Stone? Is it Stone?"

"Yes, it is."

Sir Leslie struggled to his feet and walked toward Stone, taking off his gloves. He was a small, very black man with white curls and a clean-shaven face. They shook hands. "I am so very glad to see you, Stone; I had heard you were on the island, and I had hoped you would come to see me."

"I couldn't visit St. Marks without seeing you."

"Will you have some tea?"

"Thank you, yes."

Sir Leslie waved him to a table and chairs in the garden and went into the kitchen. He came out shortly with a teapot and a plate of cookies and set them down. "How have you been? What have you been up to? Any interesting cases?"

"I've been busy doing a lot of things, but I haven't spent all that much time in court lately."

"I'm sorry to hear it; it is your natural habitat."

"Thank you, Leslie; that's high praise coming from such an eminent barrister. How about you? Any interesting cases?"

"Only the small stuff. As usual, I specialize in annoying the government in small ways."

"That must give you great satisfaction. I hear there have been a lot of changes around here."

"Oh, yes, and it has been fascinating to watch. Winston is in what you Americans call hog heaven; he is enjoying himself immensely, while turning the screws on anyone who gets in his way."

"I hope you're staying out of his way."

"Oh, yes, I just peck around the fringes, but I hear a lot of things."

"Thomas told me you are a fount of information."

"Well, if there were a St. Marks version of the parlor game called 'Trivial Pursuit,' I would do very well at it, I think. Are you looking for information, Stone?" Sir Leslie asked.

"I think I'm looking for more of an opinion."

Sir Leslie grinned. "I am full of opinions."

"Well, then, here's the situation: Some friends and I are staying in one of Thomas's new cottages, and we came home last night to find that someone had searched the place. We also discovered that all the telephones had listening devices planted in them. Now who would do such a thing? What is your opinion?"

"Oh, that's an easy one," Sir Leslie said. "Colonel Croft. Colonel Croyden Croft, who is in charge of a department called Internal Investigations—ostensibly under the Home Secretary, but he is a creature of Winston Sutherland."

"And why would he wish to bug the cottage of some tourists?"

"Because he can, and very likely because Winston wished it. As I recall, you were a tourist the last time you were here, but before you left you had caused Winston a great deal of bother. As much as I enjoyed watching it and being a part of it, I must tell you that I feared more for your safety than I let on at the time."

"Do you fear for my safety just because I'm here again?"

"Let me put it this way: I think that if Winston could think of a plausible reason to arrest you, and perhaps your friends, jail you for a few days, then throw you ignominiously off the island, it would give him great pleasure to do so." He smiled. "But I think it is unlikely that he would go so far as hanging you, as he tried so hard to do with the lovely Allison."

Stone laughed. "Then I must be careful not to do anything to excite his interest."

"There is another possibility as to why you were bugged," Sir Leslie said. "It is possible that, after Thomas built the cottages, all of them were bugged, on general principles. It's the sort of thing our Colonel Croft would do."

"So it's possible that I and my friends are not targets of Colonel Croft?"

"You should not draw that conclusion. The fact that the cottages may already have been bugged would simply be a convenience for the Colonel."

"I'm surprised Thomas has not mentioned Colonel Croft to me," Stone said.

"Thomas is in a delicate position," Sir Leslie said. "He is your friend, but he is a subject of the Colonel's and Winston's constant attention. So far, he has fared well under the new regime, but he is well aware that, should he cross Winston, he could find himself bereft. You must be careful not to put him in that position."

"I'm glad you told me this, Leslie, because I would not wish to do anything to harm Thomas or his interests here."

"Just be very careful of your conversations in the cottage."

"I'll do so. Tell me, Leslie, do you know of an Irene Foster?"

"Ah, the CIA lady, the queen of Black Mountain!"

"Exactly."

"She is quite something," Leslie said. "I believe I might be one of the few men on the island she hasn't slept with." He giggled.

"Surely she can't be that bad."

"I exaggerate, of course, but I know of four instances where gentlemen have succumbed to her tender mercies. At the moment, I believe, she has an in-house lover."

"Yes, one Harry Pitts; they knew each other back in Virginia."

"I wonder if Mr. Pitts is or was CIA, too?"

"Why do you say that?"

"Well, these intelligence people tend to stick close to their own kind, don't they?"

"I think he is probably what he says he is, a retired building contractor."

"Perhaps, perhaps not. Permit me my fantasies; they are all that is left for an old man."

"Do you know of an Englishman named Robertson?"

"Ah, the retired Englishman; he is quite new to the island, and also a denizen of Black Mountain. I understand he was in the computer business in some fashion, back in the mother country."

"Have you met him?"

"No; I meet so few people these days, but I hear a lot."

"Have you heard anything that might make you think that Mr. Robertson is not exactly who he says he is?"

Sir Leslie grinned. "No, but I suspect everyone."

Stone laughed. "Please excuse me, Leslie, but I must rejoin my friends; they will think I've been arrested."

Sir Leslie stood. "Then you must see to it that their worst fears are not realized. And Stone, if you should run afoul of the Colonel, tell Thomas to call me; I'll be happy to represent you."

"Thank you, Leslie." They shook hands, and Stone took his leave. As he went through the garden gate he looked back to see Sir Leslie back on his knees, digging in the soil.

20

Stone drove back to the inn and parked at the cottage, and he saw Holly and Genevieve stretched out on the beach, naked, a very pleasant sight. He liked Holly's slimmer body. He went inside, undressed, grabbed a towel and joined them.

"Hey, there," Holly said. "Where you been?"

"I made a stop at the airport, then I went to see my old colleague Sir Leslie Hewitt."

"And?"

"And I gleaned some useful information. Where's Dino?"

"He says the sun makes you old; he's napping inside."

"Have you spoken with Lance today?"

"Yes; nothing new."

"You may need to call him again. I began thinking about how Teddy always has an escape route planned, and if he's on the island how he might need an airplane to get out of here to where there are international connections. So I went out to the airport and had a talk with a fellow named Don Wells, who runs the FBO, and he showed me an old Cessna 140 that belongs to a recent arrival on the island, one who answers to the general description of Teddy Fay."

"Who is he?"

"He calls himself Robertson, says he's English, a retiree who was formerly in the computer business."

Holly sat up. "I like it," she said.

"And get this: he lives on Black Mountain, at number 56."

"Irene is number 100, so I guess he's halfway up?"

Dino came out of the cottage and joined them. "You woke me up," he said accusingly.

"Sorry about that. It's good that you're here, anyway; we have something to talk about." He brought Dino up to date on Robertson.

"He sounds good to me," Dino said.

"Yeah, well, we need to have Lance have his London station check him out, and thoroughly. There's something else, though."

"What?" Holly asked.

"Leslie has identified who may have bugged our cottage; his name is Colonel Croyden Croft, and he runs a department called Internal Investigations, which is part of the Home Office, but he really works for Sir Winston Sutherland."

"Why does Sir Leslie think he bugged our cottage?" Holly asked.

"Because that's what he does. Leslie thinks he might even have bugged all the cottages when they were built, but that doesn't take any heat off us."

"Heat?"

"Leslie says that Sir Winston would welcome an opportunity to throw us all in jail for a while, then expel us from the island. Apparently, he holds a grudge against me from our previous courtroom encounters."

"Well, thanks, Stone," Dino said, "for pissing off the powers that be. That's a great help."

"My point is, we've got to be very careful to be no more than tourists while we're here. And, of course, we have to be very careful what we say inside the cottage."

"I'm glad we didn't yank the bugs," Holly said. "That would have *really* pissed them off."

"I think you have to be careful, too, not to be seen using the satellite phone to call Lance. The sight of the thing by someone who reports to Colonel Croft might just give them the excuse they need to bust us."

"Good point," Holly said. "I think I'll go behind the cottage and phone Lance now; I want to get him working on this Robertson guy. If we can identify him as Teddy, then we can get out of here before Sir Winston falls on us."

"Go ahead." He handed her a slip of paper. "This is the British registration number of his airplane."

Holly picked up her towel, wrapped it around her sarong-style and grabbed her handbag. She went into the cottage, then out the back door into a fenced-in area where the gas bottle and the garbage cans were, then she dug the satphone out of her bag and called Lance's direct line at Langley.

"Lance Cabot."

"It's Holly."

"Your second call today; something new?"

She told him about Robertson and asked for a background check, then explained their situation with Sir Winston.

"For Christ's sake, don't get yourselves arrested," Lance said. "If we had to bring pressure on the St. Marks government to get you out of there, we'd have to involve the State Department, and then questions might arise as to your presence there, and we wouldn't want that."

"I understand; we'll be careful."

"I don't want you sniffing around this Robertson while I'm checking him out. It's already late in London, so it's going to be tomorrow before anything can be done. I'll call the duty officer now and leave instructions so that they can get started first thing in the morning, while we're still sleeping."

"Great, but don't call me, I'll call you."

"Why?"

"Because of the bugging in the cottage. I don't want the listeners to hear the satphone ringing or my end of the conversation. What time shall I call you?"

"Around ten o'clock; I'll know at least something by then. And remember, Holly, the last time Sir Winston got an American woman in his jail, he tried to hang her."

"Thanks for reminding me," Holly said drily. "Will you call Ham and find out how Daisy is doing?"

"Holly, the Central Intelligence Agency doesn't do dog checks."

"Can I call him on the satphone?"

"Oh, all right."

"Talk to you tomorrow." She hung up and called her father in Orchid Beach, Florida.

"This is Barker," he drawled.

"Hey, Ham."

"Hey, girl; how's it going?"

"Pretty well, I guess; tell Ginny I'm enjoying being her. I lost fifteen pounds for the job."

"That couldn't hurt."

"Watch it, Ham. How's Daisy?"

"Happy as a clam; she goes fishing with me every day and helps by lying down on the foredeck and falling asleep."

"She's eating well?"

"You ever know her to turn down a meal?"

"Well, you know, I miss her."

"By the way, somebody was sniffing around the flight school, asking questions about Ginny."

"Oh, God, I hope Ginny wasn't there."

"She was giving a flying lesson at the time. It was a black guy in a suit and tie, with some sort of accent, and being that dressed up is pretty rare around here."

"Who'd he talk to?"

"The secretary/bookkeeper in the office. She told him Ginny was out of the country on vacation, like she was supposed to."

"That's a relief to hear. We found out our cottage was bugged, and it's interesting to know that somebody's checking on us."

"Well, you watch your ass, girl; I don't want to have to come down there and bring your corpse home."

"Relax, Ham; nothing like that going on. I gotta go. You give Daisy a big, wet kiss for me."

"Yeah, sure. I'll give Ginny one, instead."

"Bye." She hung up and went back out to the beach.

"What's the word?"

"I'll call Lance tomorrow at ten for the results of the background check. There's something else, though."

"What's that?"

"A black man in a suit with an accent visited Ginny's flying school and asked questions about her."

"Oh, shit."

"Fortunately, he didn't see Ginny; she was flying. And the lady in the office gave him the ready story. I hope that satisfied him."

"So do I," Stone said. "I hope that's an end to it."

21

Everybody was dressing for dinner, and Stone was ready first. "I'm going to go up to the inn and see what Thomas knows about this Robertson character; I'll meet you in the bar."

"Okay," Holly said, switching on her blow dryer.

Stone slipped into a linen jacket and walked up to the inn. Thomas was behind the bar, in conversation with a customer, a black man in a black suit. A very nice suit, Stone thought, but an odd choice for the tropics.

Thomas waved him over. "Stone, I'd like you to meet one of our more prominent citizens," he said. "This is Colonel Croft, of our home office. Colonel, this is an old customer, Mr. Stone Barrington, from New York."

The colonel swiveled on his stool and smiled a broad smile with many teeth. "How do you do, Mr. Barrington?" he said.

He was wearing gold-rimmed dark glasses with reflective lenses, so Stone could not see his eyes, which he found a little disconcerting. "How do you do, Colonel? I didn't know St. Marks had an army."

"It's a police title," the colonel explained. "Since joining the Home Office I'm no longer a policeman, exactly, but the rank seems to have stuck. Everyone calls me Colonel."

"I'm a retired policeman myself, like Thomas," Stone said.

"You look awfully young to be retired," the colonel replied.

"Medical reasons," Stone said. "I took a bullet in the knee after fourteen years on the NYPD."

"And what was your assignment on the force?" the colonel asked.

"I was a detective, mostly investigating homicides."

The colonel smiled again. "Well, Mr. Barrington, you would have been unable to earn a living in St. Marks; we have so little violent crime and hardly any homicides."

"You are to be congratulated," Stone said. "It takes good police work to keep crime at such low levels."

"We do our best for a small country. I understand you now practice law; in fact, I've heard that you have actually practiced in St. Marks, on a previous visit."

So the colonel knew who he was; Stone was hardly surprised. "I had that honor," he said, "but quite by happenstance. Your distinguished prime minister bested me handily in court." Stone thought it best to spread the flattery on thick.

"Yes, your client was hanged, I believe."

"I'm afraid so."

"I was chief of police in Markstown at that time," the colonel said, "so I was not involved in the investigation, but, of course, everyone knew of the incident."

"Yes, I believe the trial gained some notoriety in the United States as well." Couldn't hurt to remind him that treating Americans badly engendered bad publicity. "I hope your tourist trade was not affected."

"On the contrary," the colonel said, "the notoriety seemed to give us a shot in the arm, as it were, and our tourist trade has grown steadily since then, benefitting many St. Marksians, as Thomas can readily testify."

"I can," Thomas said. "My home island has been very good to me."

"I hear rumors of a big expansion in tourism to come," Stone said, "with the arrival of casinos."

The colonel abruptly stopped smiling. "Oh? And where did you hear that?" he asked, and he seemed genuinely interested in an answer.

"Oh, just gossip on the beach. That couple who went home yesterday said something about it." The colonel was silent, and Stone felt that his eyes might be boring into him from behind the reflective glasses. "I forget their names."

"It is best not to repeat gossip, Mr. Barrington," the colonel said, and it didn't sound like a suggestion.

"Quite right," Stone said. "May I buy you a drink, Colonel?"

The colonel looked at his watch. "I'm afraid I have an engagement," he said. "Perhaps another time." He stood up.

"I hope so," Stone said.

"Will you be remaining in St. Marks for very long, Mr. Barrington?"

"Only until the weekend," Stone said. "So much work waiting back in New York."

"What a pity," the colonel replied. "It would have been interesting to get to know you better."

"Perhaps on some future visit," Stone said. He offered his hand; the colonel shook it, then departed. When he had gone, Thomas sighed. "Stone, you want to be very careful of what you say to that gentleman."

"Oh? Did I say something wrong?"

"That business about the casinos is *very* closely held information."

"The colonel did give the impression that I wasn't supposed to know about it."

"You recovered well, but still . . . Where on earth did you hear that? Not from me, certainly."

"Just between you and me, it came up at dinner at Irene Foster's house."

"Ah."

Stone shrugged. As he recalled, it had been Harry Pitts who knew about it, but he didn't say so. "I visited Leslie Hewitt this afternoon, and I heard about Colonel Croft from him. I was surprised you hadn't mentioned such an important figure."

"It was my hope that you could visit St. Marks and depart without encountering the colonel," Thomas said. "But now that you have, you should avoid further contact with him, if at all possible."

"I think I would enjoy avoiding further contact with him," Stone said. "He gives me the creeps."

"He is the second most powerful man on the island, and he seems to derive a certain pleasure from making miserable the lives of people he dislikes. And it doesn't take much to incur his dislike."

"You seem to get on well with him."

"I have made a point of it," Thomas said. "I have to make a living here, and that might be impossible if the colonel didn't wish it to be so."

"Thomas, we talked this morning about the means of escaping this island. I hope you have a way out, should it become necessary."

"You needn't concern yourself about me, Stone," Thomas replied. "I have always been a survivor and, even though I am enjoying my success, I know very well that my position here could become untenable if I make the wrong move."

Stone nodded. "If I can ever be of help, I hope you'll call on me."

"Thank you; I hope that won't be necessary."

"By the way, speaking of escape routes, I visited Don Wells at the airport this afternoon, and he told me of a new arrival on the island, one Robertson, who has an airplane in one of Don's hangars. Do you know him?"

"He has been in for dinner." Thomas looked at Stone. "Are you thinking he might be your man?"

"It's a possibility; do you have an opinion?"

Thomas shrugged. "I've seen the man only once; he spoke with a very good British accent."

Holly, Dino and Genevieve arrived in the bar, and Stone let the matter drop.

22

They ordered drinks and sipped them while Thomas tended to other guests. "Who was the man in the black suit?" Holly asked.

"That was the fabled Colonel Croft," Stone said, "and I'm glad you didn't get to meet him."

"Why?"

"A very creepy person, and by all accounts, very dangerous. He also has a bit of an accent that I can't place. He doesn't sound like the other islanders."

"So he's the one who's bugging our cottage?"

"I think we can assume that. I'm afraid I sort of put my foot in it with him."

"How so?"

"We were talking about the tourist trade here, and I told him I'd heard that it would be expanded by the arrival of casinos. He didn't like hearing me say that."

"Why not? It seems innocuous enough."

"According to Thomas, it's a closely guarded secret," Stone said.

"But Harry Pitts told us about it at Irene's; if it's so secret, how does he know about it?"

"It struck me that Harry was extremely well informed about just about everything to do with St. Marks—especially for someone who's only been here for a few days."

"Irene must have brought him up to date," Dino suggested.

"Perhaps," Stone said, "but from here on in, don't mention the casino business to anybody. I don't want to raise any more red flags with the colonel. And Holly, when you talk to Lance tomorrow ask him to find out what he can about the gentleman."

The following morning at ten, Holly called Lance. "What did you find out about Robertson?" she asked.

"Very interesting," Lance said. "Mr. Ian Robertson doesn't exist. He doesn't have a British passport, he doesn't have a driver's license, he doesn't have an airplane registered in his name in the U.K., and he doesn't have a birth certificate."

"But there must be a number of people by that name in the U.K.; it sounds like it could be very common."

"There are around two dozen," Lance said, "but none of them squares with any of the information about himself that Mr. Pemberton gave to the St. Marks housing authority when he made application to buy a house here. Foreigners have to apply for permission to buy. None of the other Robertsons are his age, which he says is fifty-seven, none of them have his middle name, which he says is Osmond, and none of them owns an airplane. All of them, however, have driver's licenses, and most of them have passports. The airplane registration number you gave me belongs to an airplane that has been removed from the British Registry and listed as destroyed in a fire."

"I see. Lance, how did you come up with the information from the St. Marks housing office?"

"That brings me to another matter," Lance said. "Write down this phone number."

Holly found a pen and paper in her bag. "Shoot."

Lance gave her the number. "It's a cell phone; call that number at twelve-fifteen P.M. sharp, today, from your satphone. A man named Bill Pepper will answer. Make an appointment to meet with him."

"Okay. Who is he?"

"He's one of ours, planted in an offshore casino there as a computer programmer. You may be of help to each other."

"Why didn't you tell me about him before?"

"It wasn't necessary for you to know about him before."

"Then why now?"

"Stop asking questions," Lance said sharply. "Meet him; see what you can do for each other."

"There's something else," Holly said.

"What?"

"Stone wants to know about a man in the St. Marks Home Office named Colonel Croft."

"Ask Bill Pepper about him. Good-bye."

Holly joined the others on the beach and reported on her conversation with Lance.

"I don't get it," Stone said. "If Lance already has a man in St. Marks, why did he send us down here?"

"How the hell should I know?" Holly said irritably.

"Take it easy; I'm curious, aren't you?"

"Of course I'm curious. I'm sorry if I was short, but Lance was very irritating. He's usually very smooth and courteous."

"Maybe something else is eating him."

"I had the impression that he was introducing me to this Bill Pepper very reluctantly."

"Well, if the guy is working undercover in one of the Internet casinos, maybe he's concerned about blowing him."

"Yeah, okay; maybe he was just in a bad mood," Holly said.

A t precisely twelve-fifteen, Holly dialed the number she had been given.

"Yes?"

"It's Holly Barker."

"My wife and I will be at the inn for dinner at eight this evening; I'll be wearing a bright green linen jacket. At nine-fifteen, before the dessert course, I'll go to the men's room. You wait until I'm gone, then walk past the ladies' room and out into the parking lot. I'll be sitting in a white Toyota Avalon; join me. Got it?"

"Got it."

He hung up.

23

Holly made sure her group was already seated for dinner when Bill Pepper and his wife arrived. They were placed three or four tables away, but the bright green linen jacket marked him well. He was in his late thirties, blondish hair, the very picture of the young American businessman.

Holly and the others talked through dinner about everything but why they were there—Robertson and the colonel. Holly was worried that even the tables might be bugged.

At nine-fifteen, Pepper rose from his chair and, ignoring them, walked out of the dining room toward the men's room. Holly waited the prescribed minute, then headed for the ladies'. At the end of the hallway, past the restrooms, she opened a door with a big red "EXIT" sign over it and stepped into the parking lot. It took a moment for her eyes to become used to the darkness, then, a few yards away, the overhead light went on in a car, then went off again. She made her way to the white Avalon and got in. "I'm Holly Barker," she said, offering her hand.

"Bill Pepper," he said, shaking it.

"Is that a trade name?"

"Probably. What do you want to know?"

"Have you found out anything more about this Robertson? Or about Pemberton or Weatherby?"

"I think—and this isn't official opinion yet, since not enough people at Langley agree—that Robertson, as he calls himself, is an Englishman named Barney Cox, who Scotland Yard believes is one of four men who robbed a shipment of money at Heathrow Airport about nine months ago. They got away with something over a hundred million pounds sterling."

"I read about that in the papers; I didn't know the police there had identified them."

"'Identified' is too strong a word. All they know for sure is that Cox disappeared simultaneously with the robbery, and they only know that because his wife made a missing persons report a day later."

"Did she have any information about the robbery?"

"No; all she knew was that her husband went to work one day and didn't come back. They had been married for more than thirty years and had two grown children."

"Did he have a criminal record?"

"No, he was an ordinary civilian; he sold computers to businesses. In fact, he was director of sales for his company."

"Why do you think Robertson is Barney Cox?"

"Description, timing, money, and the fact that he says he's retired from the computer business, which, if he is Cox, is a stupid thing to say."

"Do you have any other possible identities in mind for him?"

"Well, I don't think he's the Lindbergh baby; did you have somebody else in mind?"

"Not really."

"Then what are you doing in St. Marks?"

"I take it Lance didn't tell you."

"No, but he didn't tell me not to ask, either."

"Don't ask."

"Okay, sure."

"And what you've just told me is as much as you have for thinking Robertson is Barney Cox?"

Pepper threw up his hands. "Lance told me to tell you what I know about him; that's what I know and what I think. Oh, I forgot, he has a false identity, which is what Barney Cox would have, too. Anything else?"

"Tell me about Colonel Croft."

"Ah, now *there's* a piece of work. His real name is Maurice Benet, and he's Haitian."

"That explains the odd accent."

"It explains a lot of things. When Benet was twenty, he was a captain in Papa Doc's Tonton Macoutes. You know about them?"

"The Haitian secret police?"

"They were a happy band of murderers and torturers, whose main job was to scare the shit out of anybody who had a discouraging word to say about Papa Doc or his regime. They did this by kidnapping, torturing and murdering anybody who annoyed them, then delivering the mutilated corpse home to the family."

"How did he end up in St. Marks?"

"When Baby Doc's regime fell, Benet and a cohort of his escaped the island with a large bundle of various currencies and island-hopped for a while, ending up here, in the happy arms of Sir Winston Sutherland. Sutherland found a place in the police force for him and his buddy, and he's been clawing his way up ever since. He's been a little more restrained than when he was in Haiti, but he's matured, I guess. He still scares the shit out of people, though."

"How did you identify him?"

"I followed him into a bar and got his right index fingerprint off a bar glass. It's confirmed; there's no guessing about this guy."

"Is he wanted anywhere?"

"Sure, he's wanted in Haiti, but that place is such a mess they probably wouldn't know what to do if he turned up on a street corner in Port-au-Prince."

"How'd you get hold of Robertson's application for buying a house?"

"I've been hacking into the government computers almost since I arrived here a year ago. I can find out just about anything you'd want to know, and a great deal you wouldn't want to know."

"I want to know if Colonel Croft has any real interest in our party."

"If you're here, he's interested. I hope to God you didn't yank out those bugs on your phones, because if you did, he's going to be all over you."

"I didn't; they're still in place; we're just being careful what we say when we're in the house."

"I hear you've been up to Irene Foster's."

"Yes."

"She's probably bugged, too; did you say anything indiscreet there?"

"Certainly not, and I don't think she's bugged, because when Stone Barrington happened to mention to the colonel he'd heard that casinos were going to start opening here, Croft got tense. We heard about that from Irene's buddy Harry Pitts at her house, and if she had been bugged, Croft would already have known about our conversations there."

Pepper checked his watch. "I've got to get back," he said. "If I stay any longer, my wife's going to think I'm fucking you."

Holly laughed. "She sounds like a suspicious woman; she must have cause."

"Let's not go into that." He handed Holly a card. "That's my sat-phone number; I've got one just like yours. Have you noticed that there's a scrambler button on it?"

"Yes, but Lance hasn't told me to use it."

"When you call me, use it. You can reach me any day at twelve-thirty P.M. for five minutes. No other time."

"Got it," Holly said, tucking the card into her bra.

"Give me a minute before you go back to the restaurant." He got out of the car and returned to the dining room.

Holly waited, then joined the others. Pepper was paying his check and leaving.

"Interesting?" Stone asked.

"I'll tell you when we're out of here," she said.

24

Bill Pepper and his wife, Annie, paid their check and left the inn.

"So, did you fuck her?" Annie asked.

"I would have, if I'd had the time."

"I thought so."

They were quiet for a while.

"Did you think she was attractive?"

"You got a look at her; what do you think?"

"I think she's attractive."

"Well, I won't be seeing her again; we'll talk only on the satphone."

"Satphone sex!"

"Scrambled satphone sex!"

They both laughed. They arrived home and got undressed for bed.

"I've got to call in," he said to his wife. "Anything you want to pass on?" She was Agency, too.

"Not to Lance Cabot," she said.

"You'd better start being nice to him."

"You think he's going to get the job?"

"I think he will if this Holly Barker's assignment pans out."

"What's her assignment?"

"This is between you and me, okay? Nobody else ever hears about it."

She fluffed her pillow and got into bed. "Okay."

"Lance sent her down here to find Teddy Fay."

"You gotta be kidding."

"I kid you not."

"Lance thinks he's still alive?"

"The Director thinks he *might* be still alive, and that's enough."

She shook her head. "Hang on a minute while I connect the dots." She was quiet for a moment. "Okay, I can't connect the dots."

"The dots run all the way to the president; does that help?"

Her eyebrows went up. "Ooooh; reelection!"

"You've just connected the dots."

"Why don't they just leave well enough alone? Nobody else is looking for him."

"I'll bet you a blow job the FBI still is."

"I won't take that bet," she said. "Teddy got away from them twice; Director Bob must be pissed off."

"Yeah, and he's the kind of guy who, once he's pissed off, stays pissed off, until somebody makes him happy."

"You think they'd arrest Teddy if they found him?"

"My guess is, not until after the election. After all, it was Will Lee who pulled Director Bob out of the ranks and gave him the big job. The guy must have *some* sense of gratitude."

"You'd think."

"Ms. Barker thinks this guy, Robertson, might be Teddy Fay."

"The one you think is the escaped airport bandit?"

"I'm right; I know I am."

"Excuse me, but aren't you the guy who thought that coffee merchant in Cairo was Osama bin Laden?"

"That has nothing to do with this. Besides, the guy was *very* tall. And he had a beard."

"Right. So tell me why you think Robertson isn't Teddy Fay."

"Instinct."

"Uh-oh, instinct. You should never follow your instincts, darling. Let me guess, Robertson looks like Teddy."

"He looks like the description of Teddy that Lance gave Holly Barker."

"Isn't that the same thing?"

"Maybe, maybe not."

"Come on, Billy, use your noodle a little; just consider it. What about Robertson conflicts with what's known about Teddy Fay?"

Pepper was silent. "Teddy wouldn't be stupid enough to use an identity that couldn't be confirmed."

"Nothing else, huh?"

"Not much."

"Name some little thing about Robertson that conflicts with his being Teddy."

"His identity doesn't check out, okay? All right, nothing else, but nothing conflicts with his being Barney Cox, either."

"Tell me, in your wildest dreams, who would you rather be responsible for bringing in: Barney Cox or Teddy Fay?"

"Well, Barney Cox, of course. If I brought in Teddy Fay, nobody would ever know; Langley would sit on it."

"Lance would know, and if he gets the DDO job, that would be nice."

"Yeah, but *only* Lance would know, and suppose he doesn't get the job?"

"The director would know, and that means the president would know."

"Why do you think that? You think Lance would tell her if *I* busted Teddy? He'd see that he and his acolyte, Barker, got the credit; then he'd get credit for sending her down here. And the director wouldn't tell the president until he's out of office. He wouldn't want to know a thing like that."

"You have a point." She thought for a moment. "Maybe we'd get a nice transfer out of it?"

"What's wrong with St. Marks? I'm working practically alone—ah, with the woman I love—in my very own country; I have nobody local breathing down my neck, except the guy at the embassy. And you're having the time of your life; your tennis game has never been better."

"If we were a couple of years from retirement, St. Marks would be heaven," she said. "But we have careers ahead of us. In another year, Langley will forget we're here, and we'll be left to rot on the vine. *But* if you could make Robertson as Barney Cox, the Brits would love you for it; maybe you could join MI6."

"Sarcasm doesn't suit you. Think of some way we can make hay out of Barney Cox."

"If we were the police, we'd be world-famous in an instant, have our pictures in every newspaper in the world, but that's not who we are, is it? If we're responsible for busting Cox, only the Agency is going to know; Langley is not even going to tell the Brits."

"They'd be very pleased if we busted Cox for the Brits. They could lord it over MI6 for years."

"Well, there is that. All right, you want me to see what I can find out at the tennis club?"

"Does Robertson play tennis?"

"He's a new member; I checked."

"You've been holding out on me, haven't you?"

"I only checked today. I win the blow job!" She shucked off her nightgown.

"Hang on, I don't even remember what the bet was about. How do I know you won?"

She grabbed him by the hair and drew his face into her lap. "Trust me," she said.

They forgot about calling Lance.

25

Lance asked for and got an appointment with the director, and he presented himself at the appointed time. His morning conversation with Barker had been interesting.

"Good morning, Lance," Kate Lee said, waving him to a chair. "What do you have to report?"

"We've identified a man in St. Marks as, possibly, Teddy Fay."

"Great!"

"Stone Barrington interviewed a man at the airport who showed him a small airplane belonging to a recently arrived Englishman, calling himself Robertson. There's no British paper on this character at all, so he's obviously not who he says he is, and he more or less fits Teddy's description."

"Now what?"

"Problem is, Bill Pepper, on his own hook, has made a different identification."

"Pepper's our man in the casino down there, isn't he? The computer whiz?"

"Right."

"Who does Pepper think the man is?"

"He thinks he's one of the four men who robbed a currency-transfer company at Heathrow a few months ago, name of Barney Cox."

"I remember the incident; a hell of a lot of money, wasn't it?"

"Over a hundred million quid."

"Hard to handle that much cash, isn't it?"

"Yes, but with careful planning, it could be done. Private jet to a country with amenable banks, numbered accounts, et cetera."

"How much does a hundred million pounds sterling weigh?"

"Let's see, the biggest sterling note is fifty pounds; you could get a million in a large briefcase."

"So a hundred large briefcases would do it?"

"Or ten manageable-sized crates. As I recall, they used a large van to remove the money from Heathrow."

"They'd need a big private jet, then."

"Or a not-very-big cargo plane. Of course, the Brits would be all over that sort of flight."

"They could truck it across the channel and fly from anywhere in Europe."

"Yes, they could, if they waited for things to cool off enough."

"So you think this Robertson could be Cox?"

"It's possible."

"Just as possible as if he's Teddy Fay, then."

"I'm afraid so. The reason I came to you about this is that Bill Pepper doesn't work for me. He did me a favor and met briefly with Holly Barker to tell her what he knows about Pemberton. She was also interested in the evil Colonel Croft, né Benet, of Haiti."

"Why?"

"Their cottage is bugged, and she suspects Croft, a logical assumption."

"Have they blown their mission?" Kate asked.

"No, they've been careful. But as I was saying, Bill Pepper reports to Hugh English, through one of his deputies, and should you decide to mention this Robertson to the Brits, I don't want to ruffle Hugh's feathers by having him know that I've talked to Pepper without going through him."

"Why didn't you go through him?"

"Because I don't think he would have given me permission. This was a benign contact, nothing that would jeopardize Pepper's work down there. Also, Hugh English doesn't know about our looking for Teddy, and I didn't think you'd want him to."

"Yes, well, there is that. Pepper has cracked the government computers down there, hasn't he?"

"Yes, that's how he began his background check on Robertson; he checked the info on his application to buy a house."

"One thing about Robertson that doesn't sound like Teddy: he has no paper in Britain," Kate said. "It doesn't sound like Teddy to create a legend with no paper behind him. All his experience is in new identities with a lot of depth."

"I'll grant you that, but Teddy can't have the resources he did when he was at home, here. He may have taken a certain amount of paper with him—passports, that sort of thing—but to build an identity in depth, he'd need more than just an Internet connection. He'd need British passwords and codes that he couldn't get without the Agency's people and equipment. That may be why this identity is so shallow."

"So what do you want me to do?" Kate asked.

"Nothing. But if you decide to pass Pemberton on to the Brits for a more thorough investigation, I'd like you to conceal your source from Hugh English."

"Hasn't Pepper already reported his suspicions to Hugh?"

"Not yet; his hunch is only a day or so old. I could tell him, on your instructions, not to report it until you're ready."

"I think that's the best course for now. I'll get back to you. And Lance, thanks for bringing this to my attention, even though it's outside your purview."

Kate watched Lance leave, then sat and thought about this. She should probably discuss it with her husband, since he and the British prime minister were close. He would not want to withhold anything from the British. Well, not for very long, anyway. She'd think about it later.

26

L ance went back to his office and sat at his desk, gazing out at the Virginia landscape. He had covered his ass with Kate, but he was still worried about Hugh English.

The longtime deputy director for operations would have been gone now, retired to some gated Florida golf community, had it not been for the very inconvenient murder of his chosen successor, Dick Stone. English was not a favorite of the director, since he had opposed her promotion to that office. He had been subtle, having many contacts on Capitol Hill, and, since he had removed himself from the succession, his opinion carried real weight there, but she had been confirmed anyway because of the depth of influence in the Senate of her husband. Still, English's long history with the Agency gave him broad and deep support internally, and Lance, hoping for promotion to his job, didn't want to run afoul of the man. Now, however, he had, almost inadvertently, tossed a potential hand grenade under Hugh English's chair, and he was worried that it might go off at an inopportune moment.

His phone rang; Holly Barker was reporting in. He picked it up. "Lance Cabot."

"It's Holly."

"What have you to report?"

"Nothing; you told me to stay away from Robertson, and that's what I've done. I don't know why you'd send me down here to find Teddy, then hold me back when we've developed a hot lead."

"Robertson is not your concern, Holly, until I tell you he is. Here's what I want you to do."

Holly punched off the satphone, then walked through the house, stripped off her clothes and joined the others on the beach.

"What?" Stone asked, seeing her face.

"Lance still won't let us go near Robertson."

"Then what are we doing here?"

"Lying on the beach, apparently. He wants Pepper to check him out further."

"Great," Dino said. "I like lying on the beach better, anyway."

"I don't," Holly said. She stood up, dropped her towel and ran into the sea, swimming strongly a hundred yards out. She looked back to see that Stone had followed her to the water's edge and was keeping an eye on her. She waved for him to follow, and he entered the water and began swimming.

Holly ducked underwater and swam a few strokes, looking for the sandbar that she knew ran parallel to the beach. She found it after a moment and stood up in waist-deep water.

Stone shortly joined her. "How did you know about the bar?"

"Thomas told me. He said not to go farther out, though." She splashed water in his face.

"Stand still," he said.

"What?"

"Just don't move around. Stand perfectly still."

He was looking back toward the beach, and she followed his gaze. A large gray fin was slicing through the water inside the sand-bar, between them and the beach. "Oh, shit," she said.

"Just don't move," Stone replied. Slowly, he slid under the water for a moment, then, just as slowly, reemerged. "It's a hammerhead," he said. "A big one."

The fin went a few yards past them, then reversed course. "How big?"

"I'm guessing fourteen, fifteen feet. Tell me you're not having your period."

"I'm not having my period."

"Thank God for that; we don't need that scent in the water." She looked back toward the beach and saw Dino and Genevieve walk into the water and begin swimming toward them. "They're splash-ing," she said, pointing.

Stone turned and looked at the swimmers and began waving his arms. Dino waved back. Stone, with both hands, began making a pushing motion, waving them back to the beach. It took Dino a moment to understand, then he tapped Genevieve on the shoulder, and they began swimming back. They stood in knee-deep water and watched. Dino pointed out the shark's fin to his girlfriend.

"This is ridiculous," Holly said. "Four naked people watching a shark swim."

"Two of them in the water with the shark," Stone pointed out. "That's even more ridiculous."

"What are we going to do?" Holly asked.

"Wait for it to decide we're uninteresting."

"And if it has a different opinion?"

"Hit it with our fists in the eyes, which, I think, are at the ends of the hammer. I wish now I hadn't missed that field trip to the aquar-ium when I was a kid. I was home with the flu."

"I wish I had a gun," Holly said, looking at Stone. When she looked back at the shark, the fin was gone. "Oh, shit." She pointed.

"Oh, shit, indeed," Stone replied. He ducked slowly under the water again, and this time he was under for a full minute before he came up again.

Holly kept looking for the fin. "Could you see it?" she asked.

"No, it vanished."

"Vanished where?"

"I don't know, it's just gone."

Holly ducked under the water and did a slow three-sixty. She wished she had goggles. She wished she had a shotgun. She came up again. "I can't see more than thirty feet."

"Neither could I." Stone suddenly pointed outside the bar. The fin had reappeared, moving slowly down the beach, away from them. "I think it's time to rejoin Dino and Genevieve," he said. "No overhand swimming; breaststroke."

But Holly was already swimming steadily toward the beach. She had a weird feeling that the big hammerhead was an omen, or maybe a metaphor for what might be waiting for them on St. Marks. She tried to shake off the feeling and failed.

They walked out of the water a few minutes later and flopped down on the blanket next to their friends.

"I'm exhausted," Holly said. "Too much adrenaline; I've used it all up."

"Looked like a dolphin to me," Dino said.

Stone shook his head. "I saw it underwater; a hammerhead."

"Eeeew," Genevieve said.

"My feelings exactly," Holly replied. "I'm going to shower, then I have to make a phone call."

T wenty minutes later, she dialed Bill Pepper's satphone number. He answered immediately. "Scrambling," she said, and pushed the button.

"Okay, I'm scrambled, too," Pepper said. He sounded as if he was very far away. "What do you want?"

"I've got new instructions from Lance," she said.

"I don't work for Lance, and I don't take his instructions, unless I feel like it."

"This is handed down from the director, bypassing Hugh English."

"How do I know that?"

"Do you expect the director to call you?"

"Well, that hasn't happened so far."

"And it's not going to happen now."

"What are these instructions?"

"We've got to identify Robertson beyond question."

"Isn't a strong suspicion enough to call the cops, or Interpol?"

"The problem is, he may be someone else."

"Someone else? You mean, besides the Heathrow robber?"

"This never goes to Hugh English or anyone else."

"I don't like the sound of this."

"It doesn't matter whether you like it; this has to be done."

"All right, I agree. Now, who does Lance think he is?"

"Maybe Teddy Fay."

Pepper burst out laughing.

"No kidding."

He stopped laughing. "He's not dead?"

"I wish he were."

"This is nuts."

"Maybe so, but there it is. Prove he's not Teddy. Prove he's Barney Cox or anybody else. We have to know."

Pepper sighed. "This might be fun, if it weren't so crazy."

"I hope you enjoy the experience."

"Is that why you're on St. Marks? To track down the maybe mythical Teddy Fay?"

"Yes."

"Did Lance offer any suggestion as to how I am to proceed?"

"His view is that you're here, on the ground, you have resources, and you know best how to use them."

"Great, and what are you going to do?"

"Don't go near Robertson; those are my instructions."

"And who do I report my findings to?"

"Me. I'll report to Lance."

"This is very weird."

"I can't deny that."

"You were sent here to find Teddy, but you've been told not to pursue your primary suspect? Or is he your primary suspect? Is there anybody else?"

"What do you think of Pemberton or Weatherby as suspects?"

"Jesus, I don't know; I wasn't looking for Teddy Fay when I checked them out."

"How did they check out?"

"Okay; they had the usual paper trail; as far as I can tell, they're who they say they are."

"Have you ever seen either of them?"

"No; they're snowbirds; they don't spend all their time here."

"Are they worth my pursuing them as suspects?"

"Well, apparently, you don't have anything else to do."

"Tell me what else you know about them."

"Nothing—a criminal record, use of a false identity—has come up."

"Please let me know if you hear anything else."

"I'll get back to you."

"Bye." Holly hung up, still pissed off that she wasn't being allowed to investigate Robertson.

27

Kate Lee arrived back at the White House, shed her Secret Service detail and went up to the family quarters. Her husband was sitting in front of the big flatscreen TV he had had installed, watching Katie Couric deliver the news. A commercial came on.

She kissed him. "You gave up the guys for a girl?" she asked, mixing them a drink at the bar concealed in the bookcases.

"I alternate," he said. "If you were home in time to watch the news more often, you'd know that."

"If I were home in time to watch the news, you wouldn't talk to me until the news was over, anyway."

"You have a point, as usual." They touched glasses and drank.

"What are we doing for dinner?"

"I ordered a pizza."

"What, we're having dinner alone together *twice* in one week?"

"Amazing, isn't it?"

The commercials ended, and Katie returned. Kate knew better than to talk before the news was over. Couric wrapped up simultaneously with the arrival of the pizza.

Will opened the box and looked at the pizza. "Shit," he said.

"What?"

"Green peppers. I ordered the Extravaganza with no green peppers."

Kate began picking out the green slivers and putting them aside. "I hope the voters that depend on green pepper growing for their livelihood don't hear about this," she said. "You'd never be reelected."

"You could be right," he said, picking up a green-pepper-free slice of pizza. "George Bush the elder said publicly that he hated broccoli, and look what happened to him."

Kate went to the bar, opened a bottle of wine and returned with two glasses. "Maybe Teddy Fay is like the green peppers," she said.

"Yeah, well, I didn't order him, either."

"I mean, maybe we should just ignore him."

Will's mouth was too full of pizza to respond immediately. He chewed for a minute, then swallowed. "You really think that? I thought your people were close to nailing him."

"We're just guessing."

"Kate, the man has murdered a dozen people, among them a speaker of the house and a supreme court justice. We shouldn't catch him?"

"I don't know."

"You knew before. What's changed?"

"I don't know. I just have a bad feeling about this."

"You want to call off Lance Cabot and his people?"

"It might be the best thing."

"Look at it this way: you're testifying before a committee of Congress: you can testify, truthfully, that you did everything you could to catch him and failed. That's not a great thing, but it's not terrible, either."

"It's not terrible, if I testify to that *after* the election."

Will ignored that remark. "But if you're asked if you gave an order to stop pursuing him, and you answer truthfully, then we're both in what I believe the most eminent political scientists refer to as deep shit."

"Not if I answer that I became convinced, after a thorough search, that Teddy is dead."

"If you thought he was dead, why were you conducting yet another search? That's what Congress would ask."

"You mean, now that we've started, we're stuck with it?"

"I think we are, unless he turns up verifiably deceased." He spat out a piece of green pepper. "You missed one. Why don't you instruct your Technical Services Department to put together a device that detects green peppers on your pizza before you bite into them?"

Kate took a big bite of pizza to keep from talking, and they both ate quietly for a while.

"What happened today to make you feel bad about this?" Will asked.

"Teddy is creating internal problems for us. I've about decided to appoint Lance Cabot as DDO, but he's had to go around Hugh English to deal with the Teddy thing, and Hugh doesn't like being gone around."

"Has he found out about it?"

"No, but Lance is using one of Hugh's people on St. Marks, and it could get back to him."

"Why don't you go ahead and appoint Lance, retire Hugh English and get him out of there?"

"Because people like Hugh English don't just dematerialize when they retire. If they find out they were unknowingly slighted when they were still at work, they end up giving television interviews and testifying to Congress about what a snake pit the Agency is and what a bitch I am, and it doesn't do anybody any good."

"Welcome to Washington," Will said. "Look, all we can do with this or with anything else is to do what we think is right and let the chips fall where they may."

She smiled, then leaned over and kissed him on the cheek. "That's what I love about you," she said. "Your childlike belief that if you do what you think is right, everything will be okay."

"Maybe that's why I'm president of the United States," he replied, taking another huge bite of pizza.

"There's something else."

"Oh, God, not something else," Will muttered through his pizza.

"The Teddy thing is overlapping with a British thing."

"How so?"

"We have a suspect for Teddy on St. Marks, but our man down there thinks he could just as easily be one of the four men who robbed a currency transfer company at Heathrow Airport a few months ago. I expect you remember that."

"I remember getting a phone call from my very good friend the British prime minister, asking me to instruct the entire U.S. law enforcement community to help catch them, as if I could do that, and I remember telling him that I would do anything I could to help him."

"Yes, well . . ."

"So what I should be doing right now is picking up the phone and calling London to report our suspicions."

"Technically speaking, yes."

"Technically?"

"Sort of. I mean, we're working on a firm identification of the guy, and if he turns out to be the British robber, *then* you can call your limey buddy."

"Are we talking minutes, days, weeks or longer?"

"Maybe days. If we're lucky."

"So now I have another slice of green pepper on my metaphorical pizza."

"For only a short time, I hope."

Will spat out another sliver of green. "Kate—and this is a direct order from your president—fix this."

"The green peppers?"

"The metaphorical green peppers."

"Yes, sir," she replied.

28

Holly took a seat on the cottage patio and poured herself a glass of whatever was in the icy pitcher. She sipped it. "Mmmm, what is this?"

"Some kind of rum punch, I think," Stone said. "Thomas sent it over."

"It's delicious, but it doesn't taste alcoholic."

"Don't you believe it," Dino said. "I've had two, and it ain't iced tea."

"I think we should ask Irene to dinner," Holly said. "To repay her kindness in inviting us."

"Whatever you say," Stone replied. "Do you hope to learn more from her?"

"I think this Robertson guy could be Teddy. Or maybe, Pemberton or Weatherby."

"Who?"

"Robertson owns the Cessna 140; Weatherby and Pemberton are the Englishmen who bought the cottage that used to be Irene's guesthouse and the one next door to that."

"And why do you think one of them is Teddy?"

"Because Pemberton and Weatherby have the paper trail—passport, driver's license, credit reports, et cetera that any innocent citizen would have."

"And that causes you to suspect them of multiple murders, not to mention making a fool of the FBI, the CIA and everybody else who was after him?"

"Yes."

"Why?"

"Because Robertson doesn't have a paper trail, and Teddy would never use an identity that couldn't be verified. He would look upon that as unprofessional."

"What profession are we talking about?"

"You know—master criminal and all that."

"I didn't know master criminal was a profession. That kind of waters down the pool of professionals, doesn't it?"

"Oh, stop it, Stone, you know what I mean."

"Can I ask you a question?"

"Sure."

"How many expatriate Brits do you suppose live on this island?"

"I don't know; hundreds, maybe a few thousand."

"And how many of them do you think might have perfectly ordinary paper trails floating in their wakes?"

"How the hell should I know?"

"All right, for the sake of argument, let's say that ninety-five percent of them are who they say they are, and an investigation would back them up, and the other five percent are fleeing criminals with false passports."

"What's your point?"

"That would mean that the ninety-five percent—hundreds, perhaps thousands—would satisfy your criteria for thinking that they are Teddy Fay. Do you see where I'm going here?"

"The ninety-five percent don't live next door to Irene Foster."

"All right, I'll give you that. Now you've isolated one criterion that doesn't apply to the great mass. But it's not an incriminating criterion, and it hardly resonates like, say, a DNA match."

"Stone, Teddy through maybe years of careful preparation has ensured that we are *never* going to get a match of anything—DNA, fingerprint, photo, *anything*—because he has erased all those things from every computer that might harbor them."

"Well, then, we're left with kidnapping the three of them, locking them up somewhere and torturing them until one of them admits he's Teddy—the George W. Bush method of extracting admissions from people we hate. And, of course, under torture, anybody will admit to anything, so all three of them might admit to being Teddy."

"No, no, we're going to have to rely on deduction to make the identification."

"Ah, detective work!" Dino interjected.

"Well, yes."

"Well, a tiny problem: we have no evidence to work with to deduce that any of the three of them is Teddy. You see the difficulty?" Dino spread his hands and looked sorrowful.

"Let's get some evidence, then."

Stone sighed. "We could break into their houses and ransack them, in the hope that if one of them is Teddy, he's stupid enough to leave his old birth certificate or passport lying around."

"Stone . . ."

"What I'm trying to tell you is that Teddy has made it virtually impossible for us ever to identify him by any means known to criminal investigation."

"How about eyewitnesses?" Genevieve interjected.

"Eyewitness to what?" Holly asked.

"To Teddy. He worked at the CIA all those years; there must be dozens, maybe hundreds of people who knew him, who could identify him if they saw him. Photograph all three of them and send the pictures to Lance. Let him circulate them and see if he gets a bite."

Dino looked at his girlfriend with admiration. "I think we might have a spot for you at the NYPD," he said.

Holly looked at her watch. "I have to call in," she said.

29

H olly first called Bill Pepper.

"I'm here."

"Me too."

"Scramble."

"Scrambled."

Pepper came back with his voice-from-a-barrel. "What's up?"

"When a foreigner applies to buy a house in St. Marks, does he have to attach a photograph to his application?"

"Yes, a passport photograph."

"Can you hack into the government computers and get me the photographs of Robertson, Pemberton and Weatherby?"

"Yeah, I guess so."

"How long will it take?"

"A few minutes."

"Can you e-mail them to me in, say, an hour?"

"Probably. Is this about Teddy Fay?"

"The idea is, I'll look at them, and if one of them could conceivably be Teddy, I'll send them to Lance, and he can show them to Teddy's former coworkers for ID."

"Makes sense to me."

She gave him her e-mail address. "I'll be standing by."

"Later." He broke the connection.

Holly called Lance.

"Lance Cabot."

She explained about the photographs she was going to send.

"Excellent," Lance replied. "How soon?"

"Maybe an hour or so; check your e-mail."

"Good. Anything else?"

"Yes; I think we're about done here."

"You're giving up?"

"Our stay is nearing its end, and we have not been able to identify Teddy. Our best shot is that he's Robertson, Pemberton or Weatherby; if we can't get an ID from these photos, then we have nowhere else to go. Our well is dry."

"That's discouraging."

"Well, we're discouraged. I want to have one more dinner with Irene Foster, though. Maybe we'll glean something from her."

"And her boyfriend? Pitts?"

"I think he may have already sailed for home."

"You're satisfied that he's not Teddy?"

"He isn't, unless Teddy knows how to grow hair on a bald scalp. Pitts doesn't wear a toupee."

"All right, call tomorrow. I'll send the jet for you at, say, noon the day after."

"Good." She hung up and called Irene.

"Hello?"

"Hi, Irene, it's Ginny; how are you?"

"Very well, thanks; are you still on the island?"

"We leave on Saturday. I was hoping that you could join us for dinner tonight at the inn."

"Love to; is Harry invited, as well?"

"Is he still here?"

"He seems to like the island."

"Of course; bring him along. Seven-thirty?"

"That's grand; we'll look forward to it."

Holly hung up, went into the house, got her laptop and took it out to the patio, where lunch was just being served.

"What's with the computer?" Stone asked.

Holly glanced at the butler, who finished serving and went back inside. "Pepper is going to e-mail me the photographs of Robertson, Pemberton and Weatherby that were attached to their applications to buy a house here, and then I'm going to take Genevieve's brilliant suggestion and e-mail them to Lance, if I think one of them might be Teddy."

"Good."

"By the way, the jet is picking us up at noon the day after tomorrow."

"Regardless of what we learn?"

"These photos are our last gasp; if none of them is Teddy, we're out of here. If one of them *is* Teddy, we're out of here, too. Dealing with him is somebody else's job."

"Sounds good to me."

"Me too," Dino said. "The sight of that shark off our beach nixed the place for me. I'm not going back in the water past knee-deep."

"Oh, Dino," Genevieve said, "the shark was just doing what sharks do. We've only seen him once, and he probably won't be back."

"I'm not going in the same ocean with him," Dino said, digging into his seafood salad. He held up a forkful. "I'm happy to eat his lunch, but I'm not going to *be* his lunch."

They ate in a leisurely fashion, and after an hour had passed, Holly checked her e-mail.

There was an e-mail from Ham: "Are you coming by here on your way back to D.C.?"

"I'll see if we can stop by and pick up Daisy on the way back," she responded, "but I won't be able to stay. Give my love to Ginny." She signed it and sent the mail.

"Nothing from Pepper?" Stone asked.

"Nope."

"How long was it supposed to take?"

"He said a few minutes to hack into the government computer, and he'd have them to me in an hour."

Stone checked his watch. "It's been an hour and a half."

"Maybe he got busy at work."

A nother hour passed, then two hours, and still nothing had arrived from Pepper. Late in the afternoon, Holly called Lance.

"Lance Cabot."

"It's your humble servant; something's wrong."

"What?"

"Pepper was supposed to e-mail me the photos within an hour after we talked. It's been five hours, and I've heard nothing."

"I suppose he could have become occupied with something else at work, but still, that doesn't sound right."

"I'm only supposed to call him at midday on the satphone, so I can't communicate."

"Hang on, let me think."

"Okay." Holly waited through three or four minutes of silence.

Lance came back on. "Bill has probably already left the office for the day. And I tried his home; no answer."

"But if he didn't have the photos, he could have e-mailed me to let me know."

"I know, and it doesn't sound right. I've had a look at Bill's file, and he has a sister in Miami named Doris Pepper. She's forty-six years old, five-six, a hundred and forty pounds, blonde and pretty. She teaches sixth grade at a public school in Miami. Tomorrow morning, after nine, call Bill's office, but not on the satphone." He gave her the number. "When he comes on the line tell him you're a friend of his sister, and you promised her you'd call him for her. She's fine, et cetera, et cetera."

"And what is my purpose for the call?"

"To find out if he's okay. Don't talk long, and before you hang up, tell him his sister said to drop her an e-mail sometime. I want to know exactly what his response is. Call me on the satphone as soon as you hang up."

"Okay. Do you think something is wrong?"

"I always think something is wrong when an agent doesn't do what he says he'll do." Lance hung up.

30

Holly and her party went directly to their table at the inn, but Irene was late and without Harry.

"I'm so sorry," she said, "and Harry's even later. He had some business he had to take care of at the marina." She sat down and accepted a rum punch from the pitcher on the table.

"So Harry's sticking around for a while?" Stone asked.

She smiled. "I must admit, I'm getting used to having him here. He's good around the house, and a lot of things I was letting go are getting taken care of."

"Good around the house," Genevieve said, leering. "I'll bet he is."

"Well, that, too," Irene admitted. "It's been so long since I lived with a man, I'd forgotten what it was like."

Holly felt the same way, but she didn't say so. "What are your long-term plans, Irene? Are you going to make this your permanent home?"

"I guess it already is," she replied, sipping her drink. "I've settled in very well, which wasn't the case in St. Barts. I'm too old to start learning a language, and everybody here speaks English, and the government is stable—no bands of rebels in the hills. I think St. Marks may be heaven for me."

"Does Harry feel the same way?"

"Well, he hasn't been here long enough for that to happen, but he likes it, and he's comfortable here. He may also get on his boat and sail away; we'll see how it goes."

"That's a good attitude when dealing with men," Genevieve said. "Just see how it goes." She gave Dino a sidelong glance.

"On the other hand," Dino said, "that attitude doesn't work so well with women."

"Why not?" Holly asked.

"Well, you go along for a while, seeing how it goes, and you think you've got it all figured out, then they change everything."

Stone spoke up. "Well, if we're going to listen to Dino's theories about women, this is going to be a very long and boring evening."

"Oh, here's Harry," Irene said, waving him over.

Harry bustled in, greeted everybody, took a seat and poured himself a glass of rum punch. A waiter appeared with a fresh pitcher and took the nearly empty one away. "Man, that's good!" he enthused, taking a long draft of his drink.

"Did you get your work done at the marina?" Irene asked.

"Yep, the boat is in the best shape of its life."

"You sticking around for a while?" Stone asked.

"Maybe. I've done Virginia, and Ft. Lauderdale seemed too crowded for me, though if I stay longer that would be the best place to sell the boat." He smiled at Irene. "And nobody in either place cooks like Irene." He slapped his belly. "I've been putting on weight."

"I'm going to put you on a diet," Irene said.

Stone felt his cell phone vibrate and stood up. "Excuse me; phone call." He walked toward the bar. "Hello?"

"It's Lance."

"Hi, what's up?"

"I tried to call Ginny, but she didn't answer on either the sat-phone or her cell phone; is she all right?"

"Yes, of course; we're at dinner at the inn with Irene Foster and her friend Harry. Why wouldn't she be okay?"

"I've been unable to locate Bill Pepper or his wife, and I'm worried. I just wanted to be sure Ginny was all right."

"Has this ever happened before?"

"Standard operating procedure is for Pepper to always be reachable within an hour of the initial contact."

"I see."

"I'd like you and Holly to go to his house, get inside and call me back."

"I don't think we can do that for a couple of hours without causing suspicion. Remember, we're vacationers here; we can't just make an excuse and walk away from a dinner party."

"All right, when you're rid of Irene and her friend, go there. Got a pencil?"

Stone took out a jotting pad and his pen. "Shoot." He wrote down the address and the burglar alarm code. "Got it."

"There's a note in Pepper's file: a key is taped to the underside of the mailbox. When you leave, reset the alarm with the same code and replace the key, then have Holly call me at home on the sat-phone." He gave Stone the number.

"All right, we'll be in touch."

"Don't take Dino and Genevieve with you; tell them that if you're not back at the inn in two hours, to call me."

"Thanks, Lance, Ginny will call you later." Stone closed his phone and went back to the table. "Sorry about that; my secretary is working late and needed some client information for billing. She can't always read my handwriting."

Holly wasn't buying that, but Stone wasn't sending any signals, either. She tried to relax and get back to pumping Irene. "What's new on Black Mountain?" she asked.

"Not much."

"Do you ever see your neighbors up there?"

"Not often. The Pembertons and the Weatherbys still haven't turned up, and we hardly ever spot Sir Winston outside of his car. I think it's more neighborly farther down the mountain, where the houses are thicker on the ground. I got a letter from someone wanting to start a neighborhood association, but I can't imagine what such a group would do. After all, we have the prime minister for a neighbor, and if there were a pothole, or something like that, his people would be all over it."

"Have you ever even seen the Pembertons or the Weatherbys?" Holly asked.

"Never laid eyes on them."

Harry spoke up. "Irene says you're leaving on Saturday."

"Yep," Holly said. "I've got flying lessons scheduled for next week, and Stone claims he has to work, too."

"Nobody has ever actually caught Stone working," Dino said.

"How would you all like to come for a sail tomorrow?" Harry asked.

"That sounds like fun," Holly said. "There was talk of tennis with some other guests; can we call you in the morning and let you know?"

"Sure, that's fine. I just want to keep the barnacles off the hull."

"I'll fix us a lunch," Irene said. "It would be fun."

"We'd love it, if we're able to come," Holly said.

They continued with dinner, laughing and talking. When Irene and Harry finally said their good-byes, Stone and Holly began walking back toward the cottage.

"That was Lance on the phone," he said. "He tried you, then tried me."

"What's up?"

"We have a little job to do for Lance." He handed Dino a slip of paper. "Dino, we have to disappear for a while. If we're not back in two hours, call Lance at that number and let him know."

"Let him know what?"

"Just that we're not back. You might try my cell phone before you call him."

"Okay." Dino put the number in his pocket.

Holly followed Stone to the car. "What's going on?"

"I'll tell you on the way."

31

Stone and Holly got into the car and drove out of the inn's grounds. He handed her his jotter. "You have any idea where that is?"

"No; what is it?"

"It's Bill Pepper's house. Lance hasn't been able to reach either Pepper or his wife, and he wants us to look around the place."

"Shit, what the hell is going on?"

"I don't know, but take a look at the rent-a-car map in the glove compartment, and see if you can figure out the address."

Holly opened the glove compartment and switched on the map light. "Okay, the address is 601 Victoria Road; that starts in Markstown and seems to run out into the country. Take your next right, then the first right after that."

Stone followed her instructions. "Okay, now we're on Victoria Road; see any house numbers?"

"We just passed 720," Holly said. She dug a small flashlight out of her handbag. "Slow down, so I can see the mailboxes."

Stone slowed.

"680," she said. "It'll be on the other side of the road." She continued to read off the numbers. "Next house on the left," she said.

Stone slowed, but didn't stop. "I don't want to just pull into the driveway," he said. "Let's see if anybody else is out here tonight."

The road was very dark, and Stone continued to drive slowly. "Look for parked cars on both sides," he said.

"I don't see any cars, except ones that look like they belong to the houses," Holly said.

Stone pulled into a driveway, turned around and started back toward 601. "Is that one of those lithium-battery flashlights?"

"Yes," she said, "a SureFire."

"I'm going to turn off the headlights now. Keep the flashlight pointed down the road." It was enough to keep out of the ditches, and Stone finally turned into Bill Pepper's driveway. There was a Toyota Avalon parked in front of the garage, and the house had lights burning.

"Looks like someone is home," Holly said.

"Right," Stone said. "Let's find out." They got out of the car, walked to the front door and rang the bell. No answer. They rang it again and knocked, and still no one came to the door.

"I can see into the living room," Holly said, leaning over the porch rail and peering through a window. "Nobody there."

"Give me the flashlight and wait here," Stone said. "Lance told me where the key is." He walked back up the driveway to the mailbox, looked underneath and extracted the key, leaving the tape in place, then walked back to the house. He opened the door and stepped inside, followed closely by Holly. The burglar alarm began to beep, once a second.

"Oh, shit," Holly said. "I hope that thing doesn't call the police."

Stone tapped in the code, and it stopped beeping.

"How did you know how to do that?" she asked.

"Lance gave me the code; we have to reset it when we leave."

"Bill!" Holly called out. They walked from room to room, as she continued to call his name. The bed in the master bedroom was undisturbed. They walked into the kitchen. "I smell food," Holly said. She opened the oven door. "Pot roast, I think, and there are string beans and potatoes on the stove. Everything has been turned off, though."

Stone placed his hand on the stove. "Cold," he said. "They've been gone awhile, and I can't see that anything has been disturbed."

"They planned to come back," Holly said. "Otherwise, Mrs. Pepper would have put the food in the fridge."

"Nothing seems to have been disturbed," Stone said. Suddenly, he had a thought. He leaned close to Holly's ear. "Let's get out of here," he whispered. He grabbed her hand and towed her out of the house, then went back, set the alarm and returned the key to its home under the mailbox. He backed the car out of the driveway, avoiding using the brakes, then headed back toward the inn.

"Turn on the lights," she said. "You'll kill us."

"Not yet. Use your flashlight."

"Why did you want to leave the house all of a sudden?"

"What if Pepper's house is bugged, too?"

"Oh, I didn't think of that."

Stone looked into the rearview mirror. "Turn off the flashlight," he said. "There's a police car coming up the road from the direction of Markstown."

Holly switched off the light. "We didn't set off the alarm," she said, "so the house must be bugged. Are the cops after us?"

Stone checked the mirror again. "They're turning into Pepper's driveway." He switched on the headlights and floored the engine. "We're getting out of here."

Ten minutes later they were back at the inn. They parked in front of the cottage and went inside. He held a finger to his lips as he entered. Dino and Genevieve were watching TV. "Anybody like a drink?" Stone asked, as if he had been there all along.

"Sure, I'll have a Scotch," Dino said.

"Me too," echoed Genevieve.

"I'll have one of your bourbons," Holly said. She went into the bedroom and came back with the satphone, then took her drink and went out back.

Y es?" Lance said. He didn't sound sleepy.

"It's Holly."

"What have you learned?"

"The house is empty, lights on, dinner had been cooking on the stove, but the stove had been turned off. We think the house may have been bugged, because as soon as we left, we saw a police car coming from Markstown with its flashers on, and it turned into Pepper's driveway. We had our lights off, so they didn't spot us."

"Anything amiss in the house? Had it been searched?"

"Not that we could see. Mrs. Pepper keeps a neat house, and if it was searched, it was done by experts."

Lance was quiet for a moment. "All right, there's nothing more you can do tonight; get some sleep."

"Lance, if the place is bugged and that's why the police came, then the police must have them."

"And that would mean Colonel Croft," Lance said. "Not a pretty situation."

"What are you going to do?"

"There's not much I can do tonight. I have to contrive some plausible story so that I can get the embassy on it."

"How about Bill's sister asked me to look in on him, and when I did, I found what I found. I could call the embassy and talk to the duty officer."

"You do that, and I'll call our man in the embassy, too. Tell the duty officer you want him to call the local police and report them missing, and he should ask them if they have any knowledge of the

Peppers' whereabouts. Call from your room, so the listeners will know what you're doing. Let's see what kind of reaction you get. Call me back in the morning, as usual."

"Right," Holly said. She punched off the phone, went inside and picked up the phone. "I think something's wrong," she said loudly. "I'm calling the embassy." She started dialing.

32

The phone rang half a dozen times before someone picked up. "United States Embassy," a sleepy male voice said.

"May I speak to the duty officer, please?" Holly replied.

"I'm the duty officer; my name is James Tiptree. May I have your name?"

"My name is Virginia Heller; I want to report an American citizen missing on St. Marks."

"Have you called the police?"

"I'd rather not become involved with the police. I would much prefer it if you would speak to them."

"What is the citizen's name?"

"Two people: Mr. and Mrs. William Pepper. He works for one of the offshore Internet casinos on the island; I don't know which one."

"I know the Peppers," Tiptree said. "The American community on the island is fairly small. Why do you think Bill and Annie are missing?"

"Bill's sister is a friend of mine, and I promised to call him while I'm here. When I couldn't get Bill on the phone, my friend and I went to his home. Lights were on, and food had been cooking on the stove, but the stove had been turned off. Nothing else in the house seemed amiss, but as soon as we left we saw a police car coming from the direction of Markstown, and it turned into the Peppers' driveway."

"Did you have any interaction with the police?"

"No, and I don't think they noticed us."

"What is your business on the island?"

"I'm a tourist, staying at the English Harbour Inn, with three friends."

"I know it well."

Holly heard a phone ring on the other end of the line.

"Please hold on; I have to answer another call." He put her on hold for a good five minutes, then came back on the line.

"That was another acquaintance of mine in the States with the same news," Tiptree said. "I understand your position now; I'll contact the Markstown police and report the Peppers missing, and then I'll call Colonel Croft at home and get him out of bed, if I have to."

"That's great news," Holly said.

"I'll call you at the inn when I know more."

"Thank you very much," Holly said, then hung up and turned to the others. "Why don't we take our drinks out onto the patio?" she said. "It's a lovely evening."

They all got up, trooped outside and sat down. "That was a guy named James Tiptree; Lance called him while he was on the phone with me, so the wheels are turning. Tiptree said he'd get Colonel Croft out of bed, if necessary."

Bill Pepper sat on a hard, straight-backed chair in a room furnished only with a desk and two chairs at the Markstown police station. He had been taken from a cell and placed there nearly an hour before, then left alone. He resisted the temptation to go through the drawers of the desk. The chair was extremely uncomfortable, and he frequently stood up and stretched, but he always sat down again. He had been trained to assume that when being detained anywhere in the world, he would be watched and listened in on.

The door opened and a man in a business suit, but no necktie, walked into the room and sat down. He placed a file folder on the desk, opened it and read from it for several minutes before he spoke. "I am Colonel Croft, of the home secretary's office," he said, finally, in his slightly French accent.

"Of course, Colonel," Pepper said pleasantly. "Everyone knows who you are. How do you do?"

"I do very well, thank you, which is more than I can say for you, Mr. Pepper. You have committed very serious crimes against the people of St. Marks."

"If you're referring to the several speeding tickets I've been given over the past year, I assure you they have all been paid, and I have adjusted my driving habits so that I am always within the speed limits."

"You know very well what I am referring to," Croft said.

"I'm afraid I don't, Colonel. Where is my wife? May I see her?"

"I haven't decided," Croft said.

"I assure you my wife is entirely a law-abiding resident of St. Marks."

"Does your wife have computer skills, too, Mr. Pepper?"

"She can just barely handle e-mail, I'm afraid."

"But you—you are an absolute whiz with computers, aren't you?"

"I'm the chief technology officer for the casino," Pepper replied. "Computers are an important part of my job."

"Describe your duties, please."

"As chief technology officer, I write or supervise the writing of computer software which allows people all over the world to

SHOOT HIM IF HE RUNS

participate in online gaming, thus injecting many millions in tax dollars into the economy of St. Marks. May I call my boss, the chief executive officer of my company, please?"

"No, you may not," Croft replied. "What is your interest in Mr. Pemberton and Mr. Weatherby and Mr. Robertson?"

"I'm sorry, I'm not acquainted with anyone of those names."

"Then why were you attempting to obtain information about them from the computers at the Department of the Interior?"

"Colonel, it is a legitimate part of my work to obtain information about clients and prospective clients, but the only reason I would have to obtain any information at all about anyone would be a perfectly normal check of employment and credit records, before establishing a line of credit for a new customer. In the event that the applicant was a St. Marks citizen or resident, one of my staff would seek confirmation of the contents of the credit application. I expect that must be what you are referring to."

"And would that search for information include attempting to download applications for permission to purchase a residence on St. Marks?"

"It might. Since the credit bureau on St. Marks is fairly limited in its operation, my staff might look for other sources to confirm the address and credit-worthiness of an applicant. The ownership of property is always desirable when we are extending credit to a new customer."

"And do you have signed applications for credit from those three gentlemen?"

"All our transactions with our customers and with applicants are conducted online, so we don't have paper records."

"But you could produce printouts of online applications from Mr. Pemberton and Mr. Weatherby?"

"I'm afraid that our company policies prevent the disclosure of any information about any of our customers or applicants, Colonel. The home office was made aware of our policies and procedures when our business was first established in St. Marks, and so were the home secretary and, of course, the prime minister. Sir Winston takes a very great interest in companies wishing to do business on St. Marks." Pepper was aware that both of these gentlemen took very great bribes, as well.

"Mr. Pepper, do you see the door immediately to your right?"

Pepper looked and found the door. "Yes, Colonel."

"Go and open the door and look into the next room."

"As you wish, Colonel." Pepper got up, walked to the door and opened it. A trickle of fear ran down his bowels. The room was smaller than the office in which he had been sitting, but it was better equipped; it contained a heavy wooden chair bolted to the floor and equipped with thick leather straps for restricting the movement of whoever might sit in it.

Next to the chair was a large table on which were arrayed a variety of knives, pliers and other hardware that might be used for other than their original purpose.

On the other side of the chair, resting on two sawhorses, was a freshly constructed wooden coffin, with its lid lying on the floor next to it.

Pepper closed the door and returned to his chair.

"Now," Colonel Croft said, "let us begin again."

33

Lance Cabot was waiting in the director's reception area when she arrived at work at 8 A.M. He felt awful, having been up all night, and he was anxious about this meeting.

Kate Lee regarded him closely. "Something wrong, Lance?" she asked.

"May I speak with you in your office, Director?"

"Of course; come in." She led the way into her inner office and hung her coat in a closet. "Have a seat." She waved him toward her desk.

Lance took a chair across the desk from her, noting the difference from other meetings, when they sat in the more informal cluster of sofas and chairs across the room. "Sometime yesterday, probably in the afternoon, Bill Pepper was taken from his office by the police on St. Marks. Later in the day, police also took his wife, who is also our operative, from their home."

"Is there anything in either Bill's office or home that might compromise his situation?"

"I very much doubt it; he would have followed procedure."

"Where is he now?"

"Apparently, still in the Markstown jail. The legendary Colonel Croft is also there, and I think we must presume that he has questioned or is questioning Bill and Annie."

"And, as I recall, his interrogation techniques were learned and refined in latter-day Haiti."

"That is correct."

"Do we know the reason for their detention?"

"Not yet. We were fortunate that our man in the embassy there was also the duty officer last night, so we have not yet involved the ambassador." He glanced at his watch. "That will become necessary later this morning."

"Do we know if Colonel Croft has made any connection between Pepper and Holly Barker's group?"

"No, but I very much doubt it."

"I should have thought that Colonel Croft's interrogation practices might have produced that information by now."

"Jim Tiptree, the Agency man at the embassy, first telephoned Colonel Croft, then visited the jail, demanding to see him. He is still there, waiting. I think his presence might have had a dampening effect on the colonel's urges."

"You must have some idea why the Peppers were detained. What was Bill's most recent assignment? From you, I mean; not from Hugh English."

"He was to go into the St. Marks government computers and get copies of the applications to purchase a residence of three men we suspect of possibly being Teddy Fay—Robertson, Pemberton and Weatherby."

"You suspect *three* men of being Teddy?"

"Possibly."

"As I recall, Bill has made St. Marks government computers his playground over the past few months. How would he get caught now?"

"Croft has been working at upgrading all of St. Marks's security procedures. At some point, he would turn his attention to computer security, and we may be at that point."

"And what is our next step?"

"When the ambassador arrives at his office, Jim Tiptree is going to have to involve him in the effort to secure the release of the Peppers. That, of course, will mean the involvement of State, since the ambassador will certainly inform the Caribbean Desk, as a matter of routine."

"And we don't want that, do we?"

"No, Director."

"And how do you propose that we prevent that from happening?"

"The ambassador to St. Marks, Warren Holden, is a personal friend of the president, I believe."

"Yes, they were both Senate staffers on the Select Committee on Intelligence when they were younger. Are you suggesting that the president call Holden and prevent him from reporting this incident to State?"

"Nothing quite as formal as that," Lance said. "If he could just ask him to give us time to get the Peppers released and off the island."

"And when they're gone, then report to State?"

"Well, a delay in reporting might make it awkward to report it at a later date."

"So you want the president to call in a favor from an old friend?"

"It was a pretty big favor, on the part of the president, to appoint his old friend to a cushy Caribbean ambassadorship. I should think Mr. Holden would be anxious to repay that."

"I suppose he might, but if this should turn into an international incident, then . . ."

"I believe this will end with the release and repatriation of the Peppers."

"What, exactly, do you want Warren Holden to do?"

"I'd like him to call the prime minister, Sir Winston Sutherland, tell him that the Peppers are personal friends of his—they play bridge every Thursday, or something like that—and ask him to call Colonel Croft and have them released at once."

"Are you at all concerned about the security of Holly Barker's group? Should we get them out of there now?"

"An airplane had already been scheduled to pick them up at noon tomorrow and bring them home. I think to rush that might be counterproductive."

"Would there be room on that airplane for the Peppers?"

"There would be, if I send a larger airplane."

"How large?"

"The presently scheduled airplane is quite small; something mid-sized, like a Hawker, would be sufficient."

"All right, I'll ask the president to make the call. If we can get the Peppers off the island tomorrow, and without a fuss, then Holden can just forget any of this ever happened. I want you to take every conceivable step to see that a fuss does not occur."

"Certainly, Director."

"Because that is what I'm going to tell the president, and you'd better not make a liar of me."

"I'll get this done, Director."

"All right, I'll make the call now; go back to your office, and I'll call you when it's in the works."

"Ah, there is one other thing, Director."

"What thing?"

"Hugh English."

Kate Lee emitted a small groan.

"There was no way I could ask Jim Tiptree not to report this to him. I'm sure he'll be on the phone to me within minutes."

The Director sighed. "Hugh English is going to be more trouble than the ambassador," she said.

"I know. Unless you speak to him before he speaks to me, there will be an eruption, and I don't think we want that."

The director picked up the phone. "Get me Hugh English, please; if he's not in, try his cell or his car phone." She pressed the speaker button and waited.

Lance tried not to squirm in his seat.

"Hello?" Hugh English might have been in the room with them, his voice was so clear.

"Good morning, Hugh."

"Not really, Director; I have a problem."

"The situation in St. Marks?"

There was what seemed a stunned silence, then: "I'm very surprised that you should know about this so quickly, Director; I'm not sure it rises to your level."

"Hugh, we're not sure about this yet, but the Peppers may have been detained because Bill was trying to extract some information from St. Marks government computers at my request."

"I received no such request from you, Director."

"No, it was made through another Agency officer who is also present on St. Marks at the moment. It's my understanding that Bill Pepper has been extracting all sorts of information from those computers for months, so I believed that my request would be routine for him, and he did not indicate otherwise."

"Director, I'm sure this could have all been avoided, if you had had the courtesy to go through my office, as prescribed by the operational procedures which you yourself instituted."

"Perhaps, but we don't know that yet. He may well have been detained for something you yourself asked him to do."

Lance loved that.

"In any case, Hugh, I am personally working to have the Peppers released and returned to the U.S., perhaps as early as tomorrow, so please take no steps in that regard without consulting me first."

"As you wish, Director."

"I think we can resolve this quickly and without a fuss, so just give me some time. In the meantime, you might be thinking about a replacement for the Peppers on St. Marks."

"Don't you think that might be precipitous, Director? I mean, until we know the meaning of their detention, we won't know if they've been compromised."

"Hugh, they were compromised the moment they came to the personal attention of the infamous Colonel Croft."

"Quite," Hugh English said. "I'll begin working on a replacement. Is that all, Director?"

"For the moment, Hugh."

"Good-bye." He hung up.

"If he calls you, Lance," the director said, "stonewall him, but as politely as possible. Now, get to work on getting an airplane there tomorrow."

Lance stood up. "Thank you, Director." She was asking for the White House when he left her office.

34

Bill Pepper still sat in the uncomfortable wooden chair, and the light coming through the closed shutters on the window told him that the sun was well up; his stomach was telling him it was near lunchtime. Colonel Croft kept leaving the room and returning and asking the same questions all over again.

Colonel Croft now returned again and took his seat at the desk. "Mr. Pepper," he said, "I am growing weary of your intransigence."

"Colonel Croft," Pepper said, "I have repeatedly answered every question you have put to me; there is no intransigence on my part."

"Mr. Pepper, go to the door there and open it."

"Colonel, I have already seen your display."

"Do as I say immediately."

Pepper got up wearily, went to the door and opened it. Everything was as before, except that Annie Pepper was seated in the torture chair, blindfolded.

"Return to your chair and sit down," the colonel said.

"Annie," Pepper said, "don't worry, honey; everything is going to be all right." He closed the door and returned to his chair, this time frightened, but furious.

"Now, Mr. Pepper . . ." the colonel began.

"No, Colonel," Pepper replied, cutting him off. "Not now, not ever. I demand to see an official of the American Embassy at once, and if you so much as touch a hair on the head of my wife, I will take it upon myself to see that you will spend the rest of your days regretting it. And if you don't think I have the juice to do that, you are very much mistaken. This interrogation is at an end."

The colonel rose from his chair, opened a desk drawer and removed what appeared to be a riding crop. He strode around the desk and stopped in front of Pepper. "Now, Mr. Pepper, we will see how much influence you have." He drew the crop back so far it was over his shoulder.

I rene Foster was pushing her grocery cart down an aisle at her favorite supermarket in Markstown, thumping melons and sniffing cheeses, when her basket collided with that of another woman.

"Oh, I'm so sorry; I . . ."

"Irene?"

Irene peered at the other woman. "Margaret Tiptree? I don't believe it."

"I don't believe it, either," Mrs. Tiptree said. "What on earth are you doing in St. Marks?"

"I retired here earlier this year," Irene replied. "Is Jim based here?"

"He's the cultural attaché at the embassy," Margaret replied, winking.

"Of course he is. What a plum assignment!"

"It's a great way to ride out the three years until his retirement," Margaret said. "We like it here so much, we're thinking of staying."

"Well, you must come to dinner, soon. It would be good to see Jim again; it's been years. His work must be boring, though."

Margaret came closer and lowered her voice. "Not today, it isn't. Colonel Croft has got Bill and Annie Pepper in his jail, and Jim is worried sick. He's over there now."

"I remember Bill Pepper," Irene said, "but I don't know his wife."

"He's undercover in one of the offshore casinos, and we don't even know why he was picked up."

"That's bad news," Irene said. "That Colonel Croft is a throwback to the Middle Ages; there's no telling what he will do."

"Well, Jim's all over it, so I'm hoping for a good result."

The two women chatted a bit longer and made a dinner date for the following week. As soon as they had parted, Irene went to an isolated corner of the supermarket and dialed a cell phone number.

"Yes?"

"Teddy, it's Irene."

"What's up?"

"I just ran into Margaret Tiptree at the supermarket."

"Jim Tiptree's wife?"

"Yes; he's based at the embassy here."

"Is something wrong?"

"Do you remember a young officer named Bill Pepper?"

"Yes, I outfitted him on his first mission for the Agency."

"He's here, too, undercover, in one of the offshore casinos, and that awful Colonel Croft has arrested him."

"Oh, shit," Teddy said.

"Jim is on the job, but I'm afraid Bill is going to be hurt before they can get him out. They arrested his wife, too."

"Christ, I hate hearing that."

"You've had dealings with Croft; is there anything you can do?"

Teddy was quiet for a moment. "Yes, there is, and I should have done it sooner," he said. "I'll speak to you later."

Teddy hung up, remembering where Colonel Croft liked to have his lunch every day. He went to a shelf in his workshop and removed a slightly battered briefcase that was heavier than it appeared. He checked the contents, then closed it and headed for his car. He drove to Markstown, to a hilltop overlooking the town and, in particular, the Markstown jail. He drove up an overgrown dirt trail to a spot he knew: an old tower that had once been used for firespotting, dating to a time when there were more trees on the island.

He climbed the tower, being careful to avoid steps that were rotting, and when he reached the top he looked down onto the Markstown jail. The rambling building had been built as an outpost for the British army, and it was arranged around a parade ground, now planted with trees and flowers. It was like a little park, where employees would take their sandwiches for lunch.

Teddy wasn't sure this was going to work, but it was all he could do. He hated Croft, and he had become weary of paying his bribes. This was something he had been contemplating for weeks; he had only hoped he would get the chance.

Colonel Croft made ready to rake Bill Pepper's face with the riding crop.

"Go ahead, Colonel," Pepper said. "Mark me up; the pictures will look great in the international press."

The colonel's normally impassive face creased, ready for a snarl, and he pulled the crop back even farther. Then, as he was about to swing, there came a pounding on the door.

"Colonel!" a muffled voice shouted from the other side of the door. "Please open the door at once!"

"I told you not to disturb me!" the colonel shouted back.

"It is an emergency!" the voice shouted back.

The colonel tossed the crop onto the desk and strode over to the door. He unbolted it and yanked it open. "What is it?" he snarled. Then he saw Tiptree, whom he knew from the American Embassy, standing behind the police officer.

"I know you've got an American citizen in there," Tiptree said, shoving aside the policeman and walking into the office. He saw Bill Pepper. "Are you all right, Mr. Pepper?"

"Yes, but he's got my wife strapped into a chair in the next room!" Pepper replied, getting up and going to the door. Tiptree followed him, and they both looked into the room.

It was empty of all furniture; everything was gone.

"A few minutes ago, this place was a torture chamber," Pepper said.

"I believe you, Mr. Pepper," Tiptree said.

"Mr. Tiptree," the colonel said, placatingly, "there is nothing wrong here; I am merely questioning Mr. Pepper about his activities on the island. As you can see, he is unharmed."

"He was about to use that on me," Pepper said, pointing to the crop on the desk.

"Mr. Tiptree, please, let's talk for a moment, shall we?" The colonel took Tiptree's arm and steered him toward the door. "Sergeant," he said to the policeman, "Mr. Tiptree and I will be in the garden for a few minutes. Please send us out some lunch. And would you please process out Mr. and Mrs. Pepper? You may sign them for me."

"Yes, Colonel," the sergeant said.

"Wait here, Mr. Pepper," Tiptree said. "I'll be back for you and your wife shortly."

Pepper walked into the anteroom, sat down on a comfortable sofa and tried to slow his thumping heartbeat. "Bring my wife to me right now," he ordered the sergeant. The policeman got up and left the room.

The colonel steered James Tiptree though another door, and they stepped into the sunlit courtyard at the center of the police station. "Lovely out here, isn't it? A great improvement from when the British used it to drill their troops."

"Yes, lovely," Tiptree replied through clenched teeth. "Listen Colonel, I've been waiting here, demanding to see you for most of the night, why . . ."

"Please take a seat," the colonel said, showing him to a bench. "I want to assure you that nothing has gone on here except routine police work."

"I don't think there's anything routine about this incident," Tiptree said, sitting down. My ambassador has already spoken to the prime minister, and I assure you, there will be repercussions."

The colonel sat down next to him. "I give you my word, Mr. Tiptree, there is nothing . . ." And then the colonel's head exploded.

Tiptree leapt off the bench, flecks of gray matter dotting his dark suit, and backed away from the nearly headless corpse, now lying on the gravel path. "Jesus H. Christ!" he said aloud. He could hear doors being flung open and boots pounding on the earth. "I didn't do it!" he yelled.

35

Holly and her group were sitting on their patio having breakfast when Thomas Hardy arrived and pulled up a chair.

"Colonel Croft is dead," he said.

Holly reacted with surprise, but she was not displeased. "Oh, good," she said. "Now we can rip out those fucking bugs."

"I suppose so," Thomas said. "His people will be in such disarray that they probably won't even be listening."

"How did he die?" Stone asked.

"There is a courtyard at the police station, and word is, he was sitting on a bench there, talking to a man named Tiptree from the American embassy, when his head exploded. No one heard a gunshot."

"Single shot from a silenced rifle, explosive-tipped bullet," Dino said, matter-of-factly.

"Could be, I suppose," Thomas replied.

Holly was staring out to sea, an amazed expression on her face. "It's Teddy," she said.

"What?"

"It's Teddy Fay; this sort of thing is his specialty."

"This is the man you came here to find?"

"Yes."

"But why would he shoot Colonel Croft?"

"I can't go into that," Holly replied. She stood up. "Will you excuse me? I have to make a phone call; I think our work here is done, Stone. We can go home today, if they can send an airplane."

"Just a minute," Thomas said. "You're not going anywhere today, and maybe not for several days."

"What?" she asked.

"The airport is closed; the prime minister is furious about Croft, and he is determined that whoever killed him is not going to get off the island, which means nobody else is, either. The airport is closed."

"Oh, shit," Holly said. "No reflection on your lovely inn, Thomas, but I'm ready to get out of here. I miss my dog."

"I can understand that," Thomas replied, "but be assured, you are welcome to stay on here for as long as this takes."

"Excuse me," Holly said again, then left. She went into the cottage, got her satphone from the safe and went out back, dialing Lance's direct number.

"Lance Cabot."

"It's Holly; shall we scramble?"

"Yes, please." There was a click on the line. "How's this?"

"Fine. There has been a major uproar here."

"What's happened?"

"Colonel Croft was shot this morning by a sniper with a silenced weapon; he's dead."

There was a stunned silence. "I'm going to have to get back to you," Lance said, and hung up.

Holly stared at the phone in her hand. "What the hell kind of reaction was that?" she said aloud.

L ance hung up the phone and looked across his desk at Hugh English, who had turned a funny color. "I'm sorry, Hugh, please go on."

"As I was saying, Lance," English said with elaborate courtesy, "it appears that you have co-opted an agent of mine, the result of which is that he has been arrested and is probably being tortured by that animal Croft."

"Hugh, the director has already spoken to you about this."

"Right, and now I am speaking to you about it."

"Hugh . . ."

"What in God's name was he doing for you that would result in his arrest?"

"Hugh, he was simply retrieving some documents from the St. Marks government computers, something I understand he's been doing for months. The fact that he was doing it for me had nothing to do with his arrest."

English suddenly jumped and grabbed the vibrating cell phone on his belt. "Yes?" His face slowly grew more astonished as he listened. "Why?" he demanded. "Are you perfectly serious about this? I'll get the ambassador on it right away, and I'll talk to you later." He hung up. "That was Bill Pepper; Jim Tiptree went to the jail and effected the release of Bill and his wife, but now the police are holding Jim."

"Why on earth would they do that?" Lance asked.

"Apparently, Jim was sitting on a park bench, talking with Colonel Croft, when his head exploded."

"Single shot with an explosive-tipped bullet," Lance mused.

"Yes, but the St. Marks police haven't figured that out yet, and they're holding Jim while they mull it over. I have to go back to my office and call the ambassador," English said, standing. "Lance, did you have anything to do with Croft's assassination?"

"Nothing whatever, Hugh; I give you my word. I certainly wouldn't have done such a thing while he was sitting next to your station head, and I don't have anyone on the island who could do it."

"I'll speak to you later," English said, and it sounded like a promise.

H olly's satphone rang. "Yes?"

"Scramble."

Holly did so. "Okay."

"I've just heard about Croft's death in some detail. Apparently, Jim Tiptree, our station head down there, was sitting next to him when it happened. Of course, you didn't have anything to do with this."

"Of course not; Teddy Fay did it."

"*What?*"

"It's practically his trademark, isn't it?"

"Well, yes, but what possible motive would Teddy have for killing Croft?"

"From what I've heard, anybody on the run who wants to live on this island and not be found has to pay off Croft. Maybe Teddy didn't like him, or maybe he just did it on a whim, who knows?"

"I've got to have time to figure this out," Lance said, "but it's just as well you're being picked up tomorrow. I'm sending a larger airplane, and Bill Pepper and his wife are coming back with you."

"No," Holly said.

"What do you mean, 'no'?"

"Sir Winston Sutherland has shut down the island; nobody leaves, maybe for days, while Croft's death is investigated, so you may as well cancel the airplane."

"Swell," Lance said.

"Yeah, well . . . Do I have your permission to get in touch with Bill Pepper?"

"For what?"

"I want to find out if he got those housing applications of Robertson, Pemberton and Weatherby. They could help us identify Teddy."

"I suppose so. All right, go ahead and call him on his satphone. He should be home by now."

"He's been released?"

"Yes, but they're holding Jim Tiptree; it's a huge mess, and we're trying to sort it out now. Let me know if you're sending the photos."

"All right; good-bye." Holly hung up and called Bill Pepper's number. No answer. She went back to the patio. "Stone, can I have the car keys?"

Stone handed them to her. "Where are you going?"

"Where we were last night," she said.

"Hang on, I'm going with you."

36

Lance presented himself in the director's office for the second time that morning.

"Now what, Lance?"

"There's a bit of a flap in St. Marks."

Kate Lee massaged her temples. "Oh, God."

"Let me explain what's happened." Lance gave her the rundown on Croft's murder and Tiptree's detention.

"What a mess," Kate said.

"It gets worse," Lance replied. "Holly Barker thinks Teddy Fay did it."

"I'm sorry, my mind just boggled; I'm unable to follow her logic."

"She may have a point. First, Croft was shot in the head with an exploding bullet, apparently from outside the Markstown jail building, an expert shot, and that sounds like Teddy. Second, Holly points out that anyone hiding on the island would have to bribe Croft to remain safe, and that's a motive for Teddy."

"Could Teddy know about Bill and Annie Pepper's arrest?"

"I don't see how he could."

"I can see him being angry with Croft, if he knew."

"If Holly is right, then that settles the question of whether Teddy is on the island. Now we have to find him."

"You want to keep Holly there longer?"

"No, but I don't have a choice. Sutherland has shut down all transportation from the island; nobody can leave until he says so. If we tried to bring some sort of pressure to allow Holly and her group to leave, it might bring suspicion to bear on her."

"Do we have any idea what identity Teddy is using?"

"There are the three men I told you about. Bill Pepper was caught trying to get photos of them from government computers, so we could circulate them here to see if any of Teddy's former coworkers could make him. If somebody can, then we've got a chance of . . . detaining him. Holly is trying now to learn if Pepper downloaded the photos before he was arrested."

"From what you've told me, there's no way to connect any of these men to Holly."

"No."

"Unless she has contact with them and one of them is arrested."

"Well, yes."

"Order her to have no contact with them, to ask no questions of anyone about them."

"Certainly."

"There's another problem," Kate said.

"Yes?"

"What happens if one of these men is Teddy and Teddy is the shooter and they catch him? I'm sure that Colonel Croft was not the only man in St. Marks who knows how to extract a confession from a suspect."

"Director, do you have any reason to believe that you and I are being recorded at this moment?"

"I have every reason to believe that we are not," she replied.

"If Teddy is arrested by the St. Marks police, then we have to kill him before they can question him."

"That's pretty brazen of you, Lance."

"Think about it: if Teddy is, ah, persuaded to reveal his true identity, and if Sir Winston Sutherland chose to make an issue of a former Agency operative as murderer, then we have a flap of major proportions on our hands. If the American press got hold of that, I think it's safe to say that the outcome of the next election might be in doubt."

Kate Lee turned and gazed out the window at the Virginia landscape.

Lance waited for her to speak; he had said all he intended to.

"Lance," she said finally, "you are authorized to use whatever means you feel are necessary to prevent Teddy Fay from falling into the hands of Sir Winston Sutherland's police."

"May I have that in writing, Director?"

She turned and looked at him. "Certainly not," she said.

"I may not be able to handle this without the cooperation of Hugh English," Lance said. "May I confide in him?"

"Certainly not," she replied. "But you may use whatever resources we have on the island without Hugh's knowledge."

"I'm afraid that would not be possible; we've seen that already. Hugh would have to be . . . out of the picture. Unless he is, I would not have the freedom to operate."

Kate's face was expressionless. "You're right," she said finally. She pressed a button on her phone.

"Yes, Director?"

"Please ask Hugh English to join me in my dining room for lunch at noon," she said. "Don't take no for an answer." She disconnected and turned to Lance. "You're invited, too."

37

olly drove quickly out of the inn's grounds and toward the Peppers' house.

"Slow down," Stone said. "We don't want to attract the attention of the police."

Holly made a determined effort to drive more slowly.

"That's better; we're just a couple of tourists out for a drive."

Ten minutes later Holly turned into the Peppers' driveway. The small car was parked where it had been before, but this time the front door was ajar.

Holly and Stone got out of the car and approached the front door.

"I don't know if we can eat this," a woman's voice said from inside.

"Just heat it up, it'll be fine," a male voice answered.

Holly rapped on the door. "Hello?"

Bill Pepper came into the living room with some sort of electronic device in his hand. When he saw Holly, he tapped an ear.

"Hi, Bill," Holly said, "I'm Ginny Heller, a friend of your sister's in Miami. She asked me to drop in on you and see how you were doing."

"Hi, Ginny," Pepper said, but his attention was on the device in his hand. He walked toward the telephone in the living room, picked it up and started unscrewing the mouthpiece.

"This is my friend Stone; we're traveling together."

"Hi, Stone."

"Hi, Bill."

Pepper took a small disk from the phone and held it up, then he put it on the stone floor and stomped on it. "There," he said, consulting the meter on the device in his hand, "that's the lot. Now we can talk."

"Good," Holly said.

"I hear we're flying out of here tomorrow with you."

"I'm afraid not. Sutherland has locked down the island; nobody leaves until Croft's assassin is found."

Annie Pepper came into the room. "Hello," she said.

"Annie, this is Holly Barker and her friend Stone Barrington. You saw them at the inn earlier in the week."

"Of course," Annie replied.

"Annie and I had already left the police station when the Croft hit happened," Pepper said. "I think we were in a cab by then. I didn't hear about it until I called Lance."

"Thomas Hardy told us," Holly said.

"Thomas knows just about everything about everybody on this island," Pepper said.

"Would you like to stay for lunch?" Annie asked. "I'm heating up last night's dinner; I was arrested while I was cooking it, but it seems to be okay."

"Sure, if it's no trouble," Holly said. "Bill, business first; did you get the housing applications for Robertson, Pemberton and Weatherby downloaded before the cops came?"

"Yes, but they're on my laptop, and they confiscated it. I forgot to demand its return when we got out of jail, so I was going to call Jim Tiptree and ask him to retrieve it."

"Has he been released?"

"The ambassador is working on that now, I think. There's no way they can make him complicit in Croft's murder. The sergeant on duty heard Croft suggest to Jim that they go outside. I think maybe Croft's office is bugged, too, like everywhere else."

"Our cottage at the inn is bugged," Holly said. "We were thinking of ripping them out, as you're doing."

"What the hell? Croft's not around to listen anymore."

The phone rang, and Pepper picked it up. "Hello? Hi, Jim; are you out? Good; I didn't think they would have any reason to hold you. Listen, in our haste to get out of there, I didn't get my laptop back from them; do you think you could handle that? There's something on it that I need. Don't worry, it's encrypted; they'll never be able to get into it. They caught me downloading the stuff from the government computer from their end. Great, Jim, and thanks; give me a call when you've got it, and I'll come get it. Well, all right. Thanks again." He hung up. "Jim's going to send somebody over there for the computer and have it delivered here."

"Great; do you know when?"

"Let's have lunch, and maybe it will be here by the time we finish."

They went into the kitchen, where Annie was setting the table, and Pepper opened a bottle of wine. They sat down to eat.

"Are we all family here?" Pepper asked as we sat down.

"Yes; Stone is a consultant to the Agency, and he's aware of everything that's going on."

"Have you talked to Lance recently?"

"Not since earlier this morning."

"You need to talk to him again; things are heating up."

"How so?"

"I take it you think Teddy Fay might have killed Croft?"

"Yes, it's like him, especially if he had some motive. My guess is he may have been paying off Croft, so that he could stay on the island."

"Possibly," Pepper said. "I only knew Teddy slightly. He outfitted me for a mission earlier in my career."

"Did you get a look at the photos on the applications of Robertson, Pemberton and Weatherby?"

"Yes, and one of them could be Teddy, if he's as good at disguise as they say."

"Do you think Sir Winston Sutherland might have any reason to suspect either of them?"

"I don't know; it depends on how much Croft told Sutherland, but from what I know about the PM, he's a hands-on guy, a control freak, so I can't imagine there's much Croft knew that Sutherland doesn't. I think we have to assume that Sutherland knows everything Croft knew. Of course, he's unlikely to know that one of the Brits is Teddy. He probably thinks that Teddy is dead, like the rest of the world."

Stone spoke up. "Sutherland is not a stupid man; I've dealt with him before, and you should think of him as dangerous at all times."

"Yeah, I heard about your trial here a few years back," Pepper said, "and I tend to agree with you."

"If Sutherland goes after Robertson, Pemberton or Weatherby, then we've got to get there first," Holly said.

"Funny, that's what Lance said, which means that's what the director has said, too. He's working directly for her on this, and I think Hugh English is royally pissed off about it. Something's going to blow at Langley pretty soon."

"How do you think this is going to play out?"

"Well, I don't think Lance will want to work with English or vice versa, and I also don't think Hugh will sit still very long with Lance poaching on his turf, so the director is going to have her hands full." He toyed with his food. "There could be political implications, too."

"I can see how there might be," Holly said, "but I'm not mixing in that."

Pepper sipped his wine. "I think that if we can prove that one of the three Englishmen is Teddy, one of us in this room is going to be asked to do something about him. You'd better be prepared for that when you talk to Lance."

"My orders were to find Teddy, report back and get the hell out," Holly said.

Pepper shook his head. "Everything has changed, with Croft's killing. We're all going to be getting new orders."

38

Hugh English knocked, then entered Kate Lee's office. "Good morning, Director," he said.

"Good morning, Hugh," Kate replied. She thought he looked a little flushed and angry. "Let's go straight in to lunch, shall we?"

"Of course."

Kate led him into the small dining room off her office, where the round table was set for three and a bottle of Chardonnay was on ice. "Please take a seat."

"Is someone joining us?"

"Yes, I've asked Lance to come a little later; first, though, I want us to talk." She continued quickly, not giving him time to ask questions. "Hugh, first thing is I want to thank you again for stepping in after Dick Stone's murder and holding things together."

"I was happy to help."

"I know you had to delay your retirement plans and that it may have been expensive for you to do that, so let me assure you, the Agency will make you whole in that regard."

"Thank you, Director."

"Secondly, I want to ask you to stay on just a little longer."

"I suppose I can do that. Have you made any progress on choosing my replacement?"

"Yes, I've decided to promote Lance Cabot to the job. I realize, Hugh, that Lance would not have been your first choice, but I'm sure you know that I have my own priorities. I know you will agree that Lance has been a more than capable officer for us, winning good outcomes on a remarkable number of important efforts over the past few years."

"Well, yes," English said without enthusiasm. "I suppose you've already told Lance."

"No, I wanted you to be here for that; it's the purpose of our lunch. I also want to have a conversation among the three of us about the future of the operations directorate."

"When is Lance's appointment going to take effect?"

"Right after this luncheon," Kate said. "What I'd like you to do is to gather your deputies and assistants this afternoon, tell them of the transition and ask them to assemble summaries of the various operations, both under way and contemplated. Tomorrow, or the next day, if they need the time, I'd like them to make full-blown presentations to Lance, so that he will have the greatest possible grasp of what's happening everywhere. At your meeting this afternoon with your people, I'd like you to tell them to begin immediately to report to Lance on absolutely everything, and to cable all stations and all field agents to do so, as well. Instructions should go out before close of business today. It will be a bit of a cold shower for Lance, but I think it's the fastest way to get him up to speed. I'll make a written announcement to the building at half past four this afternoon."

"Very well, I'll get out of my office this afternoon."

"That won't be necessary, Hugh. Lance can continue to work from his temporary office until you feel the transition is as complete as you can make it. I know that Lance will want to consult with you on an hour-by-hour basis, until he has all the reins firmly in his hands. I know that moving out of an office you've occupied for as long as you have will take time; there'll be a lot of files and mementos to go through, and I'll appoint a screening committee to sift through everything as you send it home, to protect both you and the Agency from any inadvertent transfer of classified material."

"All right." English was looking a little deflated now.

"Also, Hugh, I know you'll probably want to write your memoirs, and I'd like you to do that on a secure Agency computer, which we will install in whatever home you choose. Because of the sensitivity of your work here, I want to place a moratorium of one year from today on any contact with the press or publishers. You may instruct an agent to offer your book to publishers, if you wish, but of course, we'll want to vet the proposal, which should be vague.

"I know, Hugh, that over the years you've established an outstanding network of contacts in Congress, and I hope that, at a series of lunches here at the Agency, you will introduce Lance to as many key people as you can, even though congressional approval is not required for his appointment, as it was not for yours. I must ask you, though, to refer any questions from Congress about any operations to your successor."

"Of course. How much longer do you contemplate that you will need me in the building?"

"I should think at least a few days, perhaps longer, but that will be up to you and Lance. When you both feel that Lance is comfortable in the job, then we'll send you on your way with all our best wishes."

There was a knock at the door, and the director's secretary stuck her head in. "Lance Cabot is here."

"Would you ask him to wait just a moment, please?"

The woman left, and Kate turned back to Hugh English. "Hugh, is there anything you'd like to talk about before we invite Lance in?"

"Yes, Director; I have some questions about whatever it is that Lance is doing in St. Marks."

"Hugh, I'm afraid that, in the circumstances, I can't answer your questions, at least not yet. Lance is firmly in control of his very small operation there, and this afternoon, he'll be talking with Jim Tiptree, Bill and Annie Pepper and the ambassador, just to get everybody on the same page."

"Well, certainly everybody is not on the same page now."

"I know, and I apologize for that being necessary in the circumstances. I know you felt left out of this business, but please be assured that that was not due to any lack of trust in you. It was necessary to compartmentalize, it was done on my authority, and I hope there will be no hard feelings for Lance on your part. If blame is to be assigned for anything, please assign it to me. Anything else?"

"No, Director, I think not."

"Then I'll ask Lance in," she said, pressing a buzzer. "Please send Lance Cabot in."

Lance knocked, then opened the door.

"Come in, Lance," Kate said, "and have a seat." She reached over, took the bottle of wine from the cooler and poured them each a glass. "I'd like to propose a toast," she said, and they all stood. "To the Central Intelligence Agency's new deputy director for operations."

"Congratulations, Lance," Hugh English said, mustering a trace of warmth. "I know you'll do a great job."

The director and English drank, while Lance looked stunned.

"I'm sorry if I'm speechless," Lance said.

"Never happened before," Kate said, and they all chuckled.

"Director, I want to thank you for your trust; Hugh, I want to thank you in advance for all the help I'll need from you to get a grip on the job." He raised his glass and drank.

They all sat down, and lunch was served.

39

They were eating dessert when a muffled ringing came from Holly's handbag.

"That will be Lance," Pepper said.

"It's not our regular time," Holly said, grabbing her handbag and coming up with the ringing satphone. She walked over to the window for better reception and punched on. "Hello?"

"Scramble," Lance said.

Holly punched the button. "Scrambled."

"Holly, first of all, I have news, then I have instructions."

"I'm listening."

"Less than an hour ago the director appointed me DDO, to succeed Hugh English, and with immediate effect."

"I congratulate you, Lance."

"Thank you. Where are you at the moment?"

"At Bill and Annie Pepper's house."

"Have you been discussing Agency business?"

"Yes, but Bill swept the house; it's clean."

"Can they hear you now?"

"Yes."

"Go to another room."

Holly looked at the table. "Is that a bedroom?" she asked, pointing at a door.

"Yes," Annie replied.

"May I use it for a few minutes?"

"Of course."

Holly went into the bedroom, closed the door and stood by a window. "All right," she said.

"It has become imperative that we identify and locate Teddy Fay immediately."

"Bill has the photos downloaded from government computers on his laptop; it's being delivered here sometime soon."

"I want them e-mailed to me instantly as soon as you have them," Lance said.

"I understand. Do you want me to tell Bill and Annie your news?"

"I'll tell them myself, when we're done. Have you heard anything about when the travel embargo might be lifted?"

"No, nothing."

"I'm going to get you off that island if I have to send a submarine for you," Lance said.

"You're kidding."

"Yes, I'm kidding, but getting you and the Peppers out is a top priority, right after identifying Teddy."

"If we do identify him, what are my instructions then?"

"Your instructions are to wait for further instructions, and only directly from me."

"What instructions are Bill and Annie likely to get from Hugh English?"

"None whatever; the director has effectively built a wall around Hugh, and he understands that there will be consequences if he breaches that wall. I want to know immediately if you hear that he has so much as spoken to anyone on the island."

Holly was silent.

"Do you understand? This is critical."

"I understand."

"All right; now let me speak to Bill Pepper."

Holly walked back into the living room and handed the phone to Pepper. "Lance wants to speak with you."

Pepper took the phone and walked to the window. "Yes, Lance?" His expression changed as he listened. "Congratulations," he said, then resumed listening. "Of course; I hope it will be here soon. Tiptree is having it delivered here. No, I won't be going back to the office; I've already told them that a family emergency requires me to resign and return to the States. Well, I'll look forward to that. Of course. And again, my congratulations." Pepper punched off and returned to the table.

"We have a new boss," he said to Annie.

"Lance?"

"Himself."

"What are our instructions?"

"To get the photos to him ASAP and to render Holly and Stone any assistance we can in identifying Teddy Fay."

"So it's true?" she asked. "Teddy is still alive?"

"It seems Lance thinks so," Pepper said.

"Did you ever meet Teddy?" Holly asked Annie.

"Once, in passing."

"Do you think you could recognize him?"

"I doubt it, but anyway, I hear he uses a lot of disguises."

"I hear that, too," Holly said. She turned to Pepper. "Bill, do you have any opinion on who might replace Croft?"

Pepper shrugged. "Who knows? He has a Haitian assistant, but I don't know if he has the weight to succeed his boss. His name is duBois."

"What do you know about him?"

"He came from Haiti with Croft, so my assumption is that he is of the same stripe."

"Do you think duBois is conducting the investigation into Croft's murder?"

"Possibly; that will be up to Sir Winston Sutherland, of course, and I expect he's pretty heavily involved in the investigation himself."

"If you were running the investigation, who would be your initial suspects?"

"Well, there are people in Parliament and in the government who are opposed to Sir Winston, but they keep quiet about it. Certainly, there's no violence-prone clandestine resistance that we know of, and I would doubt that any native of the island would be likely to lay his hands on the kind of weapon that must have been used— that is, high-powered and silenced. Nobody heard a gunshot."

"So they'll look at foreigners?"

"I expect so; visitors before residents, I should think."

"So Robertson, Pemberton and Weatherby would not be among the first suspects?"

"I'm only guessing, of course, but probably not. What are you thinking?"

"I'm thinking that I want us to get to them before duBois or some cop does."

"You want to just go and knock on their doors?"

"Not yet, but if we get some sort of ID of one of the photos from Langley, yes."

There was a crunch of tires on gravel from the driveway, and they heard a car door slam.

"Who would that be?" Holly asked.

"Either somebody from the embassy with my laptop or the police, take your pick." Pepper got up, went to the front door and opened it.

Holly could see a young man hand Pepper something. Pepper closed the door, walked back to the dining table and set a very small laptop computer on it. "Let's take a look at those photos," he said, switching it on.

40

Sir Winston Sutherland sat at his desk, reviewing a stack of files. His phone buzzed.

"Yes?"

"Prime Minister," his secretary said, "Major duBois is here, as per your request."

Sutherland closed the file he had been studying.

A uniformed police officer of tall stature entered, came to attention and saluted. "Prime Minister, Major Marcel duBois reporting as ordered."

"Ah, Major," Sutherland said, looking him up and down. His uniform had obviously been cut to the man's body, and he was the picture of military efficiency. "I expect you know why I have asked you here."

"I would imagine it might have something to do with the death of Colonel Croft," duBois replied.

"Quite," Sutherland said. "I have been reading your file—especially your efficiency reports, as logged by Colonel Croft, and I am very impressed."

"Thank you, Prime Minister."

"I am promoting you as his replacement, with the rank of lieutenant colonel," Sutherland said.

"Thank you, sir," duBois replied, but a flicker of disappointment showed on his face.

"Ah," Sutherland said, "I detect ambition."

"Of course, Prime Minister."

"You believe you should be given Croft's rank, as well as his responsibilities."

"I believe that responsibility and rank should go hand in hand."

Sutherland beamed. "All right, full colonel."

DuBois permitted himself a small smile. "Thank you, Prime Minister." He was pleased; after all, he had a pair of Colonel Croft's eagles in his tunic pocket.

The prime minister stood up and extended an open hand. "Allow me the pleasure of pinning on the emblems of your rank."

DuBois felt a little abashed, but he produced the eagles and stood at attention while the PM pinned them on. He watched as Sutherland turned to his desk and returned with a framed certificate. "Your commission," he said.

"Thank you, Prime Minister." He noted that the commission was for colonel; the PM had been playing with him. "I shall be constantly devoted to following your every command."

"You'd better be," the PM said, smiling. "My first command is, find the man who shot Colonel Croft."

"Yes, sir," duBois said."

"And how do you intend to go about it?" the PM asked.

"I have already taken the liberty of canceling all leaves and ordering each man to duty for the duration of the investigation, seven days a week."

"It had better not take seven days," the PM said. "What will be your first steps?"

187

"I shall order the immediate interrogation of every visitor to the island at their respective hotels, so as not to alarm the innocent; when that has been accomplished, I will start on the alien residents."

"Detach a complement of your men and interview the residents simultaneously with the visitors. Here on my desk is a file on every alien resident, and I wish you to immediately arrest the first six of them and interrogate them at police headquarters. Do not release any of them until you are entirely convinced of their innocence."

"It shall be done, Prime Minister."

Sutherland handed duBois the six files. "Are you acquainted with any of these men?"

DuBois quickly leafed through the files. "I know four of them; Colonel Croft dealt personally with Pemberton and Weatherby, the two Englishmen, so I have not met them."

"Meet them now, and report back to me," Sutherland said. "Henceforth, you will report only to me, as Colonel Croft did."

DuBois saluted and left the office.

"Congratulations, Colonel," Sutherland's secretary said. She was a tall white woman with beautiful legs and breasts, and he knew that Croft had been fucking her. "Thank you, Hazel," he said, giving her a little salute. "And I hope that when circumstances permit, you and I might find time to dine together."

"It would be my pleasure," she said, exhibiting no grief for the departed Colonel Croft.

DuBois gave her a big smile and exited the PM's offices. Before leaving Government House he walked down a floor to the offices of the Home Secretary, and in the waiting room he spoke to the male secretary at the desk. "Please tell the home secretary that I wish to meet with him at once."

The man's small eyes flicked over duBois's uniform, noting the eagles on his shoulders. He picked up a phone. "Sir: *Colonel* Marcel duBois requests an immediate conference. Yes, sir, he is here." He hung up the phone. "Please go in, Colonel duBois."

DuBois walked into the home secretary's office, strode to his desk. "Good afternoon," he said, placing the files in his hand on the desk. "I require search warrants and arrest warrants for these six men," he said, "without delay. Please make a note of the names, as I shall be keeping the files."

"What grounds do you have for these warrants?" the home secretary asked.

"The prime minister's request," duBois replied.

"I shall have them delivered to your office in an hour," the home secretary replied. "Ah . . . where is your office?"

"Where Colonel Croft's office once was," duBois replied. He waited while the home secretary wrote down the names, then took the files and left the office and Government House.

As he reached the bottom of the steps duBois noted with pleasure that his driver was standing next to a new, white Mercedes S500 sedan. His old BMW 3 was not in sight.

"Congratulations, Colonel," his driver said, opening the rear door for him.

"Thank you, Nigel," duBois replied. "Take me to my new office."

"Yes, sir," Nigel replied. He put the car in gear and sped away.

DuBois ran his fingers over the leather interior and fiddled with the rear-seat controls for the air conditioning and radio. "Nigel?" he said.

"Yes, Colonel?"

"See to the installation of satellite radio as soon as possible."

"Of course, Colonel. The phone and communications radio have already been installed; the handsets are in the rear armrest."

DuBois opened the armrest and examined the equipment with satisfaction. "Faster," he said, then felt the seat press into his back with the acceleration.

41

Holly and Stone sat and waited while Bill Pepper fired up his laptop and waited for it to boot. "Something's wrong," he said.

"What?" Holly asked.

"It's not booting properly," Bill replied. "Instead, it's crashing. Let me try again." He rebooted.

"I don't like this," Holly said. "When did they take the laptop?"

"When they arrested me at my office," Bill said. "Oh, shit, it's crashed again."

Annie spoke up. "Use your backup boot disk," she said. "It's in your desk drawer."

Pepper went into his study and came back. "Gone," he said. "They must have taken it when they searched the house." He went into the living room and removed a picture from the wall, revealing a small safe with an electronic keypad. He tapped in the code, opened the safe, removed a computer disk and rehung the picture.

"Thank God," Holly breathed.

Pepper returned to the dining table, inserted the disk and re-booted. "It's giving me a choice of start-up sources," he said. "Let's try the hard disk; if it won't boot from the hard disk, then it's going to have to go to Langley for a recapturing of all the files." He sat and watched the screen. "Seems to be booting," he said. "I'm in!"

Holly walked around the table and stood behind him. An encryption page appeared on the screen. Pepper went through three stages of typing in long sequences of numbers and letters, then, finally, the desktop appeared.

"Here we go," Pepper said. "I'll bring them up side by side." He hit some more keys. "There," he said, "Pemberton on the left, Weatherby on the right, Robertson in the middle."

"Well," Holly said, "I can tell you that Robertson isn't Teddy. He's too young by fifteen years. I don't think Teddy could fake that."

Stone came and stood next to Holly. "They look like passport photographs," he said.

"British-sized passport photos," Pepper replied. "Does either of the other two look familiar to you, Holly?"

Holly stared at both the photos. Pemberton had a military-style brush mustache, and Weatherby had a Vandyke, with mustache and goatee. "No," she said, "not immediately. Is that a toupee?" she asked, pointing to Pemberton.

"Possibly," Pepper replied.

"Definitely," Stone said. "The hairline is too low for a man his age. But Weatherby's hair looks real enough."

"Gray," Pepper said. "Pemberton's looks gray, too, but Weatherby's is whiter."

"About the same weight," Holly said, "but Weatherby seems to have had a broken nose at some point."

"Did Teddy Fay have a broken nose?" Stone asked.

"Not that I can recall," Holly said.

"You've met Teddy?" Pepper asked, surprised.

"Once, possibly twice," she replied. "Both times disguised."

"What about their chins?" Pepper asked.

"Hard to say, since Weatherby has a goatee."

"Eyes?" Stone asked.

"They both have the wrinkles you'd expect in a man in his sixties," Pepper said. "The ears aren't dissimilar, but Pemberton's stick out more."

"You're right," Holly said.

"Look," Pepper said, "we're not going to be able to analyze these pictures here; it's time to forward them to Lance; he'll have Tech Services on them immediately."

Holly shrugged. "I was just hoping we'd catch something that would give us a clue about one of them, something that would help make him Teddy. But there isn't anything."

"Shall I transfer them?" Bill asked.

"Can you print copies?"

"Sure, and in color."

"Then shoot them to Lance." She watched as Bill sent the e-mails, then printed the photos, handed them to Holly and closed the laptop.

"Nothing to do but wait, now," he said.

L ance sat behind his borrowed desk, watching the faces of a group of a dozen men and women, while Hugh English spoke to them.

"I know you've all been expecting this at some point, ever since the death of Dick Stone, and now the time has come. A short time ago, the director told both Lance Cabot and me that Lance will be the new DDO, effective immediately. For those who haven't yet met him, I'm pleased to introduce you all." He ran through the introductions, while Lance consulted a list of names and photographs on his desk that he had already memorized. When English was done, Lance got up, walked around his desk and sat on its edge.

"I'm very pleased to meet some new people and glad to see again the ones I already know," he said. "First, I want to thank Hugh English for postponing his retirement and so ably continuing in this office until the director had time to make a new appointment. Though I know Hugh is looking forward to his retirement, we're going to miss his knowledge and his wisdom, and I hope he has imparted enough of both to you all, so that you can help me find my feet in this new job. It makes it tougher on all of us that we knew and worked with Dick Stone and that we will not have the full benefit of his experience."

Hugh English stood up. "Excuse me, Lance, but I think my time to exit this stage has come." He turned to the group. "Thank you all for your hard work over the years, and I hope you'll give Lance the same level of dedication and loyalty that you have given me." English shook hands with Lance, and without another word, he left the room.

Lance gave his departure a moment's silence, then turned back to his audience. He indicated a cart filled with file folders, some of them very thick. "I've already begun to read these, and let me say that, so far, I'm very impressed with their completeness and lucidity. In a day or two, I hope to be up to speed on all operations, but I'm sure I'll have some questions for most of you before that time. Any questions for me?"

A man in the rear of the room raised his hand. "Will you be working out of this office?"

"For the moment, until Hugh has had time to make his move, and a few alterations have been made. My extension number will be the same in both offices, though, so I won't be hard to find."

His laptop beside him emitted a small chime. "Excuse me a moment," he said, turning the instrument so that he could see the screen. He looked back at his office. "Any other questions?"

"What about vacations already scheduled?" a woman asked.

"Keep them scheduled," Lance said, "subject only to the sort of last-minute emergencies I'm sure you're all accustomed to. Anyone else? No? Well, thank you all, and I look forward to working with each of you. By the way, as we speak, all stations are being notified of the personnel changes, so there won't be any surprises in your contacts with those in the field." Lance ran a finger down his list of names and photographs, looked around the room and settled on an attractive woman in her forties near the back of the room. "Mona Barry? Will you stay a moment, please?"

The others ambled out of the room, and Mona Barry rose and walked forward. "Yes, sir?"

"No 'sirs' are necessary; Lance will do," he said.

"Yes, Lance?"

"I'm told that you are our best photo analyst, Mona."

"That's very flattering."

"I expect you know how good you are." He turned the laptop so that she could see the screen. "I've just received these photos from our station in St. Marks, in the Caribbean." He pressed a button, and his printer began to work. "I'd like you to give them your closest attention, and at the earliest possible moment." He also copied them onto a DVD and handed it to her.

Mona picked up the printout, set her reading glasses on her nose and began examining the three photographs. "What do you want to know about them?"

"These are photographs submitted by three men to the government of St. Marks on applications to buy houses on the island. All three are British subjects and the photos appear to be the sort used on British passports."

"Are they wanted for something? Either by us or by the law somewhere?"

"It's suspected that one of them may be a fugitive from justice in Britain, and another may be—and this is on a strictly need-to-know basis, Mona—Teddy Fay."

She looked up at Lance. "So he's alive?"

"That's what we're trying to determine."

"Well, I never worked with Teddy, and since there are no known photos of him on record, the best I can do is clean them up, rid them of facial hair and show them to people who knew Teddy better than I did."

"That's exactly what I want you to do," Lance said, "and as quickly as humanly possible."

"I'll call you when I have something," Mona said, then left the office.

Lance went back to reading operations files.

42

D ino and Genevieve were lunching on the terrace of the beach cottage when the phone rang inside. Dino got up and went to answer it. "Hello?"

"Dino, it's Thomas; you're about to have visitors."

"Who?"

"The local police and a Colonel duBois, who is Croft's replacement. Be careful in dealing with him."

"I will," Dino said. He looked up to see a car stopping outside. "They're here; thanks, Thomas." Dino got his and Genevieve's passports and his NYPD ID from their room and went outside. Genevieve was looking up with big eyes at two uniformed policemen and a civilian. "Gosh," she said. "Are you the police?"

Dino walked to the table. "Good afternoon, gentlemen," he said. "May I help you?" He gave them a little smile.

"Yes, indeed, you may," said the civilian, who was wearing a sharply cut tan suit that set off his cafe-au-lait coloring. "What is your name?"

"I am Lieutenant Dino Bacchetti, of the New York City Police Department," he said, handing the man his badge wallet.

The man inspected the badge and ID card closely.

"May I know your name?" Dino asked pleasantly.

The man looked up at him. "I am Colonel Marcel duBois, of the Home Office."

Dino offered his hand. "How do you do?"

DuBois shook it hastily. "May I see your passports." It wasn't a question.

"Of course," Dino replied, handing them over. He waved a hand at the table. "Would you like some lunch or a glass of iced tea? It's always interesting to meet a colleague."

DuBois looked at him sharply. "Colleague?"

"We are both police officers, are we not?"

DuBois ignored the question. "What is your business on St. Marks?"

"We are here on vacation."

"For how long?"

"We had planned to leave tomorrow, but I understand travel has been interrupted because of a murder."

"What do you know of this murder, Lieutenant Bacchetti?"

"Only that it occurred and that the victim was Colonel Croft. I assume you are his replacement?"

"That is so. What other details do you have of this murder?"

"None whatever, I'm afraid. In my work in New York I have specialized in homicides for many years. If I can be of any assistance, I would be happy to do so."

"Thank you, that will not be necessary. We have the required skills and experience in our own department."

"I'm sure you do; I just thought that an outside opinion might be helpful."

"Opinion of what?"

"Interpretation of the evidence."

"We do not share evidence of crimes with outsiders."

"As you wish."

Now duBois seemed intrigued. "What would you say of this, Lieutenant? Colonel Croft was shot while sitting in the central courtyard of the St. Marks Police Station."

"From inside the station?"

"From outside."

"A rifle shot, then."

"That is our assumption."

"Then the shooter would have needed elevation."

"Quite."

"And a rifle with sufficient muzzle velocity to be accurate at a distance."

"Quite."

"I would first look for the shooter's location, and when I found it I would isolate the scene and look for evidence, such as cartridge casings and fibers from the shooter's clothing. I would also look for fingerprints."

"Of course; that will be done."

Dino waved duBois to a chair and sat down himself. "Someone loading a rifle would leave fingerprints on the cartridge casings, unless he was careful to wear gloves or wipe them clean."

"Yes," duBois said. "Go on."

Dino was beginning to get the impression that duBois had never investigated a homicide. Probably, with his Haitian police background, he was more accustomed to committing than solving them.

"Have you located the shooter's firing point?"

"We believe it to be an abandoned fire tower on a hill not far from the police station."

"Then I would also look for tire tracks and footprints, and if the tower is accessed by a ladder or stairs, I would look for prints on the rungs or banisters. I would also look for DNA evidence, if the shooter, perhaps, spat or left a coffee cup or cut himself while climbing the tower. Hairs would be helpful, too."

"All of that will be sought, of course," duBois replied.

Dino was surprised he wasn't taking notes. "Do you have the facility for DNA analysis available on St. Marks?"

"Not as yet," duBois replied. "That will be one of my first requests of my government."

"I would be very happy to have any evidence you find tested in our labs in New York, if that would be helpful."

"Thank you; I will let you know." DuBois consulted a list from his pocket. "Where are your companions, Mr. Barrington and Ms. Heller?" he asked.

"I believe they are touring the island," Dino said. "They told us not to wait lunch for them."

"When will they return?"

"I'm not sure, but certainly in time for cocktails; they never miss cocktails." Dino smiled.

"Quite."

Dino didn't know what else to say. "I would be happy to inspect the shooter's roost or the crime scene, if that would be helpful."

"Probably not," duBois replied.

"Mr. Barrington was also a homicide detective on the NYPD. We were partners for some years. I'm sure he would be glad to help, as well."

"What about his girlfriend? Is she a police officer, too?"

Dino almost said yes, but remembered. "No, she is a flying instructor; she owns and operates a small flying school in Florida."

"Yes, I have heard this; did she fly you here?"

"No, we were fortunate enough to arrive by private jet."

"Are New York policemen so wealthy, Lieutenant Bacchetti?"

Dino laughed. "Oh, no. Mr. Barrington is the one with money. He is a prominent attorney in New York, and an airplane company offered him the ride, with the hope of selling him a jet."

"And will he buy one?"

Dino smiled. "Just between you and me, Mr. Barrington is not that rich, but he neglected to mention that to the salesman."

DuBois did not smile. A car door slammed behind them.

Dino looked up to see Stone and Holly walking toward them.

"Ah," duBois said, rising, "Mr. Barrington and Ms. Heller, I presume."

"That's right," Stone said.

"Good. You are both under arrest." He made a motion and the two police officers cuffed Stone's and Holly's hands in front of them.

"Colonel duBois," Dino said, getting to his feet. "Why are you arresting my friends?"

DuBois turned and looked at Dino. "Lieutenant Bacchetti, I would advise you to mind your own business."

Dino's eyes flicked toward Stone and Holly; he saw a folded piece of paper fall at her feet, and she kicked it under the police car.

"Call the embassy, Dino," Stone said, as they got into the back of the police car.

The car drove away.

"What was that all about?" Genevieve asked.

"I don't know," Dino said. He walked over to where the police car had been parked and retrieved the piece of paper Holly had dropped. When he unfolded it, he saw the photographs of the three men. "Robertson, Pemberton and Weatherby, I presume," he said. Then he walked quickly to the phone.

43

The phone was answered by a young man. "United States Embassy," he said.

"I don't suppose you would connect me with the CIA station chief, would you?" Dino asked.

There was a brief silence. "Sir, what is the nature of your business?"

"Please give him or her a message," Dino said. "Virginia Heller and Stone Barrington have just been arrested by a Colonel Marcel duBois of the Home Office, presumably in connection with the murder of Colonel Croft."

"And your name, sir?"

"Dino Bacchetti; I am traveling with Ms. Heller and Mr. Barrington." He gave the man the phone number at the inn. "I believe this to be a secure line," he said, "since we disabled the bugs in the telephones. I can't speak for your end."

"I will pass on the message," the young man said, then hung up.

James Tiptree's phone rang, and he picked it up. "This is James Tiptree."

"Scramble," a voice said.

Tiptree pressed the button. "Scrambled."

"Jim, this is Lance Cabot; we met some years ago in London."

"Yes, Lance, I remember."

"Have you received cable traffic regarding the replacement for Hugh English?"

Tiptree sat up straighter. "Not yet."

"You should shortly. The cable will say that I have been appointed to replace Hugh."

"Ah, well, congratulations, Lance."

"Thank you. I'm calling to brief you with a situation on St. Marks."

Tiptree immediately wondered what Cabot could know about St. Marks that he, himself, did not. "Yes?"

"I have an operative in St. Marks who is investigating the possibility that Teddy Fay is alive and on the island."

Tiptree nearly laughed but decided silence was the better move.

"Are you acquainted with Teddy Fay?"

"I've heard about him, of course, but we never met."

"My operative's name is Holly Barker; she is using the cover of a real person named Virginia Heller, called Ginny, who operates a flying school in Florida, and she has a passport and other identification in that name."

"Right."

"She is traveling with two men, Stone Barrington and Dino Bacchetti, and a woman, Genevieve James. The two men are contract consultants to the Agency; the woman is just for color. They are traveling as vacationers and staying at the English Harbour Inn."

"I understand; do they require my assistance?"

"Not at the moment, but I wanted you to be aware of their presence on the island. Barker and Barrington have already met with Bill and Annie Pepper. I had hoped to remove them all from the island tomorrow, but, as you know, travel restrictions have been imposed since the murder of Colonel Croft."

"Yes, I'm aware of that; I was sitting on a bench next to Croft when the bullet struck him."

"That must have been an interesting experience," Lance said drily.

"Indeed; my clothes are at the cleaners."

A young embassy officer knocked, entered Tiptree's office and placed a sheet of paper on his desk. Tiptree nodded, and the man left.

"Lance," Tiptree said, "it appears that Barker and Barrington do require my assistance. I've just received a telephone message from Bacchetti, saying that the two of them have been arrested by Croft's successor, Colonel duBois, in connection with Croft's assassination."

"That's preposterous," Lance said. "They had nothing to do with it, but we suspect that Teddy Fay might have. Their only orders are to locate Teddy and verify his identity, then to report back to me."

"Then I had better get over to police headquarters and see what I can do about shaking them loose before Colonel duBois gets too enthusiastic in their interrogation. I regard the man as worse than Croft, a loose cannon."

"I understand," Lance replied. "Do not, repeat, *not* bring State into this. Call me when you know more." He hung up.

Tiptree hung up and buzzed his secretary. "Have my car brought around immediately," he said, then hung up. He turned to his computer and began entering the names of Virginia Heller and Stone Barrington. In less than a minute he was printing out color copies of their U.S. passports. He put them in his briefcase, closed it and walked out of his office.

"Your car is waiting," his secretary said.

"I'm going to police headquarters to try and obtain the release of two American citizens who have been detained, Virginia Heller and Stone Barrington. Alert the ambassador and tell him they are my good friends. If you haven't heard from me in an hour, get him moving on it, but tell him Langley says not to involve the State Department."

"Right."

Tiptree set off on his second journey of the day to police headquarters. He hoped to God no more blood would be spilled. Blood only complicated his life.

44

Stone sat, still handcuffed, on a very uncomfortable chair before a desk in an otherwise bare room, more angry than frightened. It was clear that the chair he sat in had been constructed with the idea of discomfort in mind, and he was sure that he was about to be interrogated. He ran over the details of Holly's cover in his mind, just to have everything straight. He stood up, walked to a wall and leaned against it.

A door opened and duBois entered. "Sit down," he said.

"Thank you, no. What is the meaning of this?"

DuBois walked over and backhanded him. "Sit down and shut up, except to answer my questions."

Stone felt a trickle of blood running down his cheek. DuBois had been wearing a ring of some sort. Stone sat down.

DuBois sat at the desk and removed a legal pad from a drawer. He took out a pen and held it poised over the pad. "What is your name?"

"Stone Barrington." He spelled it.

"Occupation?"

"Attorney at law."

"Show me identification."

It was awkward with his hands cuffed, but Stone managed to retrieve his passport from his inside jacket pocket and toss it on the desk.

DuBois looked at the photo inside, compared it to Stone and noted the passport number. "Why did you kill Colonel Croft?"

Stone blinked. "I had nothing whatever to do with the death of Colonel Croft."

"Where were you when he was killed?"

"When was he killed?"

"If you continue to be obstructive I will use unpleasant means to extract this information."

Stone shrugged. "If you do that I will, of course, confess to anything you like, then repudiate the confession at the first opportunity. I want to see someone from the American Embassy immediately, and I want to see my attorney, Sir Leslie Hewitt. Until I do I will have nothing more to say, unless, of course, you torture it from me. I also wish to speak to Sir Winston Sutherland at once. He and I are personally acquainted."

It was duBois's turn to blink. He got up and left the room without a word.

H olly, though she did not know it, sat in a room identical to the one Stone occupied. She didn't like being handcuffed. She got out of the uncomfortable chair, walked around the desk and rummaged in the drawers until she found where they had put her handbag. She unzipped an inside pocket, removed a handcuff key, opened the cuffs, then tucked the key into her bra and put her handbag back into the drawer. She tossed the cuffs onto the desk and sat down again.

DuBois entered the room and sat down at the desk.

"Why have I been arrested?" Holly asked.

DuBois raised his eyes from the legal pad before him; then he saw the handcuffs. "How did you get out of those?"

"One of your people removed them," she replied. "Why have I been arrested?"

"What is your name?"

"Virginia Heller."

"Occupation?"

"Flying instructor; I own a flying school in Florida. Why have I been arrested?"

"Give me your passport."

"It's in my handbag, which was taken from me and placed in one of your desk drawers."

DuBois opened drawers until he found the handbag; he turned it upside down and emptied the contents onto the desk, then he picked up the satphone. "Why do you have this?"

"It belongs to my gentleman friend; he loaned it to me so that I can keep in touch with him while I'm out of the country."

DuBois put down the phone, opened her passport, compared the photo to her and noted the number. "Your friend, Mr. Barrington, is being charged with the murder of Colonel Croft; you will be charged as his accessory, which carries the same penalty as murder, that of hanging."

"That's preposterous," Holly said. "We came here on vacation and for no other reason. We met Colonel Croft only once, at the English Harbour Inn. Why would we want to kill him?"

"Perhaps you were hired. Who hired you to kill him?"

"My friend is a prominent lawyer in New York; I have already told you what I do. We are not hired killers. Check out our backgrounds; that should be easy enough. Mr. Barrington is a retired New York City police officer, and I have a website that you may visit. I want to see Mr. Barrington."

"Mr. Barrington is indisposed."

"What the hell does that mean?" Holly demanded.

"Miss Heller, I caution you to be careful how you speak to me."

"Very well, I will not speak to you again, until I have seen and spoken to Mr. Barrington." She folded her arms and stared at a spot on the wall across the room.

DuBois got up so quickly that he knocked over his chair. He strode around the desk and came at Holly.

Holly stood up and faced him. He was about five-ten and slim; she was nearly as big.

DuBois drew back his right hand and swung it at her face.

Holly stepped inside the blow, grabbed his wrist, twisted his arm behind his back and, in the same motion, used a leg to sweep his feet from under him and slam him hard onto the floor. "You have no manners," she said. She took the handcuffs from the desk and cuffed his hands behind his back. She heard a door open behind her.

"What is the meaning of this?" a deep voice said.

Holly turned and saw the imposing figure of Sir Winston Sutherland filling the doorway.

"Uh, good afternoon, Prime Minister," she said, rising to her full height and leaving duBois on the floor.

"What is this, Marcel?" Sutherland demanded, "some kind of sex game?"

"Colonel duBois lacks charm," Holly said. "Apparently he enjoys beating up women."

Sutherland stepped into the room and was followed by Stone and another man.

"Ginny," Stone said, "this is Mr. James Tiptree of the American Embassy."

"How do you do?" Tiptree said, looking baffled.

DuBois attempted to get up, but Holly put her foot on his neck. "Be still," she said.

Sir Winston Sutherland smiled, then began to laugh. Stone laughed, too. Tiptree just shook his head.

45

S tone and Holly sat in the backseat of a police car, headed back toward the inn.

"What the hell happened in there?" Stone whispered.

"Not now," Holly said.

They sat in silence until they were driven to the inn and deposited at their cottage.

"Now," Stone said as the police car drove away, "what the hell happened in there?"

"I freed myself from the handcuffs, pissed off duBois and, when he came at me, I put him on the floor and cuffed him."

"So while I'm playing the lawyer and demanding to see everybody in authority, you're beating up the guy who was supposed to beat you up?"

"Pretty much."

"Do you know, I think that's what got us released so quickly? Sir Winston just loved it!"

"What was he doing there?"

"Tiptree, from the embassy, tried to reach him, couldn't, and then, as he arrived at police headquarters, so did Sir Winston. He professed to be shocked, *shocked* that we had been arrested, and you know the rest."

"Why were we arrested in the first place?"

"My guess is that we were at the top of the list of foreign visitors, so they came after us."

"DuBois said you were being charged with Croft's murder, and I was being charged as an accessory."

"That's nonsense; he was just bluffing, and you called him on it. I have to tell you, though, I'm not sure what duBois would have done to you once he got some help."

"Funny," Holly said, "I didn't think about that; I just wanted to humiliate him."

"Holly, it is not a good policy, when arrested in a foreign country, to humiliate your interrogator. That can lead to electroshock therapy, broken bones and a ruptured spleen. Didn't they mention that to you during your CIA training?"

"No, we didn't get that far; my training was interrupted by my sudden transfer to New York."

"Oh."

"They did say that I would have to return to complete the course, but I think Lance intervened."

"I think it's going to be nice to have Lance for a rabbi, now that he has the top operations job. Do you think he'll bring you to Langley or keep you in the field?"

"I haven't the slightest idea," she replied, "but I think that my future might be somehow connected to our success or failure in nailing Teddy Fay while we're here."

"What, exactly, do you mean by 'nailing'?"

"Sorry, that should read, 'finding.' I still don't know what happens after that."

"Bill Pepper thinks that either you or he is going to be asked to kill him. Are you ready for that?"

"I certainly am not ready for that; I am not an assassin."

"Well, we'd better start looking for him."

"I'd like to shower and change before we do that," Holly said. "That jail made me feel dirty."

They went into the cottage and found Dino and Genevieve watching Tiger Woods play golf on TV.

"Hey, you're alive!" Dino said, embracing them both.

"Thanks for calling in the cavalry," Stone replied. "They arrived in the nick of time." He told Dino about what Holly had done to duBois.

"Woman," Dino said, "you are lucky to be alive."

"No," Holly said, "duBois is lucky to be alive. Excuse me, I'm going to shower and change."

"Me too," Stone said.

"Oh," Dino said, holding out the photos of Pemberton, Weatherby and Robertson, "you dropped these."

Sir Winston Sutherland seated himself in duBois's chair in Colonel Croft's large office. The photos on the wall were still those of Croft with various dignitaries; nothing of his replacement's had been added. He looked up at Colonel duBois, who stood uncomfortably before the desk. "You blithering idiot," he said.

"Prime Minister . . ."

"You knew who those people were; Colonel Croft investigated them days ago, and he even sent an agent to Ms. Heller's flying school to verify her identity."

"Prime Minister . . ."

"So while you were wasting time throwing your newly found weight around, Croft's murderer is still out there, if he hasn't already left the island."

"Prime Minister . . ."

"And on top of that you somehow managed to allow a *woman* who was *handcuffed* to free herself and handcuff *you!*"

"Prime Minister . . ."

"Well, at least I got a good laugh out of that little scene in the interrogation room," Sutherland said, chuckling.

"Prime Minister . . ."

"DuBois, you are no longer a colonel. I wish you to dress in the uniform of a police captain and continue your investigation into the assassination of Colonel Croft, and you are to wear that uniform at all times when you are on duty. Is that perfectly clear?"

"Yes, Prime Minister, but . . ."

"Get out, and by the way, this is no longer your office."

DuBois saluted, executed an about-face and left the room. Back in his old office he got out his uniform, which still displayed his major's gold leaves, then changed them to his old captain's bars, then he armed himself with a pistol and an Uzi machine pistol and left.

"Your car is waiting out front," his secretary called after him.

DuBois walked out the front door of police headquarters to find his driver seated in an elderly, dusty and banged-up Land Rover.

"Good afternoon, Col . . . uh, Captain," his driver said.

DuBois got in and tried to roll up his back-seat window, but it was stuck. "Get me out of here," he said.

"Where, to, Captain?"

"*Get me out of here!*" duBois screamed. As they drove aimlessly down the roads of St. Marks, duBois entertained himself by fantasizing about what he was going to do to Ms. Virginia Heller when he found her again.

46

Teddy Fay stood on a cliff at the eastern end of St. Marks and watched the waves crash against the rocks a hundred feet below. He didn't want to do this, but he had considered the alternatives, and there weren't any. He couldn't allow himself to be caught or even questioned with it in his possession.

He went back to his vehicle, opened the case and looked at the sniper's rifle one last time. He had done all the gunsmithing on that weapon, made it into the precision tool it was, and he loved it the way some men loved an old dog.

He snapped the case shut, looked around to be sure he was entirely alone, then stood on a boulder embedded in the top of the cliff and imagined himself flinging the case as far as he could, then watching it sink in the deep water. He couldn't bring himself to do it. Teddy trudged to his vehicle, started it and began to drive back.

As he drove up Black Mountain Road, he caught a glimpse in his rear view mirror of an old Land Rover entering the road at the bottom of the mountain. It was not a police car, but Teddy automatically paid attention to every vehicle behind him. He was beginning to sweat as he continued up the mountain; there was only the one road, and his escape plans did not include a close pursuit by anybody. But the vehicle stayed well back.

Then, to his enormous relief, the Land Rover turned into the driveway of the Pemberton house. He continued to his own drive, then garaged the vehicle, removed the rifle case and let himself into his underground bunker in the house's old cistern.

Teddy did not believe that he would be caught or have his identity discovered by anyone, let alone the clown, duBois, whom he knew Croft had distrusted. Croft had been the kind of man who preferred his subordinates to be loyal but only marginally competent, and duBois fit that mold perfectly; he was the other viper in the nest of the St. Marks police, and Teddy wished he had eliminated him, too. Maybe he still would.

Nevertheless, he would make preparations. He got a small sledge and a chisel and began to cut into the concrete floor along a line only he would have noticed. Soon, he had freed a piece of plywood that had been concealed by an inch of concrete. He pulled it back to reveal a compartment that contained equipment, much of which he considered important and some of which he considered essential to his continued survival.

He removed a small, hard-shelled leather suitcase, dialed in the combinations of both locks and opened it. He chose a blade in his Swiss Army knife and carefully pried up the false bottom. Arrayed around the floor of the hidden compartment was a hundred and fifty thousand dollars in hundred-dollar bills; on top of that lay eight passports, four of them American, two British and two from New Zealand. There was also a selection of flat rubber stamps for entering various visas and entry and departure markings. Finally, there was a Colt government .380 pistol, which looked like a tiny model 1911 .45, and half a dozen loaded magazines. All of this took up a space an inch and a half deep.

He closed the hidden compartment, set the case on his work-bench and added other items: two changes of clothes, including a wash-and-wear suit, a pair of shoes and a folding felt hat. He was unaccustomed to running with such a small cache of things, but there was more in the airplane he had hangared on the island of Nevis, not so many miles away.

He had been surprised at the speed with which the police had shut down all departures from St. Marks, but he was equipped to deal with it. He removed the charger alligator clips from the battery of his new possession and made sure everything was ready to be quickly taken outside and assembled.

When he was satisfied that he was ready to run, if necessary, he stretched out on a cot and fell quickly asleep. He had always been able to do that.

D uBois rang the bell at the Pemberton house and waited impa-tiently for someone to answer it. No one came. "Bring me the tire iron from the car," he called to his driver.

The man opened the rear of the vehicle and trotted over with the tool. "Here you are, Captain."

DuBois was surprised at how long it took him to break into the house, and he made a mess of the door before he was finally able to open it. He walked into the living room, his pistol in hand, and looked around. It was all very ordinary. He checked the bedrooms and in the master found clothing for a man and a woman; the kitchen contained canned and frozen foods; there was no cellar. There was a fine coat of dust on everything, and it looked as if it had been weeks since anyone had been here, yet the immigration records he had checked put Pemberton, if not his wife, on the island.

He closed the door as best he could and got back into the Land Rover. "Next house: Weatherby, farther up the mountain," he said to the driver.

They turned into the Weatherby driveway and stopped. This was a small house, once the guest quarters for the larger house owned by the American woman at the top of the mountain. He broke into the house, just as he had the Pemberton place.

Teddy was wakened from his nap by a tiny beeping; someone was upstairs. He watched the blinking lights on the panel that told him someone was walking from room to room. He decided not to be cornered; he let himself out of his redoubt, closed it up and left at a trot.

DuBois walked through the house, surprised. The house was furnished, but there was no indication that anyone had ever lived in it—no clothing, no food. He looked under the mattresses on the unmade beds: nothing. But Weatherby was supposed to be on the island, too, according to immigration records. Why was it that neither Pemberton nor Weatherby seemed to have been in his home—in the case of Pemberton, not recently; in the case of Weatherby, never?

He went back to the Land Rover.

"Where to, Captain?"

"Let's go up the mountain; there's an American woman living there." He didn't bother to check the garage.

The driver took him the few remaining yards and turned into the drive. DuBois noted an SUV and a pickup truck in the garage. He knocked on the door, and the American woman opened it.

"Yes, officer?" she asked.

"I am Captain duBois, of the St. Marks Police," he said politely. "May I come in?"

"Of course, Captain," she said. "I'm Irene Foster." She led him into the living room, where a man was sitting in a reclining chair with a beer in his hand, watching a golf tournament on television. He picked up a remote control and pressed a button, and Tiger Woods froze in mid-drive.

"Harold," she said to him, "this is Captain duBois, of the St. Marks Police. Captain, this is my friend Harold Pitts, who is visiting from the States."

Pitts stood up and offered his hand, which duBois shook. "What can we do for you, Captain?"

"May I see your passports, please?"

"Sure; will you get mine, honey? It's in the top drawer of the dresser."

"Of course," Irene said, and left the room.

"How long have you been in St. Marks, Mr. Pitts?" duBois asked.

"Oh, less than a couple of weeks; I sailed down from Ft. Lauderdale in my boat."

"What is your work, may I ask?"

"I'm retired; I used to have a home renovation business in Virginia," he said. "Now I'm footloose and fancy-free."

"How nice for you."

The woman returned with the passports and handed them to him. "I'm a permanent resident," she said. "I own this house."

DuBois examined the passports closely, then handed them back. "They appear to be in order," he said. "Where were the two of you earlier in the day?"

"I haven't left the house all day," she replied. "Harold went down to his boat at the English Harbour Marina, then came back."

"I do a little work on it almost every day," Pitts said.

DuBois found these people boring—elderly, retired Americans with no possible axe to grind with Croft. "Have you seen the occupants of the house next door recently?"

"I've never seen them," Irene said. "I hear their name is Weatherby, but I don't know if they've ever even moved in."

"Thank you," he said, rising. "I'm sorry to have disturbed you."

The woman showed him out, then returned.

"That had to be about Colonel Croft," Pitts said to her.

"I would imagine so," she replied. "They must be checking on all the foreigners."

Pitts pressed a button, and Tiger Woods finished his drive, pulling it into the rough.

"Shit," Pitts said.

O n his way down the mountain, duBois stopped at number 56, the Robertson place, since his file said that he owned an airplane. He found it much the same as the Pemberton house. Where were all these people?

47

Will Lee was nearly dressed for a state dinner honoring the prime minister of Australia when he heard running footsteps through the master bedroom. He stuck his head out of his dressing room, but she had already disappeared into hers.

"Running just a tad late, aren't you?" he called out.

"Sorry," she yelled back. "Accident on the beltway screwed everything up."

Will came out of his dressing room, his bow tie hanging loose. "Don't I remember a helicopter in the CIA appropriations bill?"

"Two helicopters," she called back.

He walked to the door of her dressing room and leaned against the doorjamb. He liked watching her undress, even when she was in a hurry. "And they were both down?"

"Can you imagine what the press could do with a story that had me taking a helicopter so as not to be late for a dinner party?"

"Not a dinner party, a state dinner; not even nearly the same thing."

"Certainly not as much fun." She stepped into a red dress and turned her back. "Shut up and zip," she said.

He zipped. "Now you have to tie my tie. Tit for tat."

"Oh, all right, come here."

He knew how to tie a bow tie; he just liked it when she did it. She stood close, concentrating.

"What are you staring at?"

"What I stare at every chance I get."

"That is covered by a dress."

"Oh, I like your face, too."

"You're sweet."

"Even when it hasn't been washed and made up."

"Oh, God," she cried, running for her bathroom. "Why didn't you tell me?"

"I did tell you. Just as soon as you got my tie tied."

There was a sound of running water and splashing. "How much time do I have?"

Will checked his wristwatch. "Minus ten minutes."

"Shit! Are they down there waiting?"

"They're in the Oval; we're having cocktails there."

"You go ahead; I'll be there a few seconds after you."

"Someone on the staff has heard that Hugh English was seen having lunch with Cal Ferguson."

"That will have to keep until I have a face again."

Will went back to his dressing room, got into his waistcoat and dinner jacket, chose a white silk pocket square, put his glasses, pen and jotting pad, which contained his nuclear code card, into his inside pockets and started across the bedroom. "Minus twelve minutes," he called out.

"Go fuck yourself, Mr. President!"

Will laughed all the way to the elevator.

They were halfway through their first martini when Kate swept into the Oval Office. "I'm so sorry to be late," she said, shaking hands with the PM and his wife. "I wish I could blame it on national security, but it was just traffic."

"That's quite all right," the PM said. "We have traffic in Australia, too."

Will handed her a dirty martini with an olive stuffed with an anchovy. "Inhale that and relax."

"It's not like you're late for the Queen," the PM's wife said. "I was once twenty minutes late for the Queen, when we were in London. She was not amused."

"The Duke of Edinburgh was amused," the PM said. "I thought he would burst out laughing, until the Queen gave him that *look*."

Kate drew in a third of her martini. "Ahhhh," she said.

"Mr. President . . ." the PM began.

"Please, we're Will and Kate."

"And we're Geoff and Sheila," he replied.

"Sheila is the national term for female in Australia," Sheila said. "Makes it easy for people to remember my name."

"Will," the PM began again, "when I visited the Capitol this afternoon, a senator, that ginger-haired fellow, the tall one . . ."

"Senator Ferguson?"

"That's the one."

"He said something odd to me; he said, 'When you see the President tonight, ask him how Teddy is.' "

Will shot a glance at Kate. "Oh?"

"Was he talking about Teddy Kennedy?"

Will shook his head. "Sometimes it's hard to tell exactly what Senator Ferguson is talking about. You ever get any time for golf in your job?" Will asked, anxious to change the subject.

"Every Sunday," the PM said, "if the country's not being invaded. I think it gives you a sort of perspective to know that there's an activity that's more frustrating than government."

Will laughed. "Exactly."

There was a rap on the door and the chief usher opened it. "Dinner is served, Mr. President, Prime Minister."

"I'm sorry we didn't have more quiet time before this thing," Will said.

"No," Kate said, "*I'm* sorry; all my fault." She dropped back a step and took Will's arm as they followed their guests.

"What's up with Ferguson?" Will asked under his breath.

"It's Hugh English," she said. "He isn't wasting any time."

"I'm confused."

"I relieved him today; Lance Cabot has the job. I thought I had contained Hugh, but apparently not."

"Do something painful to him," Will said.

"I'll give it some thought."

"I don't suppose you have an assassin over there who could deal with Ferguson?"

"Where is Teddy Fay when we need him?" she asked, and they swept into the East Room.

48

Senator Calvin Ferguson, R-UT, sat across the East Room with his wife, Evelyn, who was twenty-seven years his junior, and gazed at Katharine Lee.

"Who are you staring at, honey?" Evelyn asked him, leaning in close, so that he could look down her cleavage. That always got his attention.

"Kate Lee," he said. "I planted a tiny bomb this afternoon, and I want to see if it explodes tonight."

Evelyn, Ferguson's former deputy press secretary, had replaced his late wife an alarmingly short time after her death; rumor had it that he had proposed to Evelyn in his wife's hospice room. She was a smart woman, knowledgeable about the political flora and fauna inside the beltway, and she was jealous of Kate Lee, because she had a real job, while Evelyn no longer did, except to the extent that Cal Ferguson was a job. "You want to go over there and look down her dress?" she asked.

"Certainly not," Ferguson replied testily. He was a bishop of the Church of Jesus Christ of Latter-day Saints, and he did not like that kind of talk—not when someone might overhear it, anyway. The Marine Band began to play some Glenn Miller. "Tell you what I do want to do," he said, as the president and his wife led everyone to the dance floor. "I want to dance with her for a minute. How would you like to dance with the president?" He took her hand, hoisted her from her chair and shuffled a beeline across the floor toward the First Couple.

"Evening, Cal," Will said as they came close.

"Good evening, Mr. President," Ferguson said. "I wonder if we might change partners for a moment?"

"Of course," the president said, gracefully steering Kate into Cal's arms while bringing Evelyn into his own.

"Good evening, Cal," Kate said, flashing a brilliant smile.

"Hey, Kate. Tell me, what's happening in the Caribbean these days?"

"The Caribbean? Well, let's see: I can't think of a thing. Were you thinking of invading some place down there?"

"I was thinking about a certain former Haitian who got his head blown off in St. Marks."

"St. Marks? Isn't that in the Mediterranean somewhere?"

Ferguson managed a chuckle. "My friend, Hugh English, tells me it's not."

Kate formed her features for tragedy. "Oh, isn't it sad about Hugh?"

Ferguson frowned. "What?"

"Of course, I replaced him with Lance Cabot the minute we began to suspect. Just today, in fact."

"Kate, you're not telling me Hugh English is a mole, are you?"

"Of course not," Kate said, shocked. "The man is a patriot!"

"Then what's sad about him?"

"I'm sorry, Cal, I shouldn't have mentioned it; I thought you already knew."

"Knew? Knew what?"

Kate looked around, as if to see if she might be overheard. "Cal, you have to promise me faithfully that you'll keep this to yourself. We don't want this to get around; we just want a happy retirement for Hugh."

"Of course."

Kate sighed. "Well, this isn't exactly a diagnosis, but some of Hugh's actions over the past few days have caused a number of people to feel that he is suffering the early stages of . . ." She shrugged and made a face.

"Nonsense," Ferguson said. "Why the man is as sane as I am."

"That's what I told everybody," Kate said, "until . . ."

"Until what?"

"Well, there was an incident a couple of days ago during a staff meeting about . . . well, about a classified matter, and Hugh suddenly piped up and said, 'We've got to get the man out, and quickly.' That pretty much brought the proceedings to a halt, and somebody said, 'Who, Hugh? And out of where?' "

"And what did Hugh say?"

"He said, 'Nelson, of course; out of East Berlin.' "

"But East Berlin as a political entity doesn't exist anymore," Ferguson said.

"Exactly," Kate replied, "and neither does Nelson, but at that moment, they both existed for Hugh. Someone had the presence of mind to say, 'Right, I'll get on it, Hugh,' and the meeting continued, but Hugh got up and left. When I inquired about it, I was told that he had been exhibiting . . . memory issues and flashbacks. Someone thought it came on after his wife died."

Ferguson looked perplexed. "We were going to call him in to testify next week." Ferguson was the ranking Republican on the Senate Select Committee on Intelligence.

"Well," Kate said, looking sympathetic, "if there's anything the committee wants to know about East Berlin . . ." She ducked under his arm, put her own around her husband's waist and, effectively, left Evelyn Ferguson to rejoin her husband.

"What was that all about?" Will asked.

"It was about neutralizing Hugh English," she said. "By tomorrow morning, no one, not even the press, is going to pay attention to anything he has to say."

"And how did you accomplish that?"

"My darling, you don't want to know."

49

Stone and Holly sat in their car on Black Mountain Road as dusk fell. Holly had produced a small pair of binoculars from her handbag and was training them, alternately, on the Pemberton and Weatherby houses, which could both be partly seen from their vantage point. They had already peered through the windows of the Robertson house and seen nothing out of the ordinary.

"What else have you got in that handbag?" Stone asked.

"Huh?"

"You keep pulling things out—a satphone, binoculars. What else is in there?"

"Oh, a couple of changes of clothing, a disguise or two, a bowling ball, a light machine gun—you know, the usual spy stuff."

"I don't think I want to walk through customs with you on the return trip."

"Don't worry; the duty is paid on everything."

"Why are we sitting here? Why don't we just go knock on both doors and see who opens them?"

"I want to see if any lights come on first," she said. "That way, we'll know if anybody's home. I don't want to approach the houses if anybody's home."

"Wait a minute; are you thinking of breaking and entering?"

"Why not?"

"I don't know, maybe alarm systems, attack dogs, security cameras. All we need is to give duBois an excuse to rearrest us."

Suddenly, lights came on in the Pemberton house.

"There you are," Stone said. "Somebody's home."

Then lights came on in the Weatherby house.

"Did you notice," she said, "that, in each house, three or four lights came on at once?"

"You're thinking they're on a timer?"

"That's what I'm thinking. Isn't it odd that both houses came on almost simultaneously?"

"Not very odd," Stone said, "if they're both set to come on as it gets dark. Maybe, instead of timers, they work on light sensors. You want to hang around and see if they go off when the sun comes up? I'd rather go get some dinner and, eventually, some sleep."

"You'd never make a CIA agent," she said.

"What, doesn't it say anything about dinner and sleep in the official spy handbook?"

"Come on," Holly said, opening the car door.

"Where are you going?"

"I want to peek through some windows."

"Do you have any memory at all of what I just said a minute ago about alarm systems and security cameras?"

"Oh, come on, Stone; don't be such a wuss."

"Tell you what, you do the spy thing, and I'll play the part of the getaway driver. If any alarms go off, you run like hell for the car, and you might catch up with me." Stone started the car, put it in gear, made a U-turn and stopped, keeping his lights off. "Don't delay, or you might have to hoof it down this mountain."

"You move from this spot and I'll kill you."

"Don't give me that; you're unarmed."

"I'm a trained killer; I don't need guns."

"Hurry up!" Stone left the engine running.

Holly took a small flashlight from her handbag, got out of the car and trotted up the drive toward the Pemberton house.

Stone waited and watched; he could see her silhouetted against the lights of the house. She looked in a couple of windows, then he was astonished to see the front door open and Holly go inside. He could see her moving about from room to room. Stone waited for the alarm to go off, but nothing happened.

Holly left the house, came down the driveway, then trotted up the road to the Weatherby driveway and disappeared. Stone took deep breaths and tried to remain calm. He glanced at his watch; she had been gone for nearly fifteen minutes.

Suddenly the car door opened, startling him, and Holly got in.

"Okay, we can go now," she said.

"You scared the shit out of me," he said, putting the car in gear and starting down the mountain. "What the hell were you doing inside that house?"

"Well, somebody got here ahead of us and forced the front door—both front doors, in fact."

"Yeah, I think duBois got here first."

"I'm glad he didn't get here simultaneously."

"Me too."

"What did you find inside?"

"Two unoccupied houses," she said. "Three, with Robertson's. The Pemberton place had men's and women's clothes and some canned food, but the Weatherby house, though it's furnished, seems never to have been occupied at all."

"Maybe they're not in the country."

"Maybe," she said doubtfully.

"Well, if they were in the country, there'd be signs that they're living there."

"Maybe," she said again.

"What are you thinking?"

"I'm thinking that I don't know what to think."

"Go for the simple explanation: neither Pemberton nor Weatherby is on the island."

"Nor Robertson."

"Can we go back to the inn and have dinner now?"

"I guess."

At the bottom of Black Mountain Road, Stone turned toward the inn. "Holly," he said, "if you say Robertson is not Teddy, and neither Pemberton nor Weatherby is on the island, and if Teddy killed Croft, then neither Pemberton nor Weatherby could be Teddy. Or more likely, Teddy didn't kill Croft, somebody else did."

"Depressing, isn't it?" she asked.

"Not really. If you think about it, the best possible outcome of this little jaunt would be that Teddy isn't on St. Marks, that he has never been on St. Marks."

"That's what depresses me," she said.

"It shouldn't. Lance is just dying to be told that Teddy isn't here. That would get him off the hook with the director, wouldn't it?"

"I guess."

"Oh, I get it: you were hoping to cuff Teddy and deliver him to Lance with a big red bow on him."

"Something like that."

"Well, at least if Teddy isn't here, you won't have to kill him."

"What makes you think I would kill him, if he were here? I don't even have a gun."

"You're a trained killer; you don't need a gun."

"Well, what makes you think I would slip a stiletto into him, or garrote him? I'm not an assassin."

"If we find Teddy, that's what Lance is going to ask you to do— or, more likely, order you to do."

"I won't."

"So you'll just tell Lance to stick Teddy up his ass?"

"I don't know."

"Or resign from the Agency?"

"I don't know; I'll think about that when I have to."

"You'd better think about it now. My advice is, tell Lance that Pemberton and Weatherby are not here, and you think somebody besides Teddy killed Croft."

"But what if I don't think that?"

"You'd better start reflecting on the consequences of not thinking that," Stone said.

Holly didn't speak for the rest of the way back to the inn.

50

Captain duBois sat at his desk the following morning and disconsolately went through a large stack of files containing all the information the police had on visitors to the island. The primary objects of his investigation had simply melted away as suspects: the Pepper couple were in custody at the time of the shooting; Pemberton and Weatherby appeared to be off the island, though he could find no record of their departure; Irene Foster's friend's alibi had been confirmed by Thomas Hardy; he was at the marina every day; plus Barrington's and Heller's backgrounds checked out in every detail, and they had been dismissed as suspects by no less an authority than the prime minister. He wished there were an underground political opposition, so he could arrest and torture them. He began casting around for some plausible theory of the assassination, and gradually an idea began to grow.

He picked up the phone, rang the prime minister's office and requested an immediate appointment, in connection with Croft's assassination. After a brief wait, he was told to come immediately. He put on a freshly pressed uniform and walked out of the building to his waiting, hated Land Rover, still formulating the presentation of his idea.

The prime minister sat, silent, behind his large mahogany desk and seemed to be reading and signing papers, while duBois stood at attention, his hat tucked under his arm, and waited.

Finally, the PM spoke. "Tell me who murdered Colonel Croft," he said.

"Prime Minister, after a thorough review of all the existing evidence, and after investigating and/or interrogating all the foreign visitors, I believe I can say that Colonel Croft's assassin arrived on the island surreptitiously by boat, probably from St. Martin, did his work and left immediately by the same means. And, by this time, he is back whence he came, beyond our reach."

"And how did you come to that conclusion?" Sutherland asked.

"First, by a process of elimination of suspects and by deduction; second, by my knowledge of certain elements remaining in Haiti."

"Tell me about your deductive process."

"First, there is no political opposition of a violent nature on the island, and if there were, they would have no way of obtaining the weapon used—namely, a high-powered sniper's rifle of great accuracy, fitted with a silencer; second, there is no foreign visitor on the island who possesses the motive, means and opportunity of accomplishing such a deed, and who has any background consistent with the shooting skills required to make that kill with a single bullet."

"Now, tell me who in Haiti would go to the trouble of eliminating Croft."

"Numerous people, Prime Minister. When Colonel Croft and I made our escape from Haiti, we only narrowly avoided assassination squads, and for more than a year afterward we had to exercise the greatest caution in our movements, because they were known to still be hunting us. It was only when we arrived at St. Marks, and after Colonel Croft made your acquaintance, that we began to feel safe."

"Captain," the prime minister said, "I am impressed with your deduction and your theory of the assassination, and I am pleased to see that you have the mental acuity to come to the same conclusions that I, myself, have."

"Thank you, sir," duBois said. "That being the case, I believe we can now reopen the country to free travel, and I think we should do so as a matter of urgency; the police have had many complaints from tourists and those in the hospitality industry."

"You may give the order immediately, Captain, and you may also prepare a public announcement for my review explaining the circumstances of the death of Colonel Croft."

"Of course, Prime Minister. Is there anything else I can do?"

"Yes, Marcel, you may reinstate yourself to the rank of colonel and resume the rank, duties and perquisites of Colonel Croft. Good day, Colonel duBois."

"Thank you for your confidence, Prime Minister." DuBois saluted smartly, executed an about-face and marched out of the office. When he departed through the front entrance of Government House, he found the white Mercedes sedan waiting for him, his driver at the wheel. It was remarkable, he reflected, how much could be accomplished, and how quickly, by telling those in power what they wished to hear.

"Where to, Colonel?" the driver asked.

"Back to my office," duBois said. On the return trip he busied himself with replacing his captain's bars with colonel's eagles.

L ance Cabot sat in his office, working on a Saturday morning, and watched Hugh English's secretary supervising the removal of her boss's personal effects from his office. When she seemed to be done he got up and walked down the corridor to the room, carrying a legal pad and a tape measure. Quickly, he made a sketch of the bookcases and computer station he would order to be constructed. He would not have a desk, he thought; instead, he would have a large, low table with comfortable chairs arrayed about it, a less formal arrangement than his predecessor had employed. He made a note of the chairs to be ordered.

Hugh English's secretary came back into the room and cleared her throat.

Lance turned and gave her a little smile. "Yes, Carolyn?"

The woman looked stonily at him. "Have you seen the Drudge Report this morning?" she asked, referring to an Internet website that many thought scurrilous, but that had a record of picking up good gossip, especially from right-wing sources.

"I'm afraid the Drudge Report is not part of my regular reading."

"Well, it says that Mr. English is leaving the agency because he has Alzheimer's disease."

Lance was surprised. "That's an outrageous assertion," he said. "I have never noted the slightest indication of that in any of my dealings with Hugh."

"I rather thought that the assertion might have come from you," she said. The woman was retiring, along with her boss, so she had nothing to lose by annoying him.

"Carolyn, I assure you that it did not come from me, nor do I have any knowledge of whom it might have come from. I have the greatest respect for Hugh. Though we were never close, any dealings I ever had with him were always conducted with the highest degree of professionalism and mutual respect, and if you wish to quote me to the Drudge Report or anyone else, you may do so freely."

She looked a bit mollified. "Thank you, Mr. Cabot; I know Mr. English would appreciate that. By the way, a cable has come in from James Tiptree in St. Marks, saying that the island is once again open to air travel."

"Thank you, Carolyn, I'm glad to hear that. I want to extract the Peppers and some other people from St. Marks as soon as possible."

"Would you like me to arrange air travel for them?" she asked.

"Thank you, yes. If you could get them a mid-sized jet, perhaps a Hawker, I'd appreciate it. There'll be six passengers and their luggage."

"I'll do it right away and e-mail you the details," she said. "And thank you again for what you said about Mr. English."

"I'll drop him a note and tell him myself," Lance said.

The woman left the office, and Lance continued to make notes about fixtures and furnishings. He also made a note to himself to add the Drudge Report to his office's morning reading.

51

Stone woke late in the morning to find the bedsheet no longer covering him. He delayed pulling it up again to enjoy the sight of Holly lying naked on her back, her legs slightly parted, her hair awry.

She opened an eye. "You're awake?"

"I seem to be." He slid toward her on the bed, and she turned on her side to greet him.

"Something I can do for you, mister?"

Stone kissed her lightly on the lips, then he rolled her on her back again and kissed her on the nipples. They stood at attention. "Just lie there, and let me enjoy myself," he said.

"Don't I get to help?"

"Not just yet." He worked his way down her body, kissing her navel and her belly. He admired her Brazilian wax job for a moment, then parted her vulva with his tongue.

Holly made a noise of pleasure.

Stone continued playfully with his work, then more seriously, until she heaved and thrashed, while running her fingers through his hair, until she climaxed with a long, loud sigh.

They lay there for a moment, both panting, Stone's head resting on her belly.

"That's a very nice way to wake up," she said, then she rolled him on his back and sat astride him, stroking his penis until it was explosively hard. She slipped him inside her and began moving.

To his surprise, Stone came almost immediately. "Wow," he said softly.

Holly leaned over and kissed him. "That was quick."

"I had a head start," he said, "so to speak. I nearly came when I was doing you."

"How long do I have to wait for a rematch?" she asked.

"Until after breakfast," he replied, reaching for the phone. "I'm hungry for more than you. What will you have?"

"It's nearly lunchtime; Eggs Benedict, orange juice and coffee."

Stone ordered the same for both of them.

Shortly before noon, Lance was sitting in his temporary office having a sandwich sent up from the cafeteria, when he looked up to see Mona Barry standing in the doorway, holding a laptop. "Good morning, Mona," he said. "Nice to see you in on a Saturday."

"I wish I could say it was nice to be here, but I've been putting in a lot of time on the photos you gave me, and I have some results, though perhaps not the results you hoped for."

"Come in and take a seat," he said, dragging a chair next to him behind his desk, so they could both look at the laptop. "What have you got?"

Mona opened the laptop and pressed a button. "Here are the three photographs you gave me; I've run multiple tests on them. I have eliminated Robertson from consideration as Teddy."

"Why?"

"First, because the Agency people I showed the photographs to unanimously agreed that he is not; too young, wrong facial features. Also, I have been able to confirm that he is, in fact, one Barney Cox, one of four British subjects sought for questioning in a robbery of cash from a company at Heathrow Airport, in London, some months ago. Confidence is extremely high, to the point of certainty."

"Thank you for confirming that," Lance said. "I'll see that the information is passed along to the appropriate authority."

"Now," Mona said, "about the other two. At first, the photos seemed to be ordinary British passport shots, the kind you'd get at a dozen photographers' in the West End of London. I analyzed them right down to the dot level, or rather, the pixel level on the computer, and there were a number of similarities, so much so that I began to think that they might have been taken by the same photographer. What kept throwing me off was that the light was different in the two shots—a slightly different color temperature and with the light coming from a different direction."

"Is there some way to identify at which studio they were taken?"

"I'm sorry, I'm not there, yet; I'm just walking you through what I found."

"Of course, go ahead."

"It turns out that where they were taken isn't really relevant, though I suspect London. They were taken with a Polaroid camera, the kind that takes four shots at once; very common in photo shops."

"Not digital?"

"No, that's what you'd expect if they were taken in a large U.S. city, where the conversion to digital photography may be a bit farther along than in England, but again, that's not the point. After I had taken that analysis as far as I could without identifying a specific shot, I started to do multiple comparisons of the faces."

"And . . . ?"

"Well, look at the two faces: you see," she said, pointing, "the man on the right, Weatherby, has had his nose broken at some point, and his jawline is a little firmer than the other man, Pemberton."

"Yes, I can see that."

Mona hit a few computer keys. "Now, here I've enhanced and enlarged the Weatherby photo: look at his Vandyke."

"Right, I'm looking at it."

"What do you see?"

Lance gazed at the enlargement. "A mustache and goatee."

"But look at what appear to be the roots of the hairs: they seem to have a tiny, thicker dot at the root of each one."

"Which means?"

"Which means that it's a false beard, though a very good one." She moved to another enlargement. "Same at the hairline; it's a wig."

"So Weatherby is disguising himself."

"Yes, but still not the point."

"Get to the point, Mona."

"Now look at an enlargement of the broken nose," she said, moving to another photo. "What do you see?"

"Come on, Mona, tell me."

"All right." She pointed at the place where the nose seemed broken. "No pores in the skin," she said.

"So it's a false broken nose?"

"Just a clever application of spirit gum, a common theatrical makeup substance."

"All right, so he has a fake broken nose, too."

"Right." She changed photos again. "Now here's the Pemberton nose, enlarged, alongside the Weatherby shot. Look at the other side of the nose."

"I'm looking."

"The other side of both noses is very like that side of Weatherby's."

"But not the chin," Lance said. "It's softer, less firm."

"It certainly is, but here's what happens when I straighten

Weatherby's nose and remove his Vandyke." She switched to two photos where the hair was cropped out but the faces were enlarged. "What do you see now?"

"They're beginning to look related," Lance said. "Brothers?"

"No, there's spirit gum on Weatherby's chin, as well as his nose. If we remove that we get . . ."

Lance furrowed his brow. "Pemberton's chin?"

"Exactly. They're not brothers; they're the same man." She clicked on two other photos, and images appeared that made the two men look the same.

"Has anybody who knew Teddy Fay seen these?"

"The only two people still in Tech Services who knew him. They both said it could be, but they couldn't say for sure. Of course, I've altered the photos to reflect what I *think* the men would look like without disguises, but since there are no known photos of Teddy, we can't be sure it's him. But I'd put the chances at around seventy-thirty that it is."

"Well, at least we can have our people hunt down these men—this man, rather—and photograph him."

"From what I've heard about Teddy, that could be awfully hard to do," Mona said. "But I've done this," she said, switching to a page of a dozen photographs, all different. "I've made up this man with various combinations of wigs, mustaches and subtle changes in the face. Why don't you e-mail this page to our people and see what they can do with it?"

"I will do so immediately, Mona," Lance said.

She handed him a DVD. "Here's everything," she said. "Let me know how it works out." She took her laptop and left.

Lance picked up the phone and dialed Holly's satphone number. No answer and no voice mail. He sat down at his computer, inserted the DVD Mona Barry had given him and transmitted it to Holly's laptop, along with an e-mail explaining what she had done.

52

Stone and Holly lay on the bed, panting and sweaty. The remains of their lunch were on the floor at the foot of the bed.

"Once more?" Holly asked.

"You're killing me," Stone said. "I'm not as young as I used to be."

"Only joking."

"Thank God." Stone changed the subject. "Have you reported in to Lance?"

"Ah, no, not yet."

"You're afraid to tell him we aren't going to find Teddy, aren't you?"

"Certainly not."

"You sound uncertain."

"I'm not uncertain, I'm lazy. I'd rather fuck you than talk to Lance on the satphone."

"Well, that would be my choice, too."

"Then you should be a happy man."

"Tired, but happy."

There was a rap on the door, and Stone pulled up the sheet. "Come in."

Genevieve opened the door. "You two feel like a swim?"

"Not since the shark," Holly said.

"Oh, come on; the shark's gone. And you don't even have to get dressed."

"That's a thought," Stone said. They grabbed towels and followed Genevieve, who was wearing only her towel, too. Dino was already in the water, waving them in.

Stone grabbed Holly's hand, dropped his towel and ran with her into the light surf.

"What a wonderful temperature!" Holly yelled. "It's just perfect!"

They swam out to the sandbar and stood up to rest for a minute.

"Look," Stone said, pointing at a sailboat leaving English Harbour, "it's Harold Pitts."

"Pretty boat," Holly said. "You think he's leaving St. Marks?"

"I don't know," Stone said. "I had the impression Harold had begun to think about staying on here with Irene." They could see a lone figure at the helm; Stone waved, and he waved back. Then he bore away, tacked and began to recede into the distance.

"I wonder where he's going," Stone said.

L ance grew weary of waiting for Holly to return his call. He tossed his satphone into his briefcase, got into his jacket and walked out of his office, running into Carolyn, Hugh English's secretary, in the hallway.

"Hi," she said. "I've booked your jet; it's the Hawker, and it will be at the St. Marks airport at noon tomorrow."

"Great, Carolyn," he said. "I'm on my way home; would you please call the English Harbour Inn in St. Marks, ask for Ginny

Heller or Stone Barrington and tell them about the jet? And ask them to let the Peppers know."

"Of course, Lance," she said. "Have a good weekend."

"Oh, I'll be in tomorrow," Lance said. "I just have to do some stuff at home this afternoon." He continued on his way.

C arolyn called the English Harbour Inn, but there was no an- swer in the room, so she left a message on the voicemail, then she went home, too.

S tone and Holly stood on the sandbar and watched the gray fin cut through the water between them and the beach. "The son of a bitch is back," he said. Dino and Genevieve were headed for the beach at top speed.

"I hate that thing," Holly said.

"It's nothing personal," Stone replied, not taking his eyes off the fin. "He's just doing what sharks do."

"Well, I wish he'd do it somewhere else."

"You want to make for the beach?"

"Not while that beast is between us and home."

"Okay, we'll just wait here for him to come out and take a look at us."

"We're not splashing; we're not bleeding; maybe he'll just go away."

"I hope so." Stone involuntarily reached down and held onto his genitals.

"Are you holding what I think you're holding?" Holly asked.

"Uh, yes."

"You think he might find it attractive?"

"I'm not taking any chances; could be a girl shark."

O nce in his car, Lance dialed Holly's satphone number again. Still no answer. He switched off the phone and tossed it back into his briefcase. There was going to be nothing for her to report, anyway; he felt it. Carolyn would get her the message about the jet, and he could go over everything with Holly on Monday.

F inally, the shark left the area, headed out to sea, and Stone and Holly made for the beach.

"I'd better go call Lance," she said, toweling herself off and heading for the cottage.

"Kiss him for me," Stone said.

Holly went into the cottage, got out her satphone, walked outside and dialed Lance's satphone number. No message, and no voicemail. She dialed his number at Langley; maybe he was working on a Saturday. She got his voicemail. "Lance, it's Holly; we're done here, and we've come up dry. No leads, no nothing. Get us out of here, will you?" She hung up, then noticed that the message light on the room phone was blinking. She pressed the message button and waited.

"Ms. Heller and Mr. Barrington," a woman's voice said, "this is Carolyn Reese, calling for Lance Cabot. Lance would like you to know that a Hawker jet will pick up your party at the St. Marks airport at noon tomorrow, that's Sunday noon, and he asks that you let the Peppers know. Good-bye."

Holly called the Peppers.

"Hello?"

"Bill, it's, ah, Ginny. We're out of here at noon tomorrow, in a Hawker; meet us at the airport?"

"Well, that's a relief. You made any progress on the other thing?"

"None, and I don't think we're going to."

"See you at noon tomorrow, then," Pepper said, then hung up.

Holly showered and put on some clothes, then went outside. Stone, Dino and Genevieve were lying on the beach a few yards away. "Hey, everybody!" she yelled. "We're out of here at noon tomorrow, and there's nothing to do but have a farewell dinner tonight!"

She got a round of applause from the beach. "I guess she spoke to Lance," Stone said.

53

Thomas greeted them warmly at the bar, produced an ice-cold pitcher of vodka gimlets from his freezer and poured each of them one, then another for himself. He raised his glass. "To a safe trip home," he said.

They all drank.

"How did you know we were leaving tomorrow?" Holly asked.

"The ban on travel has been lifted; could your departure be far behind it?"

"You're right," Holly said.

"I hope you were able to achieve the purpose of your visit."

"There were two purposes," Holly said, "and they were mutually exclusive. We achieved one of them."

"Then your visit doesn't sound like a failure."

"No," Holly said, "it wasn't. I'm satisfied, and I hope my boss will be."

"Thomas," Stone said, "are you aware that there's a large hammerhead shark stalking your beach?"

"Oh, that's just Fred; he comes and he goes. He's never attacked anyone."

"Maybe he just hasn't seen anyone tempting enough," Stone said.

"You want to lead an expedition to kill the thing?"

"Uh, we're leaving tomorrow, remember? I'll leave you to deal with the consequences of Fred's finding someone to his taste."

Thomas went to serve another customer.

"Did you talk to Lance?" Stone asked Holly.

"No, he wasn't answering. I left a message, telling him we were done, with no joy on Teddy, and he had someone call us about tomorrow's jet. It's at noon, and the Peppers are joining us."

"Well," Stone said, "I'm a little disappointed that we didn't find Teddy; that would have been exciting."

"Maybe too exciting," Holly said. "But, anyway, I think that Croft was Teddy's swan song, if, indeed, he was the one who killed the colonel. If Teddy's still alive, I think he has gone to ground and will stay there."

"Let's hope you're right," Stone said, sipping his gimlet.

The headwaiter called them to dinner.

Stone was surprised to see Irene Foster seated alone in the restaurant. He and Holly walked over. "Good evening, Irene, are you alone?"

"Yes, Harold is sailing his boat up to Ft. Lauderdale, to sell it. I think he got tired of the cruising life."

"Is he coming back?"

"I don't think so; we haven't been getting along very well the past few days; I think he'll look for greener pastures, and frankly, that's all right with me. I got tired of seeing him in his recliner, gazing at the TV."

"Would you like to join us?" Holly asked.

"Thank you, Holly, but I'm just waiting for dessert, then I'll go home. When are you leaving, Stone?"

"At noon tomorrow," Stone said. "I want to thank you for your kindness to us while we were here." He gave her his card. "If you should find yourself in New York, call me and let me take you to dinner."

"Thank you, Stone, I'll do that, though I don't contemplate that sort of travel anytime soon."

"Good-bye, then." Holly gave her a kiss on the cheek, and they joined Dino and Genevieve at their table.

Teddy sat at his workbench, cleaning and oiling the sniper rifle. He completely dismantled it and cleaned each part carefully, then reassembled the weapon and dry-fired it a couple of times. He removed the stock and the silencer and put it back into its case.

Finally, he checked the equipment he had so carefully assembled, tightening bolts and wiping any dust away, then he opened the outer doors to his workshop, carried the three pieces outside and bolted them together at the top of the long concrete drain channel that emptied into the little gorge. He did some programming to an electronic device, half the size of a toaster, then fastened it in place and tested it. All was in working order.

He went to the garage, started his vehicle and drove down the mountain, heading over the hills into Markstown. He drove through the hilly streets, his headlights off, past the apartment building where Marcel duBois lived, and up a small hill to a little park that overlooked the residence. He pushed through some bushes to a five-foot wall made of coral, checked his sight lines and walked himself mentally through the shot. All was ready, though he reckoned he would have no more than five seconds from the time duBois left his building until he entered his car.

He would be ready. He glanced at his watch. If he got to bed early, he'd get a good seven hours of sleep before the alarm went off. He got back into the vehicle and headed back to Black Mountain.

S tone and his party lingered over coffee, enjoying the pleasant
night air. Thomas came and joined them, bringing a bottle of
brandy and some glasses.

"Thomas," Stone said, "is life going to be easier, with Colonel
Croft out of your hair?"

"It's going to be cheaper for a while, until his replacement,
duBois, finds his feet, but soon enough, he'll be around with his
hand out, and I'll have to pay."

"That's a permanent condition, then?"

"The cost of doing business. You know, our native folks would be
embarrassed to ask a bribe from someone; that's why I think Sir
Winston hired the two Haitians. Their experience at extracting
blood from stones runs long and deep."

"The St. Marksian reluctance to bribe doesn't seem to extend to
Sir Winston."

"No, once political power is achieved, embarrassment vanishes.
Sir Winston just looks at the money as his due." Thomas smiled.
"But taxes are low, and so is labor, so it all evens out. I'll get by."

They all raised their glasses and drank their cognac.

54

Lance sat in the study of his new house, surrounded by boxes of unpacked books, and read one. He needed to clear his head of work, he knew, so he'd be fresh tomorrow, when he started reading operations files again. Still, Holly's non-communication nagged at him. He dialed her satphone number again and waited: no answer. Then, just on the off-chance, he called his office number and entered the codes for his voicemail.

Holly's voice came through clearly; she had done everything he'd instructed her to and had come up with nothing. Pemberton and Weatherby were dry holes. She finished with a plea for the jet to pick them up. That didn't concern Lance, since Carolyn would have already notified her. Having e-mailed her Mona Barry's photographs, he had done all he could do, too. He hung up, took a deep breath and gave himself over gratefully to Winston Churchill's account of World War II tank operations in North Africa.

Teddy woke five minutes before the alarm would have gone off. He dressed, brushed his teeth, went to his workshop, grabbed the sniper's rifle and went outside to his vehicle. Twenty minutes later, he was climbing the hill that overlooked duBois's apartment building. He parked among some other vehicles, walked into the park and looked carefully around. The sun was not up yet, and the place was deserted. He made his way through the bushes to the coral wall and opened the rifle case.

He fastened the stock to the gun and screwed in the silencer and, first making sure that no one could see him, laid the weapon on top of the wall while he set up a small tripod. Then he hoisted himself up and sat on the wall, waiting for sun.

The sunlight illuminated the top of the building first, then began working its way down as the orb rose. Teddy saw some movement inside the penthouse. He didn't know in which apartment duBois lived, but he hopped down from the wall and sighted through the powerful scope. He saw movement again, a figure crossing a room behind some sheer curtains.

Then, in an amazing stroke of luck for Teddy, a sliding glass door opened, and duBois, wearing pajamas, stepped into the sunshine striking his deck. Teddy perfected his aim and waited for the man to stop moving.

DuBois took a few steps, then stopped and spread his arms in a great stretch, yawning. Teddy squeezed off the round and saw the red plume from the chest as the tip of the .223 bullet exploded. DuBois staggered backward and fell into the plate glass door behind him, smashing it.

Teddy did not tarry. He disassembled the rifle, packed it into its case, viewed the park from the bushes to be sure he was still alone and walked unhurriedly toward his vehicle, pulling his baseball cap low over his face and donning sunglasses.

He reached the vehicle, and as his hand touched the door handle, a woman stepped out of her house a few feet away, bent, and picked up a newspaper, then glanced up at him as he started the engine. She smiled and gave him a little wave, and he waved back. She didn't know him, but he had been seen.

He drove back to Black Mountain, never going faster than thirty miles an hour. Then, as he approached the turnoff to the road up the mountain, the black Mercedes that carried Sir Winston Sutherland to his office each day turned onto the main road and passed Teddy, going in the opposite direction. Before Teddy had even had time to think, he had made a U-turn and was following the Mercedes at a distance of a quarter of a mile.

Teddy's mind began to work at top speed, calculating time and distance and plotting an escape route over a road through the hills. All this just in case the opportunity arose. He had thought about doing this many times but he had devoted his energies to eliminating Croft and duBois; Sir Winston would be more complicated, he knew, and he had not done the planning, and he was cautiously excited.

He watched as the Mercedes entered the outskirts of Markstown and came to a screeching halt. Children dressed in their Sunday finest were pouring out of a church and crossing the road toward three school buses, apparently for an outing of some sort. A nun stood in the road holding a stop sign.

Teddy stopped some distance back and watched; then Sir Winston made his decision for him. He got out of his car and waded into the group, kissing them and touching their hands. The nun remained at her station, stopping traffic, as did another nun on the other side of the children.

Teddy turned right and up a hillside, then made a left into a dirt track that ended in a small clearing. Occasionally, he caught sight of the Mercedes and the crowd. He turned his vehicle in the clearing and pointed back toward the road; then he got out, grabbed the rifle case and started back on foot, looking for gaps in the foliage. He came to one that gave him a view of the rear of the car and part of the crowd, knowing that Sir Winston was a few steps away, among the children.

Teddy was not willing to risk hurting a child, but Sir Winston would have to return to his car, and when he did, Teddy would be waiting. He knelt, opened the case and quickly assembled the weapon. It would be a standing shot, and he clipped on a shoulder strap, wound his arm through it and sighted. He had a window about a yard square, and he knew he would have only a second or two to fire.

Then Sir Winston appeared in that frame, his driver holding the door open, no policemen in sight, and he did something unexpected: he stopped at the open door, turned and stood waving at the departing children.

Teddy got off his shot, and he was reminded of the effect the bullet had had on Colonel Croft's head. He carried the rifle back to the vehicle, trying not to hear the screams of the children, tossed the weapon onto the front seat, started the truck and drove. When he came to the road, he turned left, away from the scene of the shooting, and began climbing into the hills.

The road turned to dirt, and Teddy drove through a series of crossroads, always turning right, making his way back to the main road. Along the way he stopped for a moment, disassembled and repacked the rifle, then continued on his way. He reached the main road and stopped to check for traffic. He turned left and made his way back to Black Mountain Road. In the distance he could hear sirens.

Back at the house he noticed that low clouds were moving over Black Mountain. He went over every surface of the truck with a cloth soaked in Windex, then locked the vehicle in the garage and went back to his workshop. He switched on his police scanner and began to wipe down every surface of the workshop. The scanner was alive with police broadcasts, directing cars both to duBois's building and to block off streets around the church.

He turned on the local radio station to hear the first news reports; TV wouldn't come on until seven o'clock.

S tone woke up a little before seven, got out of bed and switched on the TV; out of habit, he wanted to get the local weather before flying. He went into the bathroom, peed and brushed his teeth, then came back into the bedroom, where Holly was sitting up in bed and pointing silently at the TV.

F irst reports from the police are that Colonel duBois was standing on the terrace of his penthouse apartment when he was struck in the chest by gunfire. This recalls the death earlier this week of his predecessor in the police, Colonel Croyden Croft, who was shot by a sniper while he sat in the courtyard of the police station." The reporter accepted a sheet of paper from off-camera. "We have a report that an attempt has been made on the life of the prime minister, Sir Winston Sutherland, but no confirmation yet."

"Holy shit," Stone said quietly.

"You're damned right," Holly said.

"What do you make of it?"

"I make of it that Teddy Fay is alive and well and shooting people," Holly said.

"And what do you want to do about it?" he asked.

"I don't *know* what to do about it," she replied, "but I'm going to ask Lance." She got her satphone, switched it on and went outside for reception. No answer on Lance's satphone; no answer on his office phone, so she left a message about what had happened; no answer on his home phone, either. Where the hell was he? She looked up at the sky: looked like it was going to be a cloudy day, the first since they had arrived.

L ance had left his house, on his way to Langley, five minutes before Holly called him there. He picked up coffee, a Danish and copies of the Sunday *New York Times* and *Washington Post* at a deli near his house, then drove in a leisurely fashion, listening to local news radio, alert for any story that might involve the Agency on a Sunday. He was waved through the front gate, after showing his ID; he parked in his reserved spot in the basement garage, near the elevator, swiped his ID card at the door and went upstairs to his office, clearing three more security checks.

He put the papers and his breakfast on the coffee table and sat down on the sofa, glancing at the headlines while he sweetened his coffee and munched on the Danish, not noticing the tiny, flashing red light on the phone behind his desk. He switched on the TV, which was already set to CNN.

He had finished his breakfast and was halfway through the *Times* when he glanced at a clip of yesterday's golf tournament and, almost simultaneously, caught sight of the tape crawling across the bottom of the screen: . . . TWO POLITICAL SHOOTINGS ON CARIBBEAN ISLAND OF ST. MARKS

Lance walked around his desk and picked up his phone, noticing the flashing red light. He dialed voicemail and listened for a moment, then dialed Holly's satphone number. "You'd better answer the bloody thing, girl," he said aloud to himself.

55

Holly grabbed the ringing satphone and went outside. "Hello?"

"Where the hell have you been?" Lance demanded.

"Right here," she said. "I left a message for you."

"I just got it; do you know who got shot on the island?"

"Only what I've seen on local TV," Holly said. "A policeman named duBois was shot, and they're saying there was a reported attempt on the PM's life, but no confirmation yet."

"Jesus, that has 'Teddy' written all over it."

"I don't know what we can do about this, Lance; our search for Pemberton and Weatherby came up dry, and we don't have any other suspects for Teddy."

"Did you go over the photographs I sent you?"

"What photographs?"

"Check your e-mail; our photo analyst says Pemberton and Weatherby are the same man, and she's made up sample photos of what he might look like in different disguises."

"I'll check that out right now," Holly said.

"Forget about Robertson; he turns out to be one of the Heathrow Robbers, a guy named Barney Cox. Call me back if you have any ideas. You know about the airplane?"

"Yes, at noon; I hope he can land; they'll probably shut down air travel again."

"I'll get word to the pilot to declare a fuel emergency, if necessary; then they'll have to allow him to land. You just be there."

"Okay." She punched off the connection and ran into the house.

"What's going on?" Stone asked.

Holly switched on her computer and waited for it to boot up. "Lance had the photographs of Pemberton and Weatherby analyzed, and the analyst says they're of the same man." She typed in her e-mail password and waited. "Here we go."

"They don't look like the same man," Stone said.

Holly scrolled down. "Look at this; without the facial hair and the wigs they do," she said and kept scrolling. "The analyst has made up some others showing what he would look like in different disguises; here they are." She scrolled slowly through a dozen pictures.

"Wait a minute," Stone said, pointing. "Look at that one. Who does that look like, except for the hair color?"

"Holy shit," Holly said. "That one is a ringer for Harold Pitts! But he sailed yesterday, didn't he? I mean, we saw him."

Stone picked up the phone and rang Thomas Hardy.

"Hello?"

"Thomas, to the best of your knowledge, did Harold Pitts sail for Ft. Lauderdale yesterday?"

"Yes, he did. I was down at the marina, and I cast off his lines myself."

"Yeah, we saw him sail out of English Harbour and turn to the east. Is there anywhere along the eastern shore where he could have anchored? Another marina or a cove?"

"No, it's all cliffs on that end of the island, and there's heavy surf from the trade winds, so he couldn't anchor there, either. What's going on, Stone?"

"Have you heard about duBois and the prime minister?"

"Yes, there was just a report that Sutherland was DOA at the Markstown hospital."

"DuBois, too?"

"Yes. That pretty much cuts off the heads of the government and the police force. There's going to be chaos, and I think you should expect to be questioned again."

"Our airplane is due at noon, and they've been instructed to declare an emergency, if necessary, to get permission to land. Do you think we'll be able to get out of here?"

"I'll drive you to the airport and do what I can to help."

"Thanks, Thomas."

"Why are you asking about Harold Pitts?"

"Because we think he may be Teddy Fay."

Thomas was silent for a moment. "Well, it wasn't Harold who shot duBois and Sutherland. He'd be a hundred miles north by now."

"Could you do me a favor and call every marina and anchorage and see if his boat is still on the island?"

"Well, there's no way to call anchorages, but there are only a couple of decent ones; I'll have somebody drive to them and check, and I'll call the marinas, then get back to you."

"Thanks, Thomas." Stone hung up. "Did you get that?"

"Only your end."

"Thomas cast off Harold's lines himself and saw him leave the harbor. He's checking to see if he could have anchored somewhere else on the island."

"Let's go up to Irene's and see if he's there."

"Wait a minute; don't go off the deep end. Let's wait to hear from Thomas. Anyway, we aren't armed, and we don't want to go after Teddy naked."

Dino was standing in the door. "You want a gun?" he said.

"You have a gun?" Stone asked.

"I'm a police officer; I'm armed at all times."

"Good thing we didn't have to explain that to St. Marks customs."

"I don't mind explaining to customs," Dino said. He went away and came back with a small 9 mm semiautomatic and a spare magazine. "Here you go," he said, handing it to Holly. "I'd rather you didn't shoot anybody with it, unless you really have to; it's registered to the NYPD."

"You don't have any instructions to shoot anybody," Stone said to Holly.

"I want it for defense," she replied. "We could need it, as you pointed out."

"*We*? What's this *we* stuff?"

"Aren't you going with me?"

"Where?"

"Up to Irene's?"

"Before I answer that, I want to know your plan," Stone said.

"Well, I'm just going to go up there and confront Irene."

"And she's going to say, 'Oh, yeah, Teddy's in the bedroom closet'?"

"Well . . ."

"In the unlikely event that he's there, she's going to protect him."

"I guess so."

"I think you'd better call Lance again."

"You're right," Holly said, grabbing the satphone. She went outside and called Lance's office.

"Yes?"

"Lance, among the photographs you e-mailed me is one that looks an awful lot like Harold Pitts, Irene Foster's friend from Virginia, the one you checked out."

"And he checked out just fine," Lance said.

"Also, Pitts left St. Marks yesterday in his sailboat, bound for Ft. Lauderdale. We saw him leave; we're checking out other marinas and anchorages on the island now, to see if he didn't really go."

"When will you know?"

"Soon."

"Call me the minute you hear. In the meantime, I'm going to run another check on Pitts." He hung up.

Holly went back inside. "Lance is running another check on Harold; he wants to know when we've heard whether the boat is still here."

The phone rang, and Stone picked it up. "Hello?"

"It's Thomas. Harold's boat is *not* on the island. Not anywhere."

Stone turned to Holly. "Thomas says the boat is not anywhere on St. Marks."

"Well, I'm going up to Irene's anyway," Holly said.

Stone turned back to the phone. "Thanks, Thomas. We're going to run up to Irene's and have a word with her."

"I don't think I'd do that, Stone."

"Why not?"

"Because if Harold is the shooter and he's still there, you don't want to be anywhere near him when the police come to talk to him, and they *will* talk to him. If you're there, they'll figure you're in cahoots with him."

"Good point. I'll explain it to Holly."

"Stone, if you're going up to Irene's, let me come with you. If the police show up, I can help."

"Thanks, Thomas, good idea. We'll see you in five minutes." Stone hung up and turned to Holly. "Thomas has pointed out that if Harold is Teddy and Teddy is the shooter, we don't want to be around him when the police arrive. Thomas is going with us; he can help if the police turn up."

"Okay with me," Holly said, jamming the 9 mm into her jeans. "Dino, if we don't come back immediately, will you take our bags to the airport, and we'll meet you there?"

"Sure," Dino said.

Teddy had moved everything he needed out of his workshop, and now he turned on a fan he had rigged up that blew dust around the room. His cell phone buzzed on his belt.

"Yes?"

"It's Thomas. Stone and Holly are determined to go up to Black Mountain, looking for you. I'm coming with them."

"How much time do I have?"

"Fifteen, maybe twenty minutes."

"Slow them down if you can."

"I'll try."

Teddy hung up and took his things outside.

56

Thomas hung up and called Sir Leslie Hewitt.

"Hello?"

"Leslie, it's Thomas. Have you heard?

"Yes, it's all over the TV. I was astonished that he got Winston Sutherland. How did that happen?"

"I haven't spoken with him about it yet, but my guess is he had the opportunity and took it."

"Well, that advances things rather more than we had planned, doesn't it?"

"It certainly does, and I think we'd better get the group together tonight to discuss our options. We can't make any moves until after Winston's funeral, but we'd better be talking to a lot of people before they bury him."

"Do you have any idea where Teddy is now?"

"I just spoke to him; I assume he's either at Irene's or in his workshop. Stone Barrington and Holly Barker are going up there now looking for him, and I'm going with them."

"Will they be armed?"

"I don't know."

"Thomas, we can't let Teddy be caught."

"I'll do what I can to get him off the island."

Leslie paused for a moment. "Thomas, I'm not sure you're taking my meaning."

"I'm sorry, Leslie, what am I missing?"

"Certainly, it would be good if Teddy immediately got off the island, but if that seems in any way in doubt, then you can't allow him to be taken by the police. I don't know what the ramifications are of having him taken by this CIA woman, but I can't think that that would be to our benefit, either."

"For all practical purposes, Teddy is off the island now; his yacht sailed, and I've asked the fellow we put aboard to be sure to be seen at the western end of St. Martin, so the police can confirm that Harold left yesterday."

"I think, in view of Winston's rather sudden demise, we may have to replan a bit."

"What do you suggest?"

"First, as I said before, we cannot allow Teddy to be caught. We can't even allow his body to be found."

"His body?"

"Thomas, please focus; if he's in danger of being caught, you're going to have to kill him and get the body into the sea."

Thomas sat quietly for a moment and thought.

"Think of the ramifications of his being caught: they'll beat everything out of him. If they only have the body, they'll start to confirm every detail of his identity, and even though he told us he did a masterful job of becoming Harold Pitts, that identity will eventually unravel."

"You have a point," Thomas said.

"There's more of my point: when they find out he isn't Pitts, they'll have an unidentifiable corpse on their hands, so they'll start digging into his island connections, and that means you and me. They'll think that we hired an assassin."

"Teddy came to us, remember?"

"That won't matter. Teddy and his corpse have to disappear completely and forever."

"What about the boat? It will eventually get to Ft. Lauderdale, and there'll be someone there to meet it."

"Your man has a satellite telephone doesn't he?"

"Yes."

"Then call him and give him new instructions; we need for the authorities to know exactly what happened to the yacht and to Pitts."

Thomas was still quiet.

"Am I making sense, Thomas?"

"Yes, I'm afraid you are."

"Then what are you going to do?"

"I'm going to call Teddy and tell him to hide himself while Stone and Holly are looking for him, and that I'll get him off the island in a few days, when things have cooled off a bit."

"I hope that works. And if it doesn't?"

"Then I'll do what has to be done and take care of the disposal."

"I'm sorry it's come to this, Thomas. I know you didn't expect to have to kill anyone yourself."

"I'm sorry, too, but don't worry—I'll take care of it."

"All right. I'll call the others, and we'll meet here tonight. You bring some food from the inn, and we'll call it a dinner party, if the police should show up."

"I'll be there around seven," Thomas said.

"Good luck, Thomas, and thank you."

"Good-bye, Leslie." Thomas hung up. He went to his safe, opened it and took out the snub-nosed .38 that he had carried as a backup piece when he was a New York City cop. He strapped the holster to his ankle, checked to be sure the gun was loaded, then shoved it into the holster and secured it.

He called Teddy.

"Yes?"

"Stone and Holly are going to be there shortly. It's important that you secrete yourself while they're looking for you and, probably, for a few days after that. Do you have food in that bunker of yours, or do you want me to bring you some?"

"I'm quite self-sufficient, Thomas, and don't worry, they will not find me. I know you're worried about my being apprehended, but you may put that out of your mind; it won't happen."

"I hope not."

"I know that my capture would endanger your prospects for forming a government, and I will not put you in that position, I promise you."

"Thank you, Teddy; I'm glad you understand what's at stake for the future of St. Marks."

"I do. Give me as much time as you can; I'm nearly ready now."

"Good-bye, Teddy," Thomas said, and he meant it. One way or another, this would be their last conversation.

Thomas left his office and went to pick up Stone and Holly.

S tone and Holly were waiting outside their cottage for Thomas to pick them up when her satphone rang again.

"Yes?"

"It's Lance. Harold Pitts's house is less than ten miles from the front gate here; I sent two men to look it over, and Pitts answered the door. He returned home last night after six weeks of touring the country in an RV."

"So *our* Harold Pitts is Teddy."

"No doubt about it," Lance said. "Holly, you're not going to be able to bring him back with you, and you can't allow him to be caught."

"What do you mean?"

"I mean that if the St. Marks police get their hands on him, they'll torture him until they know everything; I mean that he's not going to get onto that airplane with you; he just won't. He knows exactly what that would mean when he's back in the States, and he'll kill you rather than allow that to happen."

"I'm armed; Dino had brought a weapon with him."

"I'm glad to hear that," Lance said. "It means that you won't have to kill him with a knife or your hands."

"Lance, I'm going to try to take him alive."

"It can't be done, Holly. The very best outcome of such an effort would be that he might kill himself, but he very likely would kill you first. He will be armed to the teeth, and he's not going to have a conversation with you before he starts shooting."

"We don't know that."

"I don't want to lose you, Holly. Quite apart from my personal loss, the Agency would be left holding a very large bag."

"That's not what I'm thinking about," Holly said.

"It's what you *must* think about. You can only prevent a horrible mess for the Agency, and perhaps for the country, by remaining alive, and that means killing Teddy at the first opportunity, do you understand?"

"I suppose so."

"These are your orders, Holly: *Kill him on sight; do not wait for him to threaten you or run.* Do you understand?"

Holly heaved a deep sigh. "I understand."

"I'll meet you at Manassas airport. Good-bye." Lance hung up.

Stone was staring at her. "Are you going to do it?"

"Yes," she said.

57

L ance had hardly hung up the phone when it rang again.
"Yes?"

"It's Kate Lee, Lance."

"Good morning, Director."

"Lance, the president wants to announce his candidacy for re-election, probably in the next day or two; he's meeting with his campaign people now. Where are we on the St. Marks operation?"

"I anticipate a resolution within hours," Lance said.

"Can you promise me that?"

"No, Director, because I'm not on St. Marks, doing it myself. But I believe that before the day is out, I can give you a conclusive answer."

"All right. I'll expect to hear from you later in the day."

"Something else, Director: Hugh English's secretary told me yesterday that an item had appeared on the Drudge Report website saying that Hugh had resigned because he has Alzheimer's disease."

"I've heard about it, and I'm shocked."

Lance thought he detected an ironic overtone to that statement. "I've told Carolyn that she can give a quote to Drudge, attributed to an inside source, but not named, that the information is false."

"Good. If I'm asked about it, I'll issue a strong denial."

"Thank you, Director. I'll call you later today."

"I'll sit by the phone, Lance. Good-bye." She hung up.

Lance leaned back in his chair and began doing deep breathing exercises to calm himself.

S tone and Holly got into Thomas's car.

"Thomas," Stone said, "can you drive us straight to the airport when we're done with this errand? I've told Dino to take the rental car and our luggage."

"Of course," Thomas said. "Please tell me what you hope to accomplish by this trip up Black Mountain."

"That remains to be seen," Holly said.

"I think it's time the two of you and I had a frank discussion," Thomas said.

"Go ahead," Stone said.

"Of course, I'll deny that this conversation ever took place, and I expect you will, too."

"All right."

"I've known for some time that Harold Pitts is Teddy Fay."

Stone's mouth fell open. "Why on earth didn't you tell us?"

"Because Teddy had work to do, work that I and some others on the island thought necessary to preserve this little country as something other than the dictatorship of Winston Sutherland."

"You mean you had Teddy kill Sir Winston?"

"No; he did that entirely on his own hook. Let me explain."

"Please do."

"Teddy came here first as Pemberton, an Englishman, some months ago. He and I met in the restaurant, and we talked a lot. Gradually, as I got to know him better, the talk turned to local politics. I told him that the island was being strangled by corruption at the top, that Winston was squeezing practically every business on the island for money, using Croft and duBois for muscle, then shipping it into an offshore account. Pemberton, as I knew him, was intensely interested in this. He intimated that he was motivated, and had the skills, to remove Croft and duBois from the picture. The words were never spoken directly; these were highly nuanced conversations."

"So you hired Teddy to kill Croft and duBois?"

"Certainly not; didn't you hear what I just said? He volunteered, and I did not discourage him. Then Pemberton abruptly disappeared and Harold Pitts arrived."

"Who is in this with you?"

"There is a group of us on the island, mostly members of Parliament, as I am, who thought that with Croft and duBois out of the way, we could go to Winston and bully him into backing off. After all, he had already accumulated enough to keep him in luxury for the rest of his life."

"From what I know of Sutherland," Stone said, "I don't think he could have been bullied."

"Neither do I, and I was prepared to go further if he resisted us. Then, early this morning, Teddy killed duBois, and I believe that he suddenly found himself with an opportunity to kill Winston, and he did that, too. I don't think it was planned."

"How long have you known that Pemberton/Pitts was Teddy?"

"I suspected it from what I had read in the international press about Teddy, but I didn't press him on it, until you arrived and told me what you were doing. Immediately after that, after he had taken on the Harold identity, I asked him, straight out, if he was Teddy Fay, and he admitted it. Irene has always known, of course."

"Of course."

"Holly," Thomas said, "you're very quiet back there."

"I'm just taking all this in, Thomas, and I'm wondering what your next move is."

"Let me ask you a question: do you believe that you and Stone can take Teddy alive, get him past the police and transport him back to the United States in your airplane this morning?"

Holly took a deep breath. "After reflection, no."

"Then you're going to Black Mountain to kill him."

"I'm not," Stone said.

"I am," Holly said. "And so are you, aren't you, Thomas? You and your people can't risk having Teddy taken by the police, just as my people can't."

"I'm afraid you're right," Thomas said.

"Are you in touch with Teddy?" she asked.

"He has a cell phone."

"Call him and tell him that I want to talk to him, just talk. Tell him I have an offer from the director that he should consider."

"Do you have an offer from the director?" Stone asked.

"No."

Thomas pulled the car to the side of the road, took out his cell phone and pressed a button.

Yes?" Teddy said.

"It's Thomas. I'm in the car with the woman you know as Ginny Heller; her real name is Holly Barker, and she's with the Agency."

"I've known that for several days," Teddy said. "It took some time for me to place the face, because she looks different from the last time I saw her, but I finally remembered."

"Holly has an offer from the director to present to you," Thomas said.

"Do you really believe that?" Teddy asked.

"Yes, I do, and I think you should hear her out. This could be the best possible solution."

"Does it involve going back to the States and being tried?"

"I don't know; you'll have to ask her that."

"Where are you, Thomas?"

"We'll be at Irene's in ten minutes."

"All right, I'll hear her out, but I'm not making any promises." He hung up.

"He says he'll hear your offer, Holly."

"All right."

Thomas put the car in gear, began humming, then softly sang the words . . . 'Gonna cut him, if he stands still, and shoot him, if he runs.' "

"What?" Holly asked.

"Just an old song," Thomas said. "An old blues."

58

Teddy left his workshop and walked up the hill to Irene's house. She was in the kitchen making a salad.

"I'm done here," he said.

"I figured you would be, after I saw the TV this morning," she replied. She wiped her hands on her apron. "Why didn't you tell me what you were doing, Teddy?"

"Surely you knew something was up, especially after I sent the yacht north."

"Knowing that something was up is not the same as knowing that you were going to take out three government officials, including the prime minister."

"Life is going to be better for you here with those three gone," Teddy said. "Their replacements are going to be of a different order."

She put her arms around his neck. "When will I see you again?"

"Until a few minutes ago I thought I could get myself to Lauderdale, sell the yacht and come back as Harold Pitts. That's not possible now."

"Why not? The identity is still good, isn't it?"

"There are some people on the way here now, and I expect they want to kill me."

"Who?"

"Thomas, Stone Barrington and the Ginny girl, whose real name is Holly Barker."

"I know that name; she works for Lance!"

"I know."

"How are you going to get out? You'll meet them going down the road."

"I've made some preparations."

They both heard the crunch of gravel from the driveway, and car doors slammed.

"Shit!" Teddy said. "You're going to have to stall them for me; give me as much time as you can." He kissed her and ran out the back door as the doorbell rang. As he ran, he looked up at the overcast, which was nearly down to rooftop level at Irene's house. This was going to be tougher than he had thought. He headed down the hill at breakneck speed.

Irene Foster opened the door, wearing an apron. "Well hello, all of you, what a nice surprise! I was just making a crab salad; can you stay for lunch?"

"I'm afraid not, Irene," Thomas said, stepping into the house. "Where's Harold?"

"He's just getting out of the shower. Why don't you all have a seat; he'll be out as soon as he's dressed." She showed them all into the living room, but nobody sat down.

"We really need to see him right now, Irene," Holly said.

"Goodness, what's the rush? Can I get anybody some iced tea?"

From outside somewhere came a loud buzzing noise.

"What's that?" Stone asked.

"Chain saw," Irene replied smoothly. "They're clearing out some trees in the ravine below the old guest house."

"There aren't any trees in that ravine, and that's not a chain saw," Holly said, and she started running.

59

Teddy sat in the front seat of the two-seater ultralight aircraft, his case strapped into the rear seat. A map image appeared on the Garmin portable GPS he had fixed to the frame ahead of him. He tapped in the identifier for Nevis airport and pressed the "Direct To" button. A line appeared on the map; all he had to do was to follow that. He pushed the throttle forward for takeoff, and the engine died. He hadn't had time to warm it up properly.

"Shit!" he practically screamed. He pulled the choke out halfway and pressed the starter button, hoping to God he wasn't flooding it. The engine began turning over again, but more weakly than the first time; the battery was a small one.

"Teddy!" he heard Thomas yell from up the hill somewhere. "Teddy!"

The engine caught and roared to life. Teddy pushed the throttle slowly forward, letting the rpms build, trying not to let it die again. Finally, it was wide open. Teddy took the knife from his belt and turned to cut the light rope that was all that was holding the little aircraft back.

H olly rounded the corner of the old guesthouse ahead of Thomas and Stone, clawing at the pistol stuck in the belt of her jeans. "Teddy!" she yelled. "It's Holly Barker! Don't do anything stupid!" She came to a sliding halt and fell on her ass. Teddy Fay was sitting in what looked like a large bird, made of aluminum and cloth, and he was reaching behind him with a knife. The noise from the propeller was deafening. Holly got to one knee and aimed carefully at Teddy's upper body. "Don't do it, Teddy!" she yelled and began squeezing the trigger.

Teddy cut whatever was holding the little airplane back, and, finally freed of its tether, it shot down the hill, as Holly fired, missing him.

T eddy concentrated on keeping the ultralight airplane in the concrete spillway, which was all the runway he had. The little craft gained speed, and as the end of the spillway rushed at him, he pulled back slightly on the stick, clearing the rough ground, but still headed downhill, picking up airspeed. He heard another gunshot, this one a little different-sounding. Two of them were shooting at him. It was now or never.

Teddy pulled firmly back on the stick, and the ultralight started to climb toward the thick clouds above him.

H olly braced herself against the corner of the house and sighted carefully. This time he was hers. She squeezed off the round, then, suddenly, the ultralight disappeared.

Teddy felt a blow on his right calf as the ultralight entered the clouds, but he couldn't let that distract him. He was going to have his hands full, keeping the wings level with no visual references. All he had was a compass, mounted at eye level, and it was moving, signaling a turn to the south. He corrected gently to his right, and the wind through the rigging began to sing louder. He was in a descent, and he yanked back on the stick.

T here!" Thomas shouted, as the aircraft partly descended from the clouds to the south, but before he could get off a shot, it climbed into the clouds again, and from the noise, seemed to be turning north. In desperation, Thomas began firing at the sound, and Holly joined in.

T eddy heard the whistle of bullets, much closer than he would have liked, and a tear appeared in the right wing. He thought he had the aircraft stable now, headed north and climbing. The firing stopped.

H olly popped out the magazine and dug in her pocket for the spare Dino had given her. "Are you out, Thomas?"

"Yes, and I don't have any more ammo," he replied.

She rammed in the fresh magazine, racked the slide and listened. The sound of the engine had grown a little fainter. "Where is the fucking thing?" she yelled.

"More to your right, I think," Thomas said. "He seems to be headed north."

Holly raised the weapon and emptied the magazine, knowing that her chances of hitting anything were remote. "That's it," she said finally. "I'm out, and Teddy is gone."

"Good," Stone said quietly.

"Whose side are you on?" Holly demanded.

"There aren't any sides now," Stone said.

The thick cloud around Teddy began growing brighter and suddenly, like flipping a switch, the airplane was flooded in sunlight. He was on top of the clouds, and he leveled off. How high was he, he wondered. He had been airborne for what, two minutes, three? The ultralight could climb at about five hundred feet a minute, so he must be a thousand, maybe fifteen hundred feet high. He kept the airplane just above the clouds, in case a helicopter or another airplane appeared. If that happened, he could duck back into the undercast and change direction. He eased back on the throttle to what seemed a decent cruise power setting, not wanting to waste fuel by running at full throttle.

The tank held five gallons of fuel, enough for about two hours of cruise. The prevailing winds were from the southeast, and that would help his speed and extend his range a bit. The GPS told him he was making forty-one knots over the ground, or the sea, whichever he was over. He did a damage assessment.

As far as he could tell only two rounds had had any effect. One had struck the wing, and the tear was getting worse. He slowed the airplane, bringing the ground speed down to thirty-five knots. He sure as hell didn't want to stall the thing at a low airspeed, but the fabric of the wing had now stopped tearing, and that was good.

He pulled up his trouser leg and looked at his right calf. He could see an entry wound and an exit wound, and the exit wound was bleeding profusely; his shoe had begun to fill with blood.

He took off his belt and made a tourniquet just below the knee, and the blood stopped flowing. That would hold him until Nevis airport, he reckoned, and he had a first-aid kit in the Cessna, which was secured in its hangar. He stopped thinking about the pain and concentrated on keeping the ultralight level and on the GPS line to St. Martin.

60

Holly grabbed a map from the glove compartment of Thomas's car and turned it over, for a display of the Caribbean, then she got out the satphone and called Lance.

"Lance Cabot."

"It's Holly; Teddy's gone."

"Gone? You mean he's dead?"

"No, though I think I hit him."

"He's on an island; how can he be gone? Does he have a boat?"

"No, he had an ultralight airplane."

"You mean one of those spit-and-baling-wire contraptions?"

"More like aluminum and nylon, but you get the picture."

"I don't understand; how far could he get in one of those things?"

"I'm looking at the map now."

Stone spoke up from the back seat. "It's probably good for a couple of hours of flying at forty or fifty knots."

"Stone's a pilot, and he says it can fly for a couple of hours. From my map, I'd say that Barbuda, Antigua, St. Kitts and Nevis are all within his range. Guadeloupe is a lot farther."

"Tell me exactly what happened."

Holly gave him a nutshell explanation. "Most of those islands have airline connections," she said. "You should check those first."

"No, he would avoid the airlines; he has to have an airplane stashed somewhere."

"I guess that's possible."

"Are you at the St. Marks airport now?"

"We're on the way; half an hour out."

"Don't let anything keep you from getting out of there."

"Thomas Hardy is with us; he'll help."

"I'll meet you at Manassas," Lance said.

"I don't know what time we'll get there."

"I'll know." Lance hung up.

Holly turned to look at Stone. "Lance thinks Teddy's got an airplane stashed on another island."

"That makes a lot of sense."

"Where could he get to in a light airplane?"

"Do you know what kind?"

"Before, he had a Cessna 182, the one he blew up."

"Well, in a similar airplane he might have a range of five to seven hundred miles. He could go north to other islands, but it would make more sense to head for South America. You say you think you hit him?"

"I know I missed on the first shot, but the second one felt right, and I thought I saw him jerk. That was just before he flew into the clouds."

Holly turned around and sat silently in her seat.

"What are you thinking about?"

"I'm thinking, I wonder if I can get our pilot to stop in Florida and pick up Daisy."

"Jesus," Stone said.

An hour into Teddy's flight the undercast was still there, and he began to invent an instrument approach for his destination. Nevis was straight ahead, another thirty-five minutes, according to the GPS, but the tear in the right wing was getting worse, and the little aircraft kept trying to turn right. One thing he didn't have, Teddy reflected, was a life raft, or even a life jacket. He was going to have to make land or die, and he was going to have to descend through the cloud cover without running into a mountain.

He loosened the tourniquet until the leg began to bleed again and feeling returned to his foot, then he tightened it again and concentrated on keeping the ultralight on course. Nevis grew larger on the GPS, but much more slowly than he would have liked. He created an approach waypoint three miles east of the airport; his second waypoint would be the end of runway 28. He meant to be under the clouds by the first waypoint.

Thomas drove into St. Marks airport with a wave at the guard on the gate and stopped in front of the terminal. Everybody got out of the car. The jet was nowhere to be seen.

Holly looked up to see Bill and Annie Pepper, in the company of James Tiptree, coming out of the terminal.

"We heard our Hawker talking to the tower," Bill said. "The pilot has declared an emergency; I hope nothing is wrong with the airplane."

"Probably not. Lance told them to declare a fuel emergency if they tried to keep the plane from landing."

"I don't like the look of that low overcast, either," Bill said. "I hope to God they have an instrument approach here."

Now two uniformed policemen came out of the terminal and marched up to them. "No airplanes landing," one of them said, "and no airplanes taking off."

"Oh, shut up, Harvey," Thomas said. "These people have a private airplane coming, and it's going to land. Sir Winston authorized it himself."

The two policemen looked at each other and said nothing.

"Look," Stone said, pointing. An airplane had just popped out of the clouds. "It's a Hawker."

They watched as the airplane touched down and taxied to the ramp. The engines were shut down, the door opened, and a pair of uniformed pilots got out.

Stone waved to them.

The two pilots walked up. "We're looking for Stone Barrington and Holly Barker," one of them said.

"I'm Stone, and this is Holly," Stone said. "This is Bill and Annie Pepper."

"Hi, I'm Ken Smith," the pilot said, and this is Bob Harkin, my first officer. Bob will get your luggage loaded while I see about refueling."

Teddy descended through the undercast and, to his delight, popped out of the clouds at his first waypoint, but the tear in the wing was now a gaping hole, and he was having great difficulty flying in a straight line; he couldn't get it to point at the runway. The ultralight was slowing down, too, and he was worried about stalling. He increased power; there was no other choice.

The drag on the right wing was moving him to the right of the airport as he approached, and he knew he would not be able to turn left without stalling. In desperation, he allowed the little plane to make a right turn, hoping to gain some ground. He made a slow 360-degree turn, and 30 degrees before he completed it, he let the craft descend toward the airport. He didn't care if it made a runway; all he wanted was level ground.

In the end, he made a taxiway next to the runway, bounced a couple of times and was finally in control again. He taxied the length of the runway toward the hangars at the other end, then turned behind a row of them, out of sight of the tower. With luck, they wouldn't have seen him at all.

He found his hangar, shut down the engine and worked the combination lock, then he got the hangar door open and pushed the ultralight inside, under the Cessna's high wing. He closed the big door behind him, switched on the lights, and unstrapped his bag and put it into the passenger seat of the Cessna 182 RG, then he got the first aid kit out of the luggage compartment and went to work on his leg. He injected a local anesthetic, then took off the tourniquet and began irrigating the wound from both ends with a squirter and hydrogen peroxide.

By the time he had cleaned the wound, the local had taken effect, and he sutured and bandaged the wounds. He checked his watch. It had been more than two hours since he had left St. Marks, and that was too much time; he had to get out of Nevis without further delay.

He opened the hangar door, picked up the towbar, which was already attached to the nosewheel of the Cessna, and pulled the airplane out of the hangar. He closed the hangar door, to hide the ultralight, locked it and got into the airplane. He could hear a siren in the distance.

He primed the engine, and it started immediately. Teddy didn't bother with the checklist but started taxiing immediately. As he cleared the row of hangars he saw a police car parked in the middle of the runway, its lights flashing, and another police car was headed his way down the taxiway. He had only one choice.

He rolled onto the taxiway and shoved the throttle forward. The airplane began to roll down the taxiway, directly toward the oncoming police car.

"One of us is going to have to give," Teddy said aloud, "and it isn't going to be me." The only question left was what the police car would do. Then it did the worst possible thing: it screeched to a halt, and its two occupants bailed out, leaving the car in the middle of the taxiway.

Teddy glanced at the airspeed indicator: forty knots; not enough. He reached over, put in full flaps and yanked back on the yoke. He didn't have enough airspeed to fly, but maybe he had enough to jump. The airplane shot up about six feet, and Teddy struggled to get the nose down again. It came down hard a few yards behind the police car, still at full throttle; he was lucky he hadn't blown a tire. Teddy reduced the flaps by a notch and after a moment he had rotation speed for a short-field takeoff. The airplane began to fly.

He looked over at the runway and saw the two policemen standing next to the other patrol car, their weapons drawn. They began firing, and he heard something hit the fuselage behind him. No stopping now.

He reduced flaps as he climbed into the overcast, then, when he was above it, turned toward the northwest, toward Puerto Rico; he wanted the police to hear the airplane going that way. He climbed to eight thousand feet and waited ten minutes, then turned back to the south. He was at optimum altitude now, and he pulled back the throttle to cruise and leaned the engine to best economy.

Now he went through the previously neglected checklist, then switched on the avionics and entered the identifier for Santa Marta, in Colombia, into the GPS. He would not fly there; instead, when the Colombian coast was in sight, he would bear to the east, toward the Guajira Peninsula, a region notorious for drug trafficking, where no questions were asked when you wanted fuel.

From the Guajira, he would head west to Central America, perhaps Panama, perhaps Costa Rica, and find a nice, rural airstrip. If that felt inhospitable, there was always Mexico, to the north.

Half an hour later, St. Marks was to the east of him, under the clouds, and he knew the airport had no radar. Teddy now had air transport, money and identification that would work anywhere in the world. He began to feel something very like peace. He had done good in St. Marks, but there were other countries that needed him. He flew on south, into the future.

61

The Hawker was refueled now, but surrounded by police-men, and Thomas's posturing and pleading was not having the desired effect.

"You know," Stone said to the others, "I don't think I want to be questioned by a new generation of cops on this island. What do you say we get on the airplane and make a run for it?"

"They'd just shoot out our tires, Ken Smith said. "Let's let your friend keep talking to them."

Then something odd happened: the cop who appeared in charge began listening to his handheld radio, then talking into it. Stone strained to hear the conversation, but couldn't. The cop walked over to Thomas and waved an arm.

Thomas smiled and walked back to the group. "The police say they have arrested the assassin," he said. "You're free to go."

Stone heaved a big sigh of relief. "Who do you think they arrested?"

"I have no idea," Thomas replied.

SHOOT HIM IF HE RUNS

Stone gave Thomas a big hug. "It was a great stay, Thomas, and we thank you for your hospitality."

"It was a pleasure having you," Thomas replied.

A moment later, they had said their good-byes, boarded the airplane and closed the door. The pilots ran through their checklist, started the engines and began to taxi.

Holly grabbed Stone's hand. "Something else is going to happen, I can feel it. We aren't out of here yet."

Stone squeezed her hand. "Shut up, Holly."

The airplane reached the end of the runway, turned and began to roll. A few seconds later they were climbing through the overcast.

As they climbed on top of the clouds, Stone looked out the window and thought he saw an airplane below them. "Look at that," he said to Holly.

They both looked out the window.

"What? I don't see anything."

"I thought I saw a small airplane, heading south," Stone said. "But it's not there anymore."

"I'm glad I didn't see it," Holly said.

L ate in the afternoon they landed at the little airport in Manassas, Virginia. As they taxied to the ramp, Holly looked out the window and saw Lance standing next to a car. Behind that was another car, a black Lincoln.

Holly was first off the airplane, with Daisy, and she walked over to where Lance stood.

"You landed the airplane in Florida for that animal?" he asked.

"I have nothing to say on that subject," she said.

The fuel truck arrived and began its work. Holly went over to Stone. "I think we're out of here," she said. "You'll be in Teterboro in an hour."

"And I'll be glad to see it," Stone said.

"So will we," Dino chimed in.

Holly gave everybody hugs and saw them onto the airplane, then it began to taxi out.

"Let's get out of here," Lance said. "We have to talk."

The Peppers got into the waiting Lincoln and were driven away, then Holly put Daisy into the rear seat of Lance's car and got in.

Lance started the car and drove out of the airport. "Let me bring you up to date on what's happened since you left the island," he said. "The St. Marks police arrested an unidentified man. He was taken to the police station where, an hour or so later, he signed a confession to the murders of Croft, duBois and the prime minister. Half an hour after that, he was shot—'while trying to escape,' as the official announcement put it."

"He was innocent," Holly said.

"He confessed, and he probably doesn't exist." Lance replied. "Let it lie."

"Did Teddy make it to another island in his contraption?"

"Two other things," Lance said. "Harold Pitts's yacht sank in three hundred feet of water off the eastern end of St. Martin, shortly after Harold got off an SOS. A search was conducted, but no sign of Harold. A life raft was found, empty."

"What's the other thing?"

"The other thing is something that *didn't* happen," Lance said. "Teddy *didn't* make it to Nevis, where he *didn't* elude two police cars and *didn't* fly off the island in a Cessna he *didn't* have stashed in a hangar there. Do I make myself perfectly clear?"

"You're buying into all of that?" Holly asked.

"Yes, I am," Lance said, "and you would be wise to accept it, too. You and I have other work to do, and we've already devoted too much time to Teddy Fay."

Holly thought it impolitic to mention Stone's sighting of the small airplane when they took off from St. Marks. "What work do we have to do?"

"I'm making you my assistant at Langley; you won't have a title for a while. There'll be some carping among the people there about your not having enough training or experience."

"Both true," Holly said.

"You have lots of training and experience, just not what Agency personnel think of in that regard. After a time, when you've had an opportunity to win over some folks, and they've decided we're not sleeping together, we'll see what work we can find for you to do."

"Working at Langley sounds very restful," Holly said, leaning back in her seat. "Shall I sell my New York apartment?"

"I wouldn't do that just yet; you never know when you might need it. For the time being, we're housing you in an old inn near Langley, where we sometimes keep visitors."

Holly glanced at Daisy.

"The inn is dog-friendly," Lance said.

"You think of everything, Lance."

"I try."

Holly put her head back on the seat and began to doze.

"Oh," Lance said, "something else happened in St. Marks while you were in the air: a woman was attacked and partly eaten by a big hammerhead shark on a sandbar just off the beach of the English Harbour Inn. Her companion lost an arm trying to rescue her."

Holly stayed awake all the way to her new quarters.

That night, Stone and Dino were having dinner at Elaine's.

"Holly called," Stone said. He told Dino about the loss of Harold Pitts and his yacht, and about the nonexistent ultralight.

"Figures," Dino said.

"Yeah."

Dino pointed at the television, which was tuned to CNN but with no sound. "Look at the crawl," he said.

Stone looked up. "WHITE HOUSE SOURCES SAY THAT PRESIDENT LEE WILL ANNOUNCE HIS CANDIDACY FOR REELECTION TOMORROW MORNING," the crawl read.

Stone smiled. "I think I'll sleep well tonight."

END

AUTHOR'S NOTE

I am happy to hear from readers, but you should know that if you write to me in care of my publisher, three to six months will pass before I receive your letter, and when it finally arrives it will be one among many, and I will not be able to reply.

However, if you have access to the Internet, you may visit my website at www.stuartwoods.com, where there is a button for sending me e-mail. So far, I have been able to reply to all of my e-mail, and I will continue to try to do so.

If you send me an e-mail and do not receive a reply, it is because you are among an alarming number of people who have entered their e-mail address incorrectly in their mail software. I have many of my replies returned as undeliverable.

Remember: e-mail, reply; snail mail, no reply.

When you e-mail, please do not send attachments, as I *never* open these. They can take twenty minutes to download, and they often contain viruses.

Please do not place me on your mailing lists for funny stories, prayers, political causes, charitable fund-raising, petitions or sentimental claptrap. I get enough of that from people I already know. Generally speaking, when I get e-mail addressed to a large number of people, I immediately delete it without reading it.

Please do not send me your ideas for a book, as I have a policy of writing only what I myself invent. If you send me story ideas, I will immediately delete them without reading them. If you have a good idea for a book, write it yourself, but I will not be able to advise you on how to get it published. Buy a copy of *Writer's Market* at any bookstore; that will tell you how.

Anyone with a request concerning events or appearances may e-mail it to me or send it to: Publicity Department, Penguin Group (USA) Inc., 375 Hudson Street, New York, NY 10014.

Those ambitious folk who wish to buy film, dramatic or television rights to my books should contact Matthew Snyder, Creative Artists Agency, 9830 Wilshire Boulevard, Beverly Hills, CA 90212–1825.

Those who wish to make offers for rights of a literary nature should contact Anne Sibbaid, Janklow & Nesbit, 445 Park Avenue, New York, NY 10022. (Note: This is not an invitation for you to send her your manuscript or to solicit her to be your agent.)

If you want to know if I will be signing books in your city, please visit my website, www.stuartwoods.com, where the tour schedule will be published a month or so in advance. If you wish me to do a book signing in your locality, ask your favorite bookseller to contact his Penguin representative or the Penguin publicity department with the request.

If you find typographical or editorial errors in my book and feel an irresistible urge to tell someone, please write to Rachel Kahan at Penguin's address above. Do not e-mail your discoveries to me, as I will already have learned about them from others.

A list of my published works appears in the front of this book and on my website. All the novels are still in print in paperback and can be found at or ordered from any bookstore. If you wish to obtain hardcover copies of earlier novels or of the two nonfiction books, a good used-book store or one of the online bookstores can help you find them. Otherwise, you will have to go to a great many garage sales.